J.A. BELFIELD | CLARE BENTLI
K.L. JESSOP | JAMES KEITH | C
FINLEY SAWYER | ELLE M THOMAS | LINDA THROSBY

Light in the DARK

Dandelion Anthologies

BRINGING AUTHORS' WORLDS TOGETHER

Front cover image and internal graphics:
Shower Of Schmidt Designs
https://www.facebook.com/groups/shower.of.schmidt.designs/
https://www.showerofschmidtdesigns.com

Formatting:
Irish Ink Publishing
http://www.facebook.com/IrishInkPublishing

Editor:
Eleanor Lloyd-Jones

A note to the reader

Light in the Dark is a collection of short stories put together by Dandelion Anthologies, with eleven different authors contributing. To keep up to date with the anthology and the authors, please follow the links:

Dandelion Anthologies
https://www.facebook.com/groups/221426099095022

J.A. Belfield
https://www.facebook.com/authorjabelfield

Clare Bentley
https://www.facebook.com/clarebentleyauthor/

D J Cook
https://www.facebook.com/AuthorDJCook/

Lizzie James
https://www.facebook.com/authorlizziejames

K. L. Jessop
https://www.facebook.com/AuthorK.L.Jessop

James Keith
https://www.facebook.com/jameskeith86

C.N. Marie
https://www.facebook.com/c.n.marieauthor

Tracie Podger
https://www.facebook.com/TraciePodgerAuthor

Finley Sawyer
https://www.facebook.com/AuthorFinleySawyer

Elle M Thomas
https://www.facebook.com/ellemthomasauthor

Lynda Throsby
https://www.facebook.com/LyndaThrosbyAuthor/

Dedicated to

...all those who struggle in the dark.
May you always find the light.

The Night Bus

J.A. BELFIELD

Chapter One

MORGAN KING STARED into darkness. She didn't need to think hard to know she'd been asleep only a moment before. Just as she didn't need to check the clock on her bedside table to know it was far from time for any normal person to be waking up, but she did so anyway, lifting her head a fraction enough from the pillow to view the glowing digits.

01:11. In the morning.

Yesterday, it had been 01:13. The day before that, 01:09.

Always the same time frame: never earlier than 01.00 itself; never later than 01:15.

As she always did, despite knowing it would never work, she forced herself to stay in place for another few minutes. Just in case.

Just in case she wasn't really awake.

Just in case she could fall back to sleep and rouse at a regular hour, like a regular gal, living a regular life.

And also as she always did, she threw back the covers on realising she had not a single chance of finding the oblivion she'd left behind before slumping from the bedroom to perform her next learned step of the night: making herself a hot chocolate in hopes that could succeed where her too-aware brain had not.

The ground floor apartment, which she'd occupied alone for the past two-ish years, felt as empty as it was as Morgan stepped along the hallway past the bathroom. On her right emerged the lounge, looking almost as lived-in as it had since the day she'd moved in almost three years earlier. Back then, though, she'd had more than her own mess to navigate. Back then, it had been the beginning of an exciting journey that had ended far sooner than anyone could have predicted.

Shaking away the images in her mind, of shoes that used to be left askew beside the sofa and music magazines that used to litter the coffee table, Morgan opened the door to the small kitchen, flipped on the light and crossed to the Tassimo in the corner. It took a minute, or so, of sleepy-eyed fiddling before the machine gurgled to life, and she leaned against the counter until it gave its final burp that let her know her steaming cup of cocoa was ready for consumption.

Taking her mug with her, she passed back into the lounge where she paused alongside the low bookcase. She picked up the small, framed photograph that always faltered her steps and demanded she stop and remember. Not that she needed the reminder. Morgan would never forget what she'd labelled snot-green eyes that'd always held such laughter—even more so at her refusal to change her description of them—or the tiny quirk of his lips that seemed to sit at a just-so angle whenever he'd looked at her.

Letting out a sigh shifted the heaviness trying to climb on top of her chest. There had been a time when a sigh would've stood no chance against the heartache, but all those who'd told her the pain got easier with time had actually known what they were talking about. It hadn't gone—maybe it never would—but it had eased.

Placing the picture back down, Morgan glanced toward the TV. Some nights, she resorted to that, but it never helped. Anyone who watched the screen in the early hours of the morning ended up either buying stuff their tired brain insisted they needed,

or even wider awake from holding their eyes open on the brightness they should've been avoiding if they wanted to sleep. No. Pointless shows and shopping channels would not fix Morgan's insomnia. She needed more.

As always, she'd just have to figure out what that was.

***

01.59. For almost thirty minutes, Morgan had stood in the same spot in the spare bedroom, staring at the blank canvas like it might propose a way forward. Sometimes, the whiteness spoke to her, demanding to be filled with colour and movement—demanding she give it a story to tell. Other nights, it stayed as eerily quiet as her mind was screeching loud.

It was definitely one of the 'other' nights.

After setting down the empty mug she'd been holding onto for too long, Morgan popped the laid-out paintbrushes back into the vase she used as a container and left the room. For a moment, she considered just going back to bed, climbing beneath the covers, and ordering her brain back to sleep.

It wouldn't listen, though. It rarely did. So she took

herself to the bedroom to prepare for the only thing that worked when all else failed.

A glance out through the window showed slush-turned snow and a sky clear enough to suggest there might be more to arrive. Knowing it would be cold out there, Morgan pulled her padded winter boots from beneath the bed, her thicker-denim jeans from the drawer, and her reindeer-patterned jumper from the back of the chair in the corner of the room. It took a few minutes to pull them all on over clean underwear, another few to work a brush through her dark hair and a smaller one over her teeth. Aside from the pale skin staring back at her in the mirror, and the even paler circles framing her hazel eyes, she labelled herself fit for public appearances and headed out for her coat.

As she stuck one arm in the sleeve, she strode through to the kitchen, her steps more purposeful with her clear plan in place. She pulled open one cupboard, closing it again on the tins inside, and then opened another, locking on the fresh bakery bag on the bottom shelf, which she drew out before working her second arm into the padded jacket and pushing back into the lounge.

By the front door in the corner, a trio of pegs held a colourful array of headwear. She skimmed over them all, already decided on the turquoise bobble hat to go with her navy coat before she got there. Once she'd wiggled it over her waves, and checked her breast pocket for her bank card, Morgan opened her front door on the awful weather outside.

Chapter Two

THE AIR SMELLED crisp and clear and cold enough to assure more snow than that left underfoot would be along within the next few hours. As Morgan stood at the bus stop near the post box on her street, she worried the regular services mightn't be operating. What if the weather had laid them off? Who the hell would get her through the night then?

She worried for only a moment, though, before shaking the thought off. The bus had been running whenever she'd needed it last winter, and it had been running the winter before that when she'd first discovered the much-needed reprieve to her newly restless mind.

Four minutes of standing there, and Morgan had taken up a dance of stomping at the ground. Not because her feet were cold—her boots made sure of that—but because her bloody legs were freezing, and her fingertips were slowly turning to ice because she'd forgotten to collect her damned gloves from the dresser before leaving. The hand holding the bakery bag had lost most of its feeling. She'd thought she hadn't time to run back in for them, not with the bus due, but with it not having turned up yet, maybe she should have.

Again, she entertained the idea that the bus might not come at all, but before she'd fully formed the argument and convinced herself to give in, headlights rounded the road's bend farther down the street and brought with them the rumble of an engine.

"Thank God for that," she muttered, sweeping her icy fingers around the plastic card in her pocket.

By the time the bus pulled to a stop, letting out a hiss as its doors opened, Morgan could no longer feel her nose—or most of her face, for that matter—and she hoped the smile she wore as she stepped up into the warmth didn't carry the look of a woman turned demented.

"'Morning, George," she called, shifting to tap her payment card. "Here again."

"'Morning," a voice responded, sounding almost hesitant—a voice that most definitely didn't belong to…

Morgan whipped up her head and stared into the eyes of a stranger. "You're not George."

"No, I'm not."

She glanced down to his chest, but the driver's cab held too little light to see a name badge, if he even wore one. "Where's George?"

"Off. Are you staying? Or are you going?"

Morgan stared hard at him, unsure what to do. Every single night bus she'd caught over the past couple of years, George had, without fail, been behind the wheel. Lovely, lovely George, who'd noticed at a glance that all hadn't been right with her world the first time he'd seen her, despite his curmudgeonly demeanour. A true gentleman who had taken her under his wing and fed her the words she'd needed to hear, time after time after time, and who'd offered an ear accompanied by patience when she'd finally been ready to talk through her woes.

"I don't mean to be rude, but in case you didn't notice yourself, I'm already running late because of this weather, so…"

Absently nodding, Morgan turned away from the scrutiny of the unfamiliar driver, but even though she fully intended doing a one-eighty and stepping back out into the frosty night, she found herself moving for the aisle.

A few feet in, and the bus doors hissed closed. The engine gave a low rumble, and her body jostled side to side as she wound her way through the mostly empty vehicle to the last low seat on the left.

She didn't know how, but that seat always seemed to be left free. She'd chosen that one on her first night-time journey and had continued to do so every other trip since, as if the universe simply *knew* when she would be coming and made sure her seat was reserved. She didn't know how she'd feel if she ever found someone else sitting there— what she'd do. Would she sit next to them? Find a new seat, start a new ritual in a completely new position? Would her expeditions under cover of darkness be the same if she did?

She didn't know.

Sliding between the gap, she lowered her rear onto the rough fabric, shuffling herself over until her shoulder hit the window. From there, she could study the vehicle's other occupants. Big guy, shoulders hunched—whether against the world, or against the cold, she couldn't be sure. Morgan had seen him before, a regular—one who kept to himself and spared nary a glance to any of the other passengers, like he hadn't the energy or wherewithal to be arsed with small talk, or even mustering up a smile.

She knew how he felt. She herself had been that way, before George had held out a virtual hand and helped her out of the lonely, dark hole.

Maybe someone should do the same for the big guy, show him he didn't have to sit alone, armour up against the world—someone who shared the bus with him for more than three stops, as Morgan always did.

Like usual, a few minutes down the bus's journey, the man heaved himself to his feet, as if it took all the effort he had in him, and lumbered from bar to bar until he slumped a shoulder against the pole near the door. His body jerked and swayed with the motion of the bus, and he planted a foot out when the brakes sent him forward a step, the readied opening of the door allowing a sound of wet sludge to roll in. As soon as the vehicle stopped, the guy barrelled outside into the cold, and as the journey continued, Morgan glanced over the few others left sitting before shifting her attention to beyond the half-misted windows.

Back when she'd first caught the bus, she'd been antsy, unsettled, irritated by life and all it'd dared throw at her. She'd spent the entire journey wanting to be somewhere else without knowing where that somewhere was. It had taken time for her to realise that it wasn't the bus she'd needed to be rid of, but her life as it was—the situation in which she'd found herself, the pain and turmoil, and the confusion over how to deal with it all. Emotions had a habit of doing that, though, didn't they? Slamming into a person with the force of a hurricane, before spinning them around and around until their minds no longer knew which way was up, leaving them a dizzied mess in the middle of a minefield they'd need to traverse before finding a safe ground upon which to function again.

Thankfully, Morgan's hurricane had been a fairly rapid one.

The minefield, though? Yeah, that'd taken quite the hike to overcome.

Outside, the pavements stood quiet and still. Very few lights shone from windows, but then very few people left their homes at such a ridiculous hour unless they had to. A new snowfall had begun, tiny flurries of whiteness floating through the air to land on the greying sogginess the previous bout had become. Morgan wasn't surprised to see it coming down—the very air had smelled of the stuff.

The bus jostled to a stop. One guy slipped out as another moved in to take his place.

That'd been something she'd noticed early on in her nocturnal adventures: how few women ventured out under the shield of night—in the week, anyway. Sunday to Thursday, Morgan rarely saw another woman. In fact, she could count on one hand the number of times she hadn't been the only one over the past couple of years, and on those times, she'd received almost pleading smiles, as if the very sight of another woman aboard the bus offered enormous relief to the other female travellers.

Weekends were another matter entirely, assuming, of course, she'd still to find solace by the time the last bus left from town. That was the bus all the clubbers piled into. Youngsters and hipsters all loud and obnoxious with alcohol, yet filled with an energy Morgan almost envied. She'd never really cared for the party life, had never really gone dancing when all her friends had begged her to join them for a night on the town.

Back then, Morgan had already been drunk on the life she'd been leading. Drunk on her creations. Drunk on warm evenings in the apartment, hot chocolate at the ready and enough marshmallows for a dozen people shared between only two ….

Drunk on Philip.

She'd had everything she'd needed. Until a piece of it had gone.

Chapter Three

FORTY-FIVE MINUTES of gentle movements, loud hisses and intermittent blasts of cold later, Morgan's people-and-weather watching had almost come to a pause, with the signs directing traffic the right way to pass through the city centre. In daytime, vehicles slowed to an agonising crawl as they navigated any others trying to muscle into the bottleneck of roads that narrowed more and more, the closer they got to the pedestrian zones. At night, the navigation held much less aggression with the lack of traffic on the roads.

As she often did, Morgan took a last look around at those who'd accompanied her on the trip, tried conjuring up reasons why they might be travelling into the heart of the area at such an hour. Was it because they, like herself, couldn't sleep? Or did their reasoning hold far more purpose than her own?

She guessed it was most probably the latter.

Around the quieter-than-usual flow of traffic along

the main bus route in, snow had begun a gradual gathering on the road outside. On the pavements, too. Morgan had always loved how the lamplight glow made it sparkle like diamonds, as if the world held secrets only the most perfect of environments could unleash for all to see—loved how a night-time snowfall could bring light to the darkness. She felt privileged to witness it as untouched as it was, before the crowds would bustle in during the more sociable daylight hours and mar its perfection with their trampling feet, uncaring for little beyond their purchasing missions.

The bus slowed to an even lesser speed than already adopted. Feet scuffed the floor as the gentle swish of movement surrounded the vehicle's interior. Morgan tore her gaze away from the wintriness of outside to watch the departing bodies trail down the centre aisle with as little enthusiasm as she had once felt for life.

One, then two, followed by three and four, passengers disembarked into the cold, the bus dancing a gentle jive with each of them. Three long seconds passed, during which Morgan held her breath. After all, she only usually travelled with George—kind and caring George, who would never dream of kicking her out into the night. She had no idea how the new driver would feel about company.

She finally exhaled at the heavy sigh of the doors closing and allowed herself to relax back into her seat. Eyes on the driver's cabin, Morgan waited. Waited for his opinion on her being there—for his opinion of *her*.

Though why she cared, she didn't know.

Maybe because a very real fear that George may never come back had ghosted through her mind—and if that happened?

Well, if that happened, she'd have to figure out a new routine, a new venture, a new way to exhaust herself when her brain wouldn't rest.

The lights of the bus went off, setting Morgan in more shadow than George usually placed the two of them in. The engine died, leaving a peacefulness in its wake. She listened to the movement up front, felt the stir of shifting about, and tensed once more when the driver's interior door clicked open.

A large silhouette appeared on the platform: broad shoulders, and tall, like he'd had to unfold himself from the confined space in which he'd been sitting. Morgan saw slight movement before the driver's door creaked shut—heard a sigh, a sniff, fabric brushing against fabric .... And then the driver began making his way down the aisle. Toward her.

In the dimmed interior, she watched his approach—wondered where his gaze roamed. Did it study her as hard as she watched him?

A few more steps brought the driver alongside her seat, and she could take the silent scrutiny no longer.

"Thanks for not kicking me off," she said.

The driver jerked backward and fell into the seat opposite. "Jesus Christ!"

She reached out a hand as if to stop what'd already happened. "Sorry."

"You scared the bloody life out of me," he said.

"Sorry," she said again. "I thought you knew I was here."

"Maybe I would if you were supposed to be here. But you're not."

"I know, but…"

"Come on." He pushed back to his feet. "I'll see you down to the door."

Morgan stared at his shadowed outline, unsure for a

moment, before she admitted, "George always lets me stay on."

"Well … George *shouldn't* let you stay on."

"No, no, it's fine," she said, shifting across the bench toward him. "He says it's okay, so long as I stay out of the way, and—"

"Doesn't matter," the driver said. "You're not supposed to be here. Don't you have some place to be?"

"Yes, here." She nodded at him. "On the bus."

"Except, you can't—"

"Listen," she pleaded, "If you kick me off, all that will happen is, I'll be standing out there freezing my cahoodles off while waiting for you to finish your break and start your return journey."

"And then where will you go?" He sounded like he frowned, although Morgan hadn't a clue if he actually did.

"Well … I'll get back on your bus."

Nothing. He was probably staring at her like she was crazy—a debatable topic, she supposed.

"See?" she said. "That's why George just lets me stay on. He says it's not safe for me to be standing around the city centre in the middle of the night. He said—"

"Fine." He took a step back, and she caught the movement of his arms as he raised his hands. "But …. Just …. No funny business, okay?"

She drew an *X* over her chest with her finger, hoping he could see. "Cross my heart."

"Sure," he muttered before retreating back down the aisle.

A moment later, low lighting flickered down the front of the bus, casting just enough glow for Morgan to catch the apprehension on the driver's face when he turned back towards her. He didn't start back her way at first, seeming somehow hesitant about doing so. What he thought she might do, she didn't know. The guy was twice her breadth and had more than a foot of height over her five-two. If anyone should've been worried, surely it should be herself.

As if finally reaching a decision, he quietly cleared his throat then wandered back between the seats, pausing alongside hers.

"George and I usually sit at the back on his break," she told him as if he'd asked the question.

Head tilted, he stared at her. With his back to the light source, shadows stole his expression, but that only made her want to see it all the more. His head started shaking. She wondered if he was about to refuse her, although she hadn't exactly asked him anything, had she?

Instead, he lifted his palm a little. "Fine," he muttered before lumbering along the rest of the bus. "But we're not sharing a seat."

Morgan couldn't help smiling at her second small—or was that big—victory of the night as she clutched hold of her paper bag and slid out into the aisle behind him. He really did take up a lot of room with his wide shoulders, even discounting the drooping rucksack hanging from his shoulder, yet he somehow managed to move with an easy grace his size belied.

At the back of the bus, he had to duck his head as he stepped up and swung to the right, where he slid his rear along the seat until, near the window, he faced the front. Complying with his stated term, Morgan climbed up to the left. She just didn't slide quite as far along the bench as he had. Assuming he'd even continue talking to her, she'd rather not have to be calling from opposing sides of the bus.

From the corner of her eye, she watched as he

dumped his rucksack down on the rear-facing bench opposite him. The slide of the zip sounded loud in the quiet between them, as did the guy's rummaging around.

Allowing herself to look at him more fully, she held out her own bag. "Croissant?"

He quit delving and twisted toward her, but he didn't reach out or speak.

"It's a thing," she said. "Between me and George." She tried for a smile, unsure if he would even see it with how dim it was up back. "If I get the bus."

"What's a thing?" he finally asked—probably to stop her waffling.

"I bring a snack," she said.

He let out a sigh like he had no idea what to do with her and turned back to his bag search.

"I mean, I bring a snack to share with George," she said, a little deflated when he appeared to be ignoring her. "And George shares his drink with me."

"You want me to share my drink with you?" he asked, his movements stilling with his hand still deep inside his rucksack.

"Oh, I'm not saying you have to. I'm just saying …" that's what George normally …" She shrugged.

"What if I don't have a drink?"

"Well, sometimes, George pops across to the all-night newsagents and grabs hot chocolates from the machine."

"Of all the buses," he muttered as if he thought she couldn't hear him. From his profile, she knew he'd raised his face to the ceiling—could just see the movement of his muttering lips. When his head dropped back down, it faced her. "How many croissants do you have?"

Chapter Four

MORGAN SMILED. YET another small barrier broken down. "Two," she said. "One each. If you want one, of course."

"Sure," he said, and despite the low grumble of his voice, Morgan decided she quite liked the sound of it.

She worked open the scrunched neck and held the paper bag out. "Help yourself."

The bag rustled with his acceptance of the offer, and with a quiet, "Thanks," he took the pastry straight to his mouth.

Morgan watched him for a second. The streetlamp outside the bus lined the edge of his jaw with light as he chewed. He had a strong jaw—not jutting, nothing too prominent, but definitely strong.

"Why aren't you eating yours?" he asked, barely breaking between bites to speak, and Morgan jerked her hand into the bag, grabbed out her own croissant, and joined him in chewing her way through the buttery goodness. She'd barely gotten halfway through when he dusted his empty hands against each other.

"It was a good croissant," he said.

She nodded. "I get them from Sprinkles Of Joy. Corner of Chumbrey High Street?"

"I know the one. Never been there myself."

"You're missing out."

"So it seems." From his bag, he withdrew a flask, its metal flashing as it caught the light outside. For a moment, he stared down toward it in his hand—seemed to be contemplating if he should make an offer in return—before his face lifted toward her. "Did you …?" He wiggled the flask in her direction.

"What have you got?" she asked, wiping crumbs from her mouth.

He seemed to grimace. "Green tea, I'm afraid."

"With honey?"

"Manuka, yeah."

She smiled. "I loved green tea with honey."

He shook his head, and what sounded like a low chuckle carried across the bench seat, making Morgan smile even wider. Another barrier booted, another small victory. How many could she wheedle her way through and over before her journey was through?

She watched as he poured the liquid into one of the flask's cups before twisting to hand it to her. "Thanks." Taking the hot drink, she breathed in the warmth and sweetness of it.

"Can I ask you something?" he said, pouring a second drink.

Morgan nodded. "Sure." Anything to keep him talking, especially as he'd done so of his own accord.

"Why are you even catching the bus at this ridiculous

hour?"

Her shoulders stiffened slightly, a reaction she'd never been able to control.

"If you don't have somewhere you're actually going to, I mean."

She let out a slow breath, nodding as if to encourage herself to continue. "I lost someone."

He paused in re-lidding the flask, his body seeming to tense as much as her own had. "I'm sorry."

"Thanks."

"Was it … recent?"

"No, not recent." She gave a small shrug. "Not really. Just …"

"It was a tough one to let go of." Not a question, but an understanding.

"Yeah."

"Must be hard, if it doesn't let you sleep."

"I sleep," she said. "Just a little bit unsociably."

"That's hard in itself."

She took a sip of her drink before agreeing with him.

He tapped the side of his plastic cup. "Too much time to think of a night, I guess. Fewer distractions."

"Actually, I think it's just that we had a routine, you know?"

"Routines are hard to break out of," he said.

"He worked the late shift," she said. "At a parcel sorting centre."

"Late hours are hard."

"They are," she agreed. "He started at six in the evening. Worked through until midnight. By the time he'd finish packing up there for night and gotten himself home, it would be just past one."

"And what about you? Your work?"

"Oh, I work for myself," she said, waving him off. "But I'd be in bed when he came home." Her lips curved, though she wasn't sure why. "And I'd wake every time. Right before he walked in the door."

"Like you knew he was there."

"Weird, right?"

"Sounds nice, not weird. You must have had a strong connection."

"We did."

"How long has it been since …"

"Just over two years now."

"And you're still waking up for him."

"Not for him. Not anymore, anyway. I think …" She cupped her drink, suddenly needing the warmth. "I kind of moved on from constant mourning a little while back, you know? I still miss him, but not to the extent that I can't get on. Or can't move on. I just …"

"Can't seem to stop the body clock from doing its thing."

"Yeah."

His shoulders hunched around his chest as he sat with his elbows resting on his knees, palms grasping his cup as if he needed warmth as much as she did. Though he hadn't looked at her once as she'd spilled her story, he leaned in towards her then. "But I still don't get why you're catching the bus in the middle of the night."

"Seems my body just loves routines," she said, letting out a small laugh. "A good while back, I caught the bus one night when I really couldn't get back to sleep. At least when Philip was still … you know. At least then, I fell back to sleep quite easily. Now?" She shook her head. "Anyway, I decided to go for a walk one night, and as I got to the bottom of my road, I saw the bus coming and figured *What the hell?"*

"And you've been getting the night bus ever since."

"Blame George."

"Why George?" he asked.

"Because he …. I don't know. He was *there* for me that first night I caught the bus. And I *really* needed someone to be there for me. I mean, obviously I have friends and family, but there's only so much they can listen to, and only so many times you can hear their same placations over and over again in the exact same tones as all the other times. Which makes me sound really ungrateful for them—"

"You just needed a fresh talking to from someone who didn't know him."

"Yes," she said, nodding. "Yes, you're right."

"George is your personal shrink." He said it deadpan, but she heard the humour in his voice.

"My shrink," she said, laughing. "He'd love that."

"Do you see your shrink every night? Is he expensive?"

"Around the cost of a pastry plus the bus fare," she said, grinning. "And not every night. Just when I can't find a distraction, or feel edgy, or … I don't know. If I'm just *bored*, I guess."

"Ah, boredom. The destructive town in which negative thoughts are bred."

"See?" she said. "You know."

"Sadly, yes." He screwed his emptied cup onto the top of his flask before looking to her. "Finished?"

She swigged down the last inch of her tea and handed him the cup. "Thanks."

"My break finishes in about two minutes," he said as he fed the flask back into his rucksack.

31

"Does it really?" It'd gone really fast—even faster than with George.

"'Fraid so. But ..." He clipped his bag shut and dragged it onto his lap. "It's been nice having the company for a change." With that, he hauled himself up off the seat and wove through the benches to the front of the bus.

Morgan watched his retreating back, trying to find something a little more discernible than what the dim lighting had given her during their talk. Just as he reached the driver's door, he turned back to her beneath the dull lamp and smiled. And oh, what a lovely smile he had, all tiny dimples at the corners of his lips, and crinkles at the edges of his warm eyes. After running a hand through chestnut brown hair, he pulled open his door and disappeared out of sight.

Chapter Five

01:03. THE NUMBERS GLOWED from the bedside clock bright enough to pierce Morgan's eyes.

She'd had nowhere near enough sleep since the night before—since finding someone else in place of George behind the wheel of the bus.

Someone whose name she had no idea of, for which she probably should've asked.

Someone who might've been to blame for her lack of rest.

As she'd stood at the front of the bus, waiting for it to brake at her stop, she couldn't help studying him out the corner of his eye. With a streetlamp sinking through the window from a different angle, she'd been able to see him slightly better and drank in as many details as her brief stolen moment had allowed: the slight flick of hair that hung over the left side of his brow, the sharpness of his nose, but in a proud rather than pompous-looking way—a Roman nose, her gran would call it.

And then, when the bus had stopped and the doors had opened, he'd turned and almost caught her staring, but his smile had lit up any remaining darkness.

"Thanks for the company," he'd said.

"You're welcome," she'd told him and stepped back out into the night.

You're welcome.

Why the hell had she said that, when there were a *host* of departing words she could've chosen instead.

I'm Morgan, by the way.
Sorry, I didn't catch your name.
So, what bus do you usually drive?

But no, just a simple *'You're welcome'*.

Once she'd let herself back into the apartment, she'd shed her outerwear by the front door and headed straight through to the kitchen, suddenly fancying a cup of the green tea she hadn't touched in a long while. From there, she'd gone straight through to the spare bedroom, where she'd picked up a paintbrush, squirted out a blob of raw sienna, another of cerulean blue, and a few others: titanium white, Payne's grey, burnt umber. With her tea in one hand, her brush in the other, she'd set about putting colour to canvas for the first time in weeks.

It had been three hours later that she'd stripped herself of her remaining clothing—uncaring that she'd need to replace what had become paint-spattered items—and climbed beneath the covers. Ordinarily, that would be the point where she'd sleep. Ordinarily, her routine wouldn't have been altered, and she'd have offloaded to George, instead of a stranger with warm eyes and a smile that didn't seem to want to leave her mind.

There was so much she hadn't got to tell him. Like, how Philip had died at the claws of a forklift when the driver hadn't been paying enough attention to what he'd been moving toward, and how they'd thought Philip must've been sleeping on his break for him to not have realised the danger moving his way. Or how she'd spent almost an entire year unable to move on from the life she'd had, unable to let go of the future she'd hoped to live. She'd never got to tell him how far she'd come since then—how much easier she found life, and how she didn't find the thought of moving forwards alone as completely terrifying as she once had.

Would she have told him, even if she'd had the chance, though?

He was one guy. She'd met him only once, completely by chance, and had spent a grand total of twenty-two minutes with him before he'd left her sitting at the back of that bus.

Maybe that might've been too heavy a topic for a chance meeting with someone she didn't even know. He'd have probably shifted about all uncomfortable with her openness, like most people tended to when faced with the topic of death. He'd probably have looked at her with relief at her departure rather than the smile he'd allowed. But then again …

Balling her hands into fists, she squashed them into the dips of her eyes and let out a groan. Obsessing. Re-enacting. Obsessing again. Rewriting the script.

Did other folk fixate on circumstances it was too late to alter like she did? Her gran said it was the downside of her creative mind—an over-imagination, she called it.

Morgan wondered if the bus driver had been thinking about *her* since she'd stepped from the bus as much as she'd been thinking about him.

Inside her tummy, butterflies kicked up, unbidden and uncontrolled, flitting about against the walls of her abdomen. She knew immediately what they represented: excitement at having met a man who'd seeped inside her brain as much as Philip had the first time she'd met him—alongside dread, guilt, fear, all for exactly the same reasons.

Lying there in the dark, her open curtains allowing branched shadows to dance across her ceiling, she reminded herself again—tortured herself again.

You didn't even ask his name.

Knowing she would never, ever sleep with her mind rolling over everything so stupendously, she flung back the covers and climbed from the bed, and as she did so, she had a thought she should've considered sooner.

What if George had another night off?

Chapter Six

SHE'D BEEN RIGHT about the weather she'd forecasted. Although the central section of the pavements had been trodden down and sullied, the outer edges had formed into small mounds of whiteness, only the occasional blip to their perfection created by people having stepped closer to the kerb. In both directions, tiny diamond-like sparkles bordered the road as Morgan stood stomping her booted feet, surrounded by a mist of her own departed breath. At least she'd remembered her gloves.

She half expected the bus to be late again—after all, the weather had worsened since the early hours of the night before—but almost smack on time, she caught the tiny growl of its engine, chased by the appearance of headlights up at the corner.

As it slowed near the stop, small sprays of melting slush arced up onto the kerbs. Morgan took a small step back, putting the tiny tingles running beneath her skin down to the cold, and waited until the bus had stopped completely before moving forwards again. With their usual hiss, the doors flapped open, and she climbed up into the warmth of her haven, barely able to control the grin trying to take over her face.

"'Morning," she called, bakery bag held at chest height lest he miss her intention.

"How you doin', kid?"

Going from the darkness of outside, it took a fraction of a second for her eyes to adjust and confirm who the voice belonged to.

"Oh … George. Hi."

"Who were you expecting? George Clooney?"

"George Clooney is a little old for me, don't you think?"

"You young uns." He jerked his chin over his shoulder. "Go on and sit down now. You're letting in all the cold."

With a nod, Morgan drifted off down the aisle, her chest filled with a deflation she had no idea how to interpret. She never got disappointed about seeing George—George was her whole reason for catching the bus in the middle of the night, and had been for the past couple of years—so why was she suddenly wishing he was somebody else?

A certain someone else with a small flop of brown hair and a smile that changed his entire face when he showed it.

Barely even seeing the other passengers, Morgan moved toward her regular seat, even twisted to wiggle in, but halted when her eyes connected with those of a tired-looking guy and an expression that said he'd rather she stopped right there and turned herself around.

It had finally happened.

First, she'd caught the bus and George hadn't been

driving.

And now somebody has stolen my seat.

How many changes could the world expect her to adapt to within the same week?

"Sorry," she muttered, turning away. On seeing the opposite seat free, she paused. She could, she supposed, have asked the intruder to take that seat instead—explained to him that she usually sat where he'd chosen and how much she liked her routines and didn't really like having to change the details of her life without a little forethought.

Obsessing, more like, her gran would say.

Yes, the rational part of her brain knew he wouldn't understand the workings of her mind—not when she didn't 'get' them herself. That, or he wouldn't care. So, taking a deep breath, she sank into the seat that *was* free, and settled herself in for the ride.

***

The hat Morgan wore protected her temple from the cold window against which she rested her head. Half-heartedly watching the streets pass by between glancing up at new arrivals and those getting off, she solemnly counted down the stops between her and the city centre.

Would she stay on, as usual? Chat to George, as she always had?

Or maybe she needed to leave and try a new experience before getting the bus home. After all, occurrences were said to come in threes, and that would complete the trilogy of routine breaks for her, right?

In its usual fashion, the bus slowed nearer the end of its route. As usual, everyone but her started fidgeting, some already climbing from their seats to make their way towards the exit.

Morgan had always liked 'usual'—normal, patterns, and order. They counteracted the disorder she often displayed in her art and calmed the too-present chaos of her mind.

The night before had been the first blip in that order, and if anyone had asked her prior to it happening, she'd have told them she'd hate it—that people had routines for a reason and that needed to be respected.

Except, she hadn't hated it. Not a single bit.

The bus finally stopped, the doors swinging aside and creating an opening over the same piece of pavement they always did. Morgan stared down toward where the handful of passengers climbed from the bus and slunk off into the gloom of the city. She was still staring that way when the doors secured her inside, and George emerged from his space, the low light at the front of the bus all that remained to show the way.

He ambled his almost sixty-year-old body along the aisle, flask in hand, coming to a stop beside the bench where Morgan sat. "Why so blue tonight, kid?"

"Not blue," she said, moving only her eyes to look at him. "Just …" She shrugged.

"You better come tell me all about it," he said, and he carried on along to the back of the bus, leaving Morgan to follow behind.

With a grunt and a heavy sigh, George climbed up onto the rear bench and patted the seat beside him as he always did.

Accepting the invitation, Morgan settled herself where he'd indicated and held up her paper bag. "Custard doughnut do you?"

"It'll more than do."

"What's on your menu?" she asked, as he set his flask

down on the facing seat.

"Hot chocolate. Anything else just wouldn't have worked against all this snow."

Morgan smiled. George always said odd little things like that. Maybe that was why she enjoyed his company. It meant she didn't have to be slightly odd all on her own.

"What happened to your jeans?" he asked, tapping just the tip of a finger against a blob of cerulean blue paint.

"Art happened."

"Ah." Twisting towards her, he studied her for a moment before lightly tapping that same fingertip against the rim of her hat. "And what happened to your head?"

"I got last night's bus," she said.

He lifted his chin in acknowledgment of her words, offering another, "Ah."

Reaching over to the opposite seat, he unscrewed the mugs from the flask, carefully placing them down on the fabric before, equally as carefully, pouring a portion of steaming hot chocolate into each.

"I know you might find it hard to believe," he said, handing her one of the mugs, "but I do occasionally need time off, you know."

She sighed. "I know."

He lifted his mug and took a sip. "Did he kick you off—the other driver?"

"No, thankfully." Her lips curved at the memory. "He was going to, but …"

"You talked him 'round. Aye," he said, nodding. "You're good at that."

"It didn't take much effort, to be fair."

"*I* didn't take much effort."

"You didn't take any effort, at all."

He raised his mug as if in toast. "Like I said."

Morgan released a quiet laugh.

"So, what has that pretty face of yours looking all dour, then?"

"Oh, nothing really."

"It ain't nothing when you come onto my bus all frowning on seeing me."

"I didn't frown." She frowned then. "Did I?"

With a wry smile, he gave a nod of his head.

"Sorry. It's just …. God, I don't even know."

"Was he mean to you—this chap from last night?"

"No, he was nice."

"He was, eh?"

"Yes, he sat at the back with me when I asked him. Although, he did insist on sitting way at the other side of the bench."

"Yeah, well … you can be quite terrifying."

"Hey!" She lightly elbowed his side before sighing and thinking back to the night before.

"Talk to me." George gently nudged her with his own elbow. "And get the doughnuts out if you ever planned to share."

The bag rustled as she offered it to George first, but she didn't reach in for her own. "The driver last night was nice," she said.

"We covered that one," George said around his mouthful.

"I don't know what else to say."

"I take it he talked to you?"

"He did, yes. Reluctantly at first, but he seemed to … just give in, I guess."

"Or maybe he quit trying to figure you out and just went with it."

"Maybe."

He took another bite of his sugary ball, chewing before asking, "So, what did the two of you talk about?"

Morgan shrugged. "Mostly just about why I was catching buses in the middle of the night when I don't actually go anywhere other than back home again."

"Did he run away at that point?" George asked, a hint of laughter in his tone.

"No, actually."

"I'm impressed."

"Hey!" she said for a second time, needling his ribs again.

"I meant with *you*."

Her half-smile faded. "Why me?"

"Okay, maybe him, too."

She wobbled her head, eyebrows raised in question.

"Well, you must've told him all about yourself within, what? Five, ten minutes of talking?"

"I told *you* all about myself when we just met."

"Actually, it took until about your fourth journey with me before you finally opened up and talked."

"No, I—" she started, but stopped at his nodding. "Surely not."

"Surely so."

"Wow," she muttered. That was *not* how she remembered it. At all.

"Must've been a pretty special driver manning my bus last night."

"Maybe." Another mutter.

"That, or you're not quite as lost as you once were." He nudged her with his knee as he climbed to his feet. "Come on now, back to your seat." Scooping up his flask, he brushed past her and stepped down into the aisle. "You can give your cup back when you leave. And *eat* something," he added as he walked away.

Morgan watched George all the way back to the front of the bus, where he ducked back into his driving kiosk and knocked the lights back on. Then she hauled herself up and back to where she was sitting before. For a moment, she considered climbing up into the seat she'd occupied every other time she'd caught the bus, but she'd survived the deviance of having to move, hadn't she? Something had forced her out of a habit, and she hadn't freaked out, or had a meltdown, and didn't feel full of distress at the idea of sitting somewhere else. Not anymore, anyway.

Ignoring the pull towards the last low bench on her right, she stepped up into the one on the left, settling herself in with her hot chocolate with one hand while reaching for her doughnut with the other.

A moment later, the bus rumbled to life, gave a slight wobble, then started off on its loop around the island to the first stop of the journey across the street.

As two passengers climbed aboard, Morgan allowed them each a cursory glance before tucking into her meal. Neither of them looked her way. That was the trouble with commuting. Some might call it social travel, which was pretty ironic really, considering so few who used it wanted to make eye contact, let alone fully engage. A lonely existence while surrounded by others.

It was a lifestyle Morgan had come to know well—a lifestyle she might have, at one time, embraced. A lot had changed in her over the past year, though, and even more had changed in one night.

One by one, passengers boarded along the route before hopping off later down the line, and before Morgan knew it, George pulled up at the stop nearest her apartment.

His door clicked open, and he poked his head out. "You going, or staying a while?"

She thought about it for a moment before shifting from her seat. "Going."

Ignoring the curious stares of the passengers—because anything different to their considered norm could get them looking, apparently—she edged her way to the front and handed over her empty mug. "Thanks for the hot chocolate."

"Thanks for the doughnut," he said, taking the cup.

"And thanks for listening. As always."

"The guy who covered me last night?"

At George's serious tone, she lifted her eyes to his.

"His name is Tom Michaels."

"Tom Michaels." The name sounded almost angelic floating past her lips.

"He usually drives the eighty-seven bus. Mornings 'til early afternoon."

Morgan stared at him, unsure why he'd told her, until he smiled and winked.

"Now, go get some sleep. Freshen up. You're going to need it."

"Thanks, George," she said and hopped down from the bus onto a wintry street that no longer felt quite so cold.

Chapter Seven

MORGAN HADN'T JUMPED out of bed the next morning and raced to the eighty-seven stop. As much as she'd wanted to, the same brain sending encouragement also paralysed her with nerves and worry, and two days passed before she managed to ignore her inner stress and kick her own arse out into the melting snow and lingering cold.

The queue at Sprinkles Of Joy reached to the door, which was nothing unusual, and Morgan took the time to carefully consider the menu. Usually, she just ordered whatever looked the most tempting from the display, but she needed to be sure for once—sure that she made the right choice to accompany the boldness she hadn't cared to display for too long.

"What'll it be?" Claire, the bakery owner, asked. "Cinnamon roll? Cookie? Or something savoury, for a change?"

Morgan smiled at the blonde woman, knowing she'd

likely surprise her. "Two fresh cream red velvet cupcakes please."

That earned her a sidelong glance. "Going for the big guns today."

"In a box," Morgan added.

Claire's eyebrow lifted. Probably because Morgan had requested more formal packaging than her usual paper bag. "Well, well, well," she said, already unfolding the cake box and shaking her head. "I hope these aren't both for you. They're much more filling than your usual."

"They aren't," Morgan admitted, even though Claire had likely already figured that out.

"Atta girl." With a wink, she popped two of the indulgent cakes into the box and handed them over. "You'll have to tell me how you get on."

"I will. And keep the change," she said, leaving a fiver on the counter.

From the bakery, she headed away from home for a short way, taking a turn onto Merryway Road and heading for a stop she'd never had much use for before, not with its far more direct route to the city centre's edge before continuing on to the next county over.

A small queue had formed at the stop—probably because the bus was near due, which was information Morgan had looked into prior to leaving the apartment. Joining the back of it, she found herself humming along to *Anti-Lullaby* by Karen-O, a song she found soothing, despite the underlying darkness to it.

As one minute passed, followed by two, she dipped into the dangerous territory of questioning her plan. What if she got on the bus and he wasn't even driving?

What if he was driving but had no idea who she was?

She glanced over her shoulder, considering making a

hasty getaway before she'd be confronted with a definite decision, but more people had joined the queue, boxing her in from behind. She'd have to weave her way around everyone else just to leave.

"Henry, come on now. The bus is coming."

Morgan spun back around to see a young boy sliding in close to what must have been his mother and taking her hand, and beyond them, the front of the bus loomed large and intimidating as it squealed to a halt at the bus stop's exit.

Bodies around her hustled in tighter, giving her little choice but to be carried forwards on their wave of movement. Before she even had chance to fully panic, she'd reached the entryway to the bus's steps, and with a passenger to her side and another at her back, she stepped up onto the platform and raised her face.

Warm eyes met hers. Hazel ones, she realised— something she'd missed in the limited light a few nights previous. That same lock of wavy hair still clung to the one side of his brow.

Just to be sure, she lowered her gaze to his name badge, also more visible than before.

"Erm … hello, Tom."

"Hey."

"I, um … I don't know if you remember, but—"

"I remember," he said, a skewed smiling forming.

For a moment, she just stood there. She'd have been quite happy simply looking at that wonky smile of his for a while, but someone cleared their throat behind her.

"Come *on*," someone else said.

Ignoring them, she held up her bakery bag. "I have snacks."

His smile grew. "I have green tea."

"Perfect," she said.

"My break's not for over an hour."

"I can wait."

He breathed out a laugh and shook his head like she amused him. "You better take a seat, then."

"I guess so," she said.

THE END

Screaming in Silence

CLARE BENTLEY

Before

THE COLD WINTER night starts to close in around me and my two friends as we hang out on the swings at the park. It's our usual haunt, and unlike in the summer, we're the only ones there. None of us have been home yet: we came here straight after school. It's something I've started doing since my mum's shop extended their hours because I don't want to be at home, alone, with him. Elyssa and Amelia have only been joining me for the past week after finding me here on their way to the shop one night.

My friend, Elyssa, looks at her watch, her long, deep auburn hair falling off her shoulder. "I'd better get home. Mum will kill me if I'm late for dinner," she says, climbing off the swing she's spent most of the night on.

Elyssa is the oldest of us by three months. She's a natural blonde but prefers bright colours on her hair—pinks and reds usually. She shocked me and Amelia when she went for a toned-down version of the latter on her last visit to the hairdressers. She and Amelia are next-door neighbours and have been friends since they were born. I'm the outsider so to speak, moving to the area six years ago.

I feel the curls of my dyed, jet-black hair bounce against the middle of my back as I jump off the brick wall I'm sitting on and land on my feet in her path. "It's Friday night, Lys. Can't you stay out a bit longer?" I know I'm begging, but I really don't want to go home yet.

Though Elyssa squints her bright blue eyes at me, it's Amelia who speaks. "What's going on with you lately, Bonnie? It's like you don't want to go home."

I hadn't thought they'd noticed. I'd thought I was better at disguising my hatred for being at home, but Amelia rarely misses a trick. She's the one who pays the most attention out of the group, so I don't know why I'm surprised she's seen through the façade I put up every day.

I shake my head and overt my dark blue eyes. I can't tell them; I can't tell anybody. "It's nothing. I just wanted to hang out for longer."

Amelia, the short-haired brunette with emerald eyes, is the youngest of us by a month, and she's the only one with older siblings: one sister and two brothers. She picks up her schoolbag and slings it over her shoulder. "I can't, Bon. My uncle's coming over tonight."

"Yeah, me neither. If I'm late for dinner again this week, Mum's going to ground me," Elyssa adds, putting her bag over her head to cross over her body and untucking the hair trapped by the strap.

I shrug as though it isn't a big deal, picking my rucksack up off the floor. "Yeah, I should get back anyway."

Amelia pulls the hood of her coat and starts to walk away with Elyssa. "See you tomorrow?"

"Sure."

I stand and watch them get further away, prolonging my arrival home. When they disappear around the corner, I turn and head through the park to get to my street. I shove my earphones in and hit play on my iPod. I plan to take my time; I'm in no rush to get back.

As Twenty One Pilots start to fill my ears, I shuffle along the pavement at a pace that's half my usual speed. If I had elsewhere to go, I wouldn't hesitate, but my dad is overseas serving our country in the army, and I'm not sure when he's coming home; everything is top secret.

By the time I get to my front door, it's taken me twice as long as it usually would. I take a deep breath to prepare to come face-to-face with what's awaiting me inside, and I put my key in the lock.

Pushing the door open, my mum appears in the hallway as soon as I'm inside, and the smell of food makes my stomach ache.

The petite woman, with beautiful bright green eyes and pixie cut brown hair, takes my coat from me as I shake it off and hangs it on the hook.

"Just in time for dinner," she almost sings.

"I'm not hungry. I'm just going to go to my room," I say, breezing past her on my mission to get up there. I'm starving; I just don't want to be around *him*—not if I can help it.

But Mum gently grabs my arm before I reach the bottom step. She pleads, whining like I used to when I didn't get my own way. "C'mon, love. You haven't eaten with us all week. It'd be nice to see you for more than five minutes."

The sadness in my mother's eyes weakens my resolve and I feel a twinge of guilt. I miss spending time with her like we used to, just the two of us—but he ruined everything when he came along.

My parent's split up six years ago, when I was ten, and I've always hoped they'd get back together. Even when mum brought home a boyfriend a year later, I still had hope. Though when she married Trevor six months later, I had to face the fact that my parents would never be a couple again.

It made me sad more than angry, and I blamed myself for the longest time, even though they both told me it wasn't my fault—they were bound to say that. I still don't know the real reason; I doubt I ever will.

I gave my stepdad a chance at first—there was no point fighting them being together after the wedding—but that lasted a month before he shit all over it at his first available opportunity.

"What are we having?" I ask, letting her know she's won.

***

I keep my eyes down to avoid looking across the table where he's sitting because I can't bear to look at him. He makes me sick to my stomach. I scoff the food on my plate down—the quicker I'm finished, the quicker I can disappear to my bedroom—but he's not content with my silence: he wants to torture me more than he already has. His dirty little secret is in jeopardy if he isn't seen to be acting normal; he's got to make it seem as though *I'm* the problem.

"How was school today?" He asks, and I ignore him, unable to bring myself to be civil—even for the sake of my mum.

An unmistakeable tension instantly falls around the table between us, and my mum speaks to try and cut through it.

"Trevor asked you a question," she says as if I haven't heard.

My eyes stay fixed on the food in front of me, what little is left, and I reply with the minimum words I can muster. "All right."

I can feel the disappointment projected my way from my mother. She thinks I don't like her husband because he's not my dad, but it's for reasons far more twisted than that—ones Mum can *never* find out about.

Finishing the last morsel of food, I stand to put my plate in the sink before I've even swallowed. "Thanks for dinner." I turn to leave the room.

But Mum stops me. "Hey, where are you going?"

"I've got homework," I lie.

"Can't you do that over the weekend? I was hoping we could watch a film tonight as a family."

I hate it when she calls us that. "We're not a family, Mum: Dad's not here."

She sighs. "C'mon, Bonnie. It's time you stopped punishing Trevor for getting in the way of what you want and face the fact that this is it. Me and your dad are over."

I'm bolstered with anger at her assumption of why I'm acting the way I am. I can't believe how blind she is to what's happening to me.

"It's not that, Mum." I glance at her husband and swear I can see him holding his breath, worried about what I'm going to say.

"Then what is it?" I hear Mum say, but I continue to stare at him.

I'm reminded of the words he's repeated over and over.

"No one will believe you. If it's a choice between me and you, it's me they'll listen to; I'm the adult. All you'll do is break your mother's heart and you'll be taken away from her."

I've been living with the weight of those words for the last five years, and I don't want to believe him. But what if it's true?

I swallow down the confession on the tip of my tongue, too scared to tell her. "Never mind; it doesn't matter."

The interrogation doesn't go any further and I'm relieved yet a little disheartened that she's willing to let it go so easily. Why doesn't she see that the way I've changed over the years is out of character and demand answers? I heard her once tell a friend of hers that she thought it was just because I was a teenager, but surely there's a part of her that knows me better than that.

I see the hope in her eyes. "Then you'll join us for a film?"

My shoulders drop with the weight on them. "Yes."

***

Sitting in the armchair across the room with my knees pulled up to my chest, I can feel his dark brown eyes on me. I've chosen this seat purposely because it's the furthest I can be from him while still being in the same room. If I had my way, I wouldn't be here at all. I'd be hiding out in my bedroom, but I can't stand to disappoint my mother again.

I'm trying to concentrate on the film playing, but I can feel my skin crawling under his gaze, and I wonder if my mother has noticed the way he looks at me, but surely if she had, she would have had questions. Did she even notice when I'd started to avoid being left alone in a room with him? I wonder if she cares.

Shouldn't she have seen the sadness across my face the morning after the first time? Shouldn't she have been able to tell how tense I was whenever I was around him? Isn't a mother supposed to notice these things? Isn't a mother supposed to know when their only child isn't acting like themselves? Isn't that part of being a mother?

I wish she'd ask me about it; I'd find a way to let her know. At least if I thought she had her suspicions I could be a little more certain that she'd believe the horrors of what I had to tell her, but she loves him, and I think that makes her blind to my suffering.

I watch my mum pick up her glass of red wine and I wonder—not for the first time—if Trevor has been drugging her with sleeping pills so she doesn't wake in the night. It is the only thing that would make sense.

Before Trevor moved in, my mum could be dead to the world and still hear me if I tried to sneak out. I didn't know how she did it, but now she doesn't even hear me scream, and I've tried more than once recently. The only way for me to know if her husband is slipping her pills would be to take a sip of her drink, and I need to stay alert.

As soon as the credits roll on the film, I jump up to my feet to make my escape.

"Night, Mum," I say, applying a kiss to her cheek on my haste out of the room.

I hear her respond in her usual way. "Night, babe. Love you."

I detour to the kitchen on my way upstairs and grab something I have a feeling I'm going to need. After a quick shower, I prepare myself for what's to come. It's inevitable that he'll show up: it's Friday and my mum has had a few glasses of wine.

I was eleven the first time he came into my room. I had no idea what he was doing there or what he wanted, at least until he showed me. He said I was special, that it was how I could show him how much I loved him. It was a kiss on the mouth at first, then he would make me touch him over his pyjama bottoms.

It took a year for him to be certain I wouldn't tell, and that's when he first made me have sex with him. The visits were sporadic at first, maybe once a month, but then his appetite grew, and after a while it was every fortnight. By the time I turned fifteen, he was sneaking into my room once a week.

I'd almost told my father so many times when I spent the weekend with him, but I'd been petrified that he would think I was making it up in an attempt to get him and my mother back together, so I'd kept the secret, sure that Trevor and I had a special bond as he claimed. I hadn't known any better back then.

When I got older, I'd been scrolling through Twitter and saw a news story about a YouTuber, who had been grooming children online. Suddenly, the previous five years had made sense: what Trevor is doing to me is wrong, though I think on some level I'd always known.

Trevor had been "grooming" me.

I'd read the story with interest.

I'm not the only one this is happening to. I'm not alone.

I'd wanted to tell someone then, to tell everyone, but I hadn't known how to begin, and it's easy to have the strength to confess in the darkness after he's gone back to bed.

I can't keep quiet anymore, and I can't tell my parents either. I have to stop him the only way I know how.

I climb into bed. Pulling the duvet up under my chin, I feel sleepy, but I fight to stay awake. I need to be ready. Tonight, will be the last night he sneaks into my room.

I'm close to dropping off when I hear the unmistakable creek of my bedroom door as he slinks inside. The sound makes me tense, and I'm immediately wide awake, but I lie still, pretending to be asleep. Maybe if I'm unresponsive it'll deter him from what he's here for—though it never has before.

The floorboard at the foot of my bed alerts me to how close he is, and I wait for the inevitable whisper of my name.

As I feel his weight on the bed next to me, I slip my hand under my pillow and grip the handle of the knife I've taken from the kitchen. It fills me with a superhero complex but I'm going to need the confidence radiating through my body if I'm going to do this effectively. I wait until the time is right to strike.

I open my eye slightly to glance at the camera I've set up on my bookshelf. He won't be able to see it—hell, I put it there and I can't see it. It's there though, recording every move.

"Bonnie." His whisper fills the silence.

I can feel the bile rise in my throat. I wonder how far I need to let his depraved act go before I have enough evidence to stop it.

Gripping the handle of the knife, being careful not to show it to him, I slide it slowly under the duvet and down to the mattress in front of me. I mimic being woken and turn on my back to look up at him.

"I don't want you here." I refuse him for the first time,

strengthened by the fact I have a weapon.

The light streaming in through my window from the street makes it easy to see the shock of my resistance on his face, and I feel a small victory.

I can hear the underlining anger in his response. "C'mon, Bonnie. It's too late to say no now."

I push myself up off the mattress, so that I'm sitting, and I pull my knees up to my chest. I'm still holding the handle of the knife down by my side.

"You can't do this to me anymore."

"This is how you show me you love me."

"I *don't* love you." My voice is louder than I had been expecting.

Despite the venom I project, Trevor smiles and he stands up. It seems my resistance hasn't deterred him; he's already erect. "Don't be silly. Just lie back. It'll be over soon," he says, untying the string on his pyjamas bottoms and pushing them down over his hips so they puddle on the floor at his feet.

I glance in the direction of the camera, not long enough for him to notice, and then look back at him. "I said no." I grip the handle tight and reveal the knife. The blade isn't big—just 4-inches—still, I feel strong for the first time since he's been violating me.

That passes when I see his reaction.

Instead of fear, I see a glint of amusement in his eye. "What are you going to do with that?"

My hand shakes as I point the knife at him. "If you don't leave now, I'm going to use it," I threaten, and that makes him laugh.

"You're not strong enough to use that, little girl," he patronises.

I'm pissed off that he's underestimating my

strength—I told him no after all. "I just have to stab in you in the right place, and you won't be able to hurt me again."

"Hurt you? I don't hurt you. What we have is special."

"No, it isn't. I don't want you to touch me anymore."

Suddenly he gets nasty. "You don't have a choice," he says, lunging for the knife.

I'm quick like a cat, springing from my bed the other side before he can reach the weapon, and I back up in a circle towards the door. Without looking, I reach behind me for the handle, but I·can't find it. I glance down and he's there, pushing his weight against the door to stop me leaving. I duck under his arm and back away from him.

I shout my demands, hoping my mum hears and comes to my rescue. "Leave, Trevor. Get out of my room and don't come back or I will use this."

But he doesn't seem worried that my mum is going to find him in my room as he turns and grabs for the knife.

I'd been hoping that just showing him I was willing to hurt him, would mean he'd leave me alone, but I'm afraid I'm going to have to use the blade in order to make my point.

I drop to the floor in front of him and unconsciously thrust the knife up at any part of his body. It's steered with all the pent-up pain he's caused me since the first time he violated my body and a scream that starts deep down in my lungs leaves my mouth with an unexpected force that can't be contained.

The blade pierces through his skin like a knife through butter, and I'm amazed at how easy it is to do.

As his pained cry shakes the room, I look at where my hand is—still holding the blade—being covered in thick blood, gushing out of his wound. I've stabbed him in the crotch, and it occurs to me that maybe my attack wasn't as random as I initially thought. Maybe it's the area I meant to target.

Pulling my hand away, I remove the blade and it makes the bleeding worse. Trevor drops to the ground, covering his injury the best he can. There's blood everywhere and I panic, but there's still no sign of my mother.

Picking up my phone from where it's charging on my bedside table, I unplug it and dial 999. I slowly lower to the floor, my back against the bed watching Trevor bleed out.

Considering what I've just done, I'm surprised how calm I am as I answer all the operator's questions and tell her what he's been making me do. It feels good to finally tell somebody the truth. And judging by the gasp she tried to disguise once my confession is out, she believes me. It's as if a weight has been lifted from my shoulders: someone knows. She may be a stranger, someone I'll never meet, but she knows.

I feel lighter, as if I'll float away any minute, but I can hear sirens getting closer, and I know they're coming for me.

After

IT HAD BEEN a few weeks since my attack on Trevor. I look across at my mum as we sit in front of the television. Her eyes are fixed on the screen, but I doubt she's watching what's on because I know I'm not. She hasn't been able to look at me since I stabbed him, and she's barely spoken to me either. My mother hates me, I can feel it. I took away the man she was supposed to grow old with, and I'm sure she'll never forgive me. My heart hurts thinking that one of the two people supposed to love me unconditionally could wish I don't exist.

How do I put right what I didn't make wrong? How do I make her love me again?

I feel more alone now than I ever had when keeping the secret of what Trevor was doing to me. At least then my mum could stand to be around me. I want to scream that she was the one who brought him into our lives—that she married him without knowing what kind of man he was—but I would just be saying those things to hurt her and get a reaction because I don't blame her, not anymore.

In my darkest times, dealing with the abuse, I'd blamed her for not seeing it and saving me, but, after just a few weeks of therapy, I know that the abuse wasn't her fault. He was the one who did this to us—him—and she's as much of a victim as I am.

I want to talk about it and start healing our relationship, but it seems she's happy to brush it under the carpet. Maybe being by my side when I was interviewed by the police and hearing all the details had been hard for her, but doesn't she understand how hard they were to verbalise after hiding them for so long? Maybe it's too painful for her to think about, although I can't imagine she's thought of anything else. Doesn't she know how much I need her?

Or maybe it's that she still doesn't believe me.

Naturally, Trevor is denying it all—even though I have his last attack on video. Once the hospital had saved his life and he'd recovered from surgery, he'd told the police that *I* seduced *him*. It's ludicrous that he expects anyone to believe his version of events, but does my mum?

Picking up the remote, I turn off the TV, hoping to force her into talking to me. She looks at me, and I can instantly see the pain in her eyes. I'm curious what's caused it.

"What are you doing?" she asks, as though it isn't obvious.

I shuffle closer to her on the settee. "We need to talk."

"What about?" I can tell by the darkening colour of her eyes that she knows exactly what I want to talk about, she's just trying to dodge it.

I'm upset that I have to spell it out. "What do you think? Trevor."

"Bonnie, I can't." She picks up her cup off the coffee

table and makes her way to the kitchen to avoid the conversation.

I follow her; I'm relentless. Although I'm scared about what she'll say, I need her to tell me how she feels so we can start to mend.

"C'mon, Mum. Talk to me," I beg, but when she doesn't say anything, I voice my fears. "Do you hate me?"

She puts her cup in the sink. "God, no. I love you, Bon Bon."

She rocks forwards on her feet and reaches her hand out in my direction; before she touches me, she pulls her hand away and rocks back.

Hearing her use the nickname she gave me when I was a toddler makes me feel warm inside, but I think she's afraid to touch me.

I frown. "Don't you believe me?"

"What? Of course I do."

"Then why aren't you talking to me?"

"What do you want me to say?"

"I dunno, anything."

She drops her gaze to the floor. "I'm sorry, Bonnie."

"What for?"

When she looks up, I can see the tears streaming down her face.

"For bringing him into our home. If I'd have known…" I suddenly realise that she feels guilty; she never disbelieved me. My heart crushes at the fact that I've spent all the years of abuse blaming my mum for not stopping him when she couldn't have known the kind of monster he was because it would have been too awful to consider.

Seeing her crying makes me emotional, and tears start to roll down my cheeks. "You didn't know. How could you?"

"I should have seen the way he looked at you or spoke to you; I should have sensed something wasn't right."

I rush to hug her. "It's not your fault, Mum. You can't blame yourself."

She pulls out of our hug, her tears seeming to dry up instantly. "Who else is there to blame? Not your father, he knew something was off about him."

That's news to me. "He did?"

"Yeah, he didn't know what it was, but your dad didn't like Trevor from day one." There was suddenly a look of realisation on her face. "God, how do I tell your father?"

I raise my eyebrows and voice my thoughts. "I think Uncle Dom will probably have covered that." My uncle Dominic is my dad's younger brother, and he'd showed up at the police station while I was being questioned. He's felt a sense of obligation with my dad being out of the country and has popped in to check on me every day since, so it's logical that if he's been able to get word to my dad—wherever he is—he will have filled him in to save me from having to go through the details again.

My mother's tears seem to be instantly replaced with anger. "I could kill Trevor for what he's put you through."

I feel so much more at ease knowing it's not me she's mad at.

"I'm going to be okay," I say with more conviction than I feel. "I'll be okay; *we'll* be okay."

But when my mum's eyes meet mine, I can see her trying to make sense of our relationship. "Why didn't you tell me what he was doing?"

"I didn't know how, and Trevor told me that no one would believe me." I consider my question carefully. "Would you have?"

She thinks through my question, and I'm not sure she knows the answer. "I wish you'd have given me a chance to."

Hindsight makes me wish I had, too.

The door knocks, breaking up our heart to heart. I wipe away my tears. "That's probably Uncle Dom."

Making my way to the door, I open it, but instead of my uncle the other side, it's my dad.

"Daddy!" I scream out as I thrust myself towards him. I throw my arms around his neck, tiptoeing to reach, and start to sob into his chest. I feel him wrap me in his big, strong arms, and I instantly feel safe—safer than I have for years. He squeezes me tighter and for longer than usual, and I can almost feel his remorse radiating through me.

"When did you get back?" I ask once he let's me go and I notice he's still wearing his uniform.

"Just." His answer is sullen as he steps inside and closes the door. "I got emergency leave once your uncle Dom told me what was going on."

When my mum appears in the doorway, I can feel the tension between them. They have been awkward around each other since the split, but this has made it worse.

"Sally." He nods in her direction.

"Hey, Kyle." She leans against the frame with her shoulder and her eyes drop to the floor; I can sense her shame.

"Uh, Bon, can I get a minute alone with your mum?"

"Dad—"

"Just a minute please, Bon." His voice is stern, the way it always is when he's trying to get me to follow instructions.

My head drops and I do as I'm told, but I'm barely at the top of the stairs when I hear him start to rip into Mum.

"How could you not see what was going on? It was happening right under your nose." His voice projects as though he is talking to a subordinate.

"It's not as if he was wearing a sign, Kyle."

I'm heartbroken that he's blaming her for what Trevor did. I hate what he's done to my family: everyone is blaming themselves. They're tiptoeing around me in case I break, and I'm stronger than they're giving me credit for—stronger than I thought I was. I will see this through and make Trevor pay for breaking my family.

I rush back downstairs, barrelling into the kitchen. "Stop it! You can't tear into each other because that's how he wins. We have to be strong, as a family."

I can't listen to them blame one another.

***

I haven't been to school since the stabbing: Mum thought it was for the best—give me chance to *recover*. Today is my first day back, and I'm nervous. Everyone's going to know what has happened because the newspaper printed a story with his picture. It hadn't been front page, but they're bound to make the connection, even though they hadn't printed my name. I know the kids in school won't have read it, but we listen when our parents have hushed conversations while we're in the room. We're not as stupid as adults think we are, and my name is bound to have been mentioned.

I head towards the corner where I usually meet Elyssa and Amelia, but they're nowhere to be seen. They'd known I was coming back to school today because we've texted each other every day. Then a thought pops into my head: what if all their texts have been a cover to try and get information about what's going on? What if the two people

I rely on heavily for emotional support have turned their backs on me? How do I get through this without them? Having my parents as support is great, but I need my friends, too.

Suddenly, I see them up ahead, and I breathe a sigh of relief. Maybe it's not as bad as I think it is.

As they get closer and smile in my direction, I relax. It's a good sign.

"Hey, skiver." Elyssa greets me grinning, and I see Amelia nudge her in the ribs with her elbow.

I sigh and look down at my feet. They know. It had been too much to hope that they wouldn't. I can see the pity in Amelia's eyes, and I'm thankful that Elyssa had been willing to pretend she knew nothing.

"How are you?" Amelia asks.

I'd be happier to not have it mentioned, but I understand that they're trying to be supportive. I shrug. "You know, doing better now."

Elyssa raises her eyebrows to convey the understatement of my reply. "Do you have to testify?"

"Yeah, but I shouldn't have to do it in person."

"Well, that's something."

"How many people at school know?" I dare to ask. I don't want to be blindsided: I'd rather know before I get there.

"Everyone, but we haven't heard your name being mentioned for days now," Amelia replies.

"What were they saying about me?" I know that even though I'm the victim, the kids at school are cruel and will say anything to get a reaction out of me.

"You don't need to worry about that. Lys and I have threatened to kick their arses if they even look at you funny."

71

I smile, appreciating the sentiment. "I missed you guys." I say, putting an arm around each of them and pulling them into a hug. I know I can face the day knowing they're on my side.

***

Testifying is hard, even though it's six months after I was forced to defend myself and I am able to do it via video link. It only takes a day after closing arguments for Trevor to be convicted and sentenced to seven years behind bars for what he's done to me—although I am told not to expect him to serve the full sentence.

It's a blow, but the fact he's been convicted means he will be put on a register of sex offenders, which carries certain restrictions he will have to abide by.

It's a small victory that Mum decides to celebrate. She cooks bacon and eggs for breakfast and takes me shopping for new clothes. I've told her it isn't necessary, but she is trying to make up for Trevor—not that she could, or should.

"Did you see that guys face as you tried on that bra over your clothes?" I ask with an uncontrollable laugh. "I thought he was going to explode in his pants."

My mum laughs, a sound I love and have missed so much during this process. "That's given him a thrill to take home with him tonight," she says, linking my arm as we move on to the next shop.

I turn sentimental. "I've missed this."

"Me too, Bon Bon. Me too."

We are going to be okay and that's all that matters.

THE END

Wrapped in Lights

D J COOK

September 2014

ADULT LIFE WAS no easy task. The older I grew, the more I wished I could just rewind—back to the days where I wasn't considered weird or sweaty, where I could play with an imaginary friend and not be judged or, better yet, walk up to someone and ask to be their friend. Being an adult made that difficult. My social anxiety was something I struggled with daily, creeping up at times I'd least expect it, and honestly, I was lonely. The more I locked myself away from the outside world, the less I was able to fight the isolation that surrounded me like the black of night.

University was my chance for a fresh start and to overcome my demons in order to be the person I'd dreamed of—to be someone's best friend, even.

I'd been practically invisible in high school and college, but for those who did know me, I was the weirdo. I'd had no friends. In-fact, the only thing I could rely on other than my parents was my shadow.

As much as I wasn't fond of being called Weirdo, it

was better than being called Fatty. However, I couldn't deny the nicknames had an element of truth. I wasn't the skinniest, and I didn't hang out with mates and watch reality TV or play footie with the lads on the fields behind school. Instead, I was overweight and spent half my time singing along to Musicals.

Music was an escape, my way out of the cruel world I lived in, where if I wasn't being verbally beaten up, I'd be torturing myself mentally. Music allowed me to close my eyes, the sounds filling my ear drums, the beats taking me to any place I could conjure up in my dreams. As much as I loved being in my bubble, and enjoyed my own company, I knew I had to make an effort to survive the next three years of my life. I knew I had to push myself to blend in and make friends because if I didn't, I'd be lonely forever.

I'd spent the whole of summer ecstatic at the thought of moving away. I loved the thought of the freedom I'd have, being able to do the things I wanted to do when I wanted to do them. I was an adult after all. What I didn't know at the time was that the reality of adulthood would revolve around drinking copious amounts of alcohol, an insane workload for my degree and cupboards full of packet noodles.

Still, I had my accommodation to look forward to: a spacious, semi-detached house on Bromley Street that I'd be sharing with five other students. These were the people I was meant to form a friendship bond with and be friends with for the rest of my life—that's what I was told anyway. However, we couldn't have been more different.

All my housemates were third years and had their own life and friends. Becky spent all day on her phone talking to her friends. Mike and Pete spent most of their time either watching football or playing football. Andy was only seen to be out of his room to get food and the rest of the time he would play on his games console. Finally, there was Joanna. Quite frankly, she could have been lying dead in her room for all I knew. I'd still not met her a few days into living there and only knew about her because my landlord had mentioned her.

I was surrounded by people, peers my age, yet somehow, I felt lonelier than ever before.

"Hey, Andy, what're you playing?" I stood underneath the door frame, looking into his room. He must have left the door open by accident; it had been shut the past couple of days I'd lived there.

"Oh. Hi Ryan. COD. Wanna play?" He chucked a controller across his bed towards his door as he stuffed a handful of crisps into his mouth. I had no idea what COD was or how to play, but I wanted to give it a go.

It was violent.

I spent sixty percent of the game waiting for someone to bring me back to life after being shot and the other forty percent of the game on a loading screen.

I sat in silence, wanting to try and make conversation as Andy pressed his tongue against his lips in concentration, shouting 'die' as he bashed the buttons on the controller.

"I'm not very good at this, am I?" I asked in an attempt to make some form of conversation.

"Nah, you'll learn, though."

Good talk, Andy. Real good talk.

"We like to drink with Ryan, 'cause Ryan is our mate, and when we drink with Ryan, he downs his drink in eight. Seven. Six…"

A quirky song I'd heard far too many times already,

77

and factually incorrect. I didn't feel like their mate at all. Another night, another drinking session before going out to house parties and nightclubs. My stomach couldn't take much more of the life of a fresher, but I had to suck it up if I wanted these people to like me.

I gulped a fishbowl concoction made up of five different varieties of alcohol even an alcoholic wouldn't dream of putting together, all mixed in a large metal pan because Mike and Pete couldn't find a bowl big enough.

The dark red liquid dripped from my mouth, leaving a stain in its place. I mean, who thought red wine, whiskey and tequila together was a good idea?

"That's disgusting." I gagged, unable to hide the displeasure on my face. All the others seemed pretty pleased with themselves.

"Becky. Your turn to pick a card," Pete said in a boisterous, drunken state.

I had to push myself each day to involve myself and ask to be part of their games when all I wanted to do was shy away in my room. The thought of having friends I could truly count on felt like a marathon away, but I knew I had to give them time to warm to me—time to get to know them properly. I'd given myself until Christmas to decide if being in accommodation was right for me. I desperately wanted friends but there was no point in paying close to five thousand pounds a year for somewhere to sleep when I lived twenty minutes away on train.

I could save money and be lonely in the comfort of my own home.

The next morning, I called my parents in a hungover state. They'd been surprised the first time, especially as I'd barely drunk at home, never mind with other humans, but after four nights on the run, they were used to it now.

I plucked courage from within my alcohol pouch, commonly known as the stomach, and told them my decision: I'd move home at Christmas if things didn't get better and they gave me the most adult response there ever was.

"We'll love and support you no matter what you decide to do."

They did however tell me to keep trying and asked if I had any course mates—which I didn't, although someone did ask me for a pen after they'd walked into a lecture late, smelling of booze. I probably smelt just as bad as them.

I'd spent the day in lectures and printed PowerPoint slides for those the day after. Any reason not to go home and put far too much undeserved effort into those that lived with me.

I was excited for food though.

After eating all things noodle-based for a week, I couldn't wait for a Fray Bentos pie that my mum had sent in a care package. It was one of the few things I knew how to cook: there wasn't much that could go wrong with a pie in a tin.

The taste pulled childhood memories to the forefront of my mind, of the times my parents had to work late. I'd pop a pie in the oven and crank the music up full blast.

A small amount of saliva leapt from my mouth and landed on a library book I was about to check out. I needed to get home.

It was already getting dark, and as I walked from the campus back to my house, I cautiously flinched and looked back at every slight noise. The sound of my own stomach gave me a fright as it growled in anticipation for food.

Walking through into the kitchen, I was barely acknowledged by Becky as she mindlessly scrolled through her phone with the television blaring in the background. I opened the tin and placed my pie on a baking tray and into an oven that didn't have the chance to pre-heat and then sat down with Becky and the very little company she gave me.

I must have sat with her for around fifteen minutes, my pie just starting to warm up nestled in its tin, when the house filled with darkness.

Pitch black.

Just the green glow of the emergency light.

"Oh my god," Becky squealed, panicking as she fumbled on her phone to find the torch.

"What's happened? Surely we can't have run out of electricity?" I asked as the rest of my housemates walked into the lounge, including a girl I presumed to be Joanna.

"It must be the fuse? There's literally no electricity in the house. I'll get onto Ray," Pete said, trying to calm Becky down as he searched for our landlord's number in his phone. Alarms could be heard in the distance, even though all the doors and windows were shut in the house. As Pete listened to the repetitive buzz of the calling sound, Joanna leapt to the front door to investigate the alarms.

"Guys, the whole street's out. It must be a blackout."

I headed towards her and the door to see for myself. All the lights were out and people crowded on Bromley Street. My housemates seemed pretty excited, but all I could think about was my un-rescuable Fray Bentos pie sinking in the now cooling oven.

The Blackout

A GLOW OF lights surrounded our street. It took my eyes a little while to adjust, but the night sky looked brighter than I'd ever seen it. The stars twinkled brighter and the moon beamed. In the distance, I could see a glow-in-the-dark football being kicked from one side of the street to the other, along with students wearing the weirdest light up items I'd ever seen.

A group of girls came out of the house directly opposite ours. One girl wore light up bunny ears that she'd clearly bought from a concert and held a cigarette in one hand. Two of the other girls wore battery powered fairy lights around their necks and another tried to create light just by flicking their lighter.

They gave a friendly exchange with a wave and smile from over the road.

They were waving at me.

I waved and stepped forwards.

They were coming over.

To speak to us.

"Hey. We can't believe there's a blackout. It's so weird, isn't it? Sophie got scared thinking someone was going to come out of the basement." She laughed, speaking in a posh southern accent, pointing to one of the girls next to her.

"I'm gutted. I was cooking my food but now its gonna have to go in the bin." I laughed at myself in misery. I could already feel the sweat beginning to drip off my back as I tried my best to interact.

"That's hilarious. I'm Roxy by the way; I'm a third year. This is Sophie; she's in her second year. Then that's Hailey and Amelia. They're both first years," she said, taking a drag of her cigarette, the smoke lit by the rays from the moon. The smell clung to her clothes like a top note against her sweet-smelling perfume.

"Ryan," I said confidently, trying to bottle the nerves that tried desperately to creep out of my body. "I'm a first year, too."

Four days prior, I was almost certain I didn't like my housemates and that they weren't fond of me. The blackout made it clearer as they retreated back to their rooms and didn't even bother introducing themselves.

I wanted to pretend that being invisible to them didn't affect me, but it did. Each day, I'd tried to fit in, battling with what seemed like my natural instincts.

I wanted to feel normal, even more so after hearing about the girl's house. They had regular movie nights, went for food together, clubbed together on the shopping bill and shared each other's streaming services. It was the house I'd expected to be living in at university—the home I'd dreamed to be a part of.

The girls asked about my housemates, and I wanted

to pretend we were the best of friends, but I couldn't lie. Their happiness had envy growing inside me as I watched them huddle as a family in the midst of the darkness.

Amelia wrapped herself tighter in the blanket she'd borrowed from their house. The fairy lights shone so bright it was hard to truly see what she looked like. Her hair was light, and she was wearing a pair of slippers that resembled some form of animal. Amelia was the quietest of the girls. She stood and listened, mostly, with an occasional laugh here or there.

"What do you study, Amelia?" It was the only thing I could think of that I knew would warrant a simple response.

"I do nursing. You?" she squeaked with nerves. She had my accent, so she couldn't have lived far from here.

"Mathematics. It's the only thing I'm good at."

"Oh really? I hated maths. I mean, what the hell is Pythagoras' Theorem?" She giggled a little, pulling her blanket even closer.

"I get that a lot. To me and you it's pretty useless, but in construction it's vital. You can't build a bridge without using the three-four-five rule."

Oh god, I'm talking about bridges. That's not cool.

"Do you want my coat?" I asked forwardly, trying to redeem myself after the talk of math.

"You're a star! Thanks, love; I'm freezing me tits off here," Sophie interrupted in a clearly intoxicated state, answering for Amelia. She was a Scouser, the twang was unmistakeable.

I passed over my jacket after wrestling it off myself. It hung off Sophie like a tent hung off its pole. I looked to

Amelia as she shied away from the boisterous personality that was Sophie. She grabbed onto her fairy lights that were starting to dim and huddled closely to Hailey.

"You're lovely you are. Come to ours for our next movie night, yeah?" Sophie said with the other girls nodding in agreement. Before I could answer, the street filled with light. Streetlights made a clinking noise as they turned themselves on, and lights poured from the houses. The street was no longer filled with a silence but, instead, cheers from the residents and the buzz of electricity.

I didn't have time to say anything in response. Before I knew it, their door was shut and I stood in the cold of Bromley Street.

I didn't even get my coat back.

October 2014

A FEW DAYS had passed since the blackout. I felt empty of courage, full of anxiety and even more ready to leave university accommodation. It had also been a few days since I'd met Joanna, who'd been on holiday.

Apparently, every year as soon as her student loan's paid in, she'd hop on a plane instead of partaking in any kind of fresher week fun. Part of me wished she'd stayed abroad. All of me, actually. Her and Becky had loud music streaming from the room next door until ungodly hours of the morning, and not even the good kind. I was barely able to drift off to my happy place and wasn't liking the reality of being awake and living with them either. I just wanted to escape. I'd go to lectures nearly an hour early in hopes I'd bump into someone new to talk to and to escape the house that was fast becoming my prison. Things had to get better.

I sat on the edge of my bed daydreaming, looking out across the street as thuds of music slammed against my bedroom wall.

I gawked at number sixty-three in a daze when the door opened.

Roxy came out wearing a tightly wrapped dressing gown, a cigarette in her hand. She sat down on the step and started puffing away. It were as if she'd just woken up, yet it was already six in the afternoon.

I wish I could sleep that long.

Sleeping itself was hard enough without the blaring music, not to mention the whirlwind of thoughts that swirled around in my head. I'd sit there for hours, wanting to tell them to switch off the music, convincing myself I could do that, but I always failed myself.

They'd dislike me even more.

They were probably playing the music to annoy me, anyway.

I must have sat there for a minute or so, pushing myself to go out and speak to Roxy, battling thoughts that something would go wrong.

I can do this.

I had to get over to Roxy. I just had to walk out the door; the rest would happen naturally.

I pulled on my shoes, ran down the stairs and casually stepped out onto the front doorstep, offering an awkward yet friendly wave.

"Ryan! Hey, you alright?" she yelled as smoke billowed from her mouth.

"Hiya! I'm good, are you? Just heading to the shop to get away from my awful housemates. It's literally none stop,"

"Is that them playing the music? There's no fucking need for it to be that loud."

"You're telling me. Try being in the next bedroom over," I said, looking back at my house and pointing to my bedroom window.

"I'll tell them to shut up." Without hesitation, she hopped up and marched over to my house, banging continuously on the door until someone heard her knocking over the music. The coward in me hid around the corner, nestled between the front window and the front door.

"Oh, hi." Pete answered the door.

"Can you tell whoever is playing the fucking music to turn it down? It's been constant and I'm not having it anymore. It's so loud I can hear it in my bedroom across the bloody road," Roxy screamed, smoke rising from her cigarette as if it was coming from her in rage.

"Woah, okay. Chill," Pete said in shock as Roxy let her temper loose.

"Good. If it's not off soon, I'll be reporting it to the university and the police." Roxy turned and strutted back across the road, looking smug. I waited until my door slammed before catching her up.

"That was incredible." I wished I could have done that. Minutes later the music had been switched off.

"You're welcome, honey. You want to come in?"

Roxy put her cigarette out, scraping the ash on the paving stone beneath her foot.

I skipped over the door ledge into their hallway. It smelt fresh and clean, like Zoflora had been sprayed throughout the house instead of a bottle of vodka.

As I was about to close their front door behind me, I looked back to my house to see Becky, standing at her window looking right at me. She knew I had something to do with it, and honestly, I couldn't bear the thought of the consequences.

December 2014

LIVING ACROSS THE street from the girls wasn't so bad. I spent all my time over there hiding from Becky and Joanna and only travelled back to my house to sleep, if then.

Since Roxy had marched over there, I'd barely seen them, but my newly acquired friends were paying for it.

It was clear Becky and Joanna weren't happy. The number of times we'd woken up to Sixty-Three covered in toilet paper, or flour and egg. Just a week later and a window was smashed at the back of the house. It didn't take a genius to realise who was behind it. The girls got their fair share of revenge though, although Roxy did have to stop Sophie from wanting to post animal poo through the letter box.

After a while, the childish games died down. Whether they ran out of ideas or whether it was their third year demands, I didn't know.

University was full on and I was missing my parents. I wasn't the only one, either. Amelia and I got the train together nearly every weekend to travel back home to our parents as hers lived only two towns away from mine. Amelia and her housemates were fast becoming my second family—a family I hadn't asked for but one that I was welcomed into like no other.

I couldn't leave university, not now. I may not have been in the house of my choice, but that wasn't going to stop me. Not when I'd made such great friends—real friends I could count on.

"Mum, Dad, this is Amelia," I said, introducing her to my parents. I'd convinced her to visit for the day before going to see Wicked in the theatre. The worried phone calls had increased over the past month, so I had to show my parents I was doing alright—that I had made real friends.

Amelia hadn't seen the show before, but somehow had learnt the entire soundtrack within a week of us booking the tickets.

"Amelia, I'm Andrea and this is Graham. We've heard so much about you. Let me grab your coat and you go make yourself comfortable," my mum flustered around us both as if she'd not met another person before.

"Thanks so much. It's lovely to meet you both," Amelia said with a huge smile.

The more I got to know Amelia, the more I realised she wasn't quiet at all. She'd be the first to crack open a bottle of wine and try and race me to the bottom. She'd always talk over the television, repeating the characters words like she'd memorised the screenplay. The minute the television was flicked on, an episode of Miranda flashed on screen and off she went, word for word.

"Ryan. Do you have a second?" my dad mumbled from the corner of the kitchen.

"Sure, what's up?"

"She's pretty, isn't she? Is she…you know, your girlfriend?"

"Dad! No, it's not like that. We're friends." I raised my voice accidentally and quickly tried to keep quiet as my voice echoed through our open-plan house.

"Okay. I was just checking." He smiled innocently and walked over to Mum who was sitting at the dining table. No doubt she'd put him up to that. I did worry that bringing a girl back would prompt questions, but my friendship with Amelia was entirely platonic.

"Okay. You were right. Absolutely the best show I've seen. Everything about it was just…" she said, fighting through a crowd of people freshly poured from the theatre.

"I told you. I know. It's just magical," I said, feeling smug. For once in our friendship, it had been me mouthing to the words of the actors and not her. She had sung *all* the songs though.

"It really was. Next time we're going to see Avenue Q. You'll love that. It's really controversial but political and the songs are hilarious. No matter how many times I tell the girls they'll like it, they won't come," she begged as we walked down the street to the train station.

"Oh, well count me in. I love a good play."

"It's with puppets, by the way."

It could have been a show about torture and I'd still get tickets to see the show with her. She was infectious to be around.

Every second, I'd find myself growing as a person.

Every minute, we'd find a reason to laugh.

Not one hour went by without the thought of Amelia and the girls.

"Look. I've been speaking to the girls, and we all agree. You spend far too much time at our house and the knocking is really annoying," she said with a straight face. She wasn't laughing any more.

"Oh…I'm sorry." My heart sank quicker than it ever had before. Of course, it had to be too good to be true. I wasn't meant to have friends. I was destined to be lonely.

"That's why we're making you our honorary housemate." A smile grew on her face.

"What? Seriously?" Amelia handed me a key with a keyring attached, a picture of the girls and me sitting proudly within it. I could have wept.

"Serious. Now you don't have to knock anymore," She linked my arm and walked by my side.

Just a few months before, I'd thought about moving back home, I'd struggled to string a sentence together with new people and my confidence had sat in the pits of hell.

I knew these girls were going to be the making of me, especially Amelia. Adult life was already seeming far from lonely.

March 2015

"YOU GIRLS ARE gonna be the death of me," I said, grinning whilst drawing another card as we sat in a circle playing a drinking game. "I got an ace."

"Eek, it's truth or dare," Amelia screamed at the top of her lungs. Thankfully their neighbours were students, too, so noise was expected.

"It should be waterfall. I rue the day you girls came into my house and made me change the game just because you can't down a drink." Roxy laughed whilst mocking Amelia and Hailey.

They couldn't down their drinks, but neither could I. We weren't seasoned drinkers. Roxy had had three years to practice the art.

"Shhhh," Amelia was already half cut as she took another sip of wine. She was going to be fragile in the morning. She could never handle her booze.

"So, go on then. What do you choose? Truth or dare?" Roxy asked. She'd just handed in her dissertation and had finished university for good. The rest of the girls and I had strung banners on every bare space in the house we could find. We'd bought cases of donuts, the fancy kind, with what little money we had left from our student loans.

Although she wasn't moving back home just yet, we had to give her the send-off she deserved and allow her to celebrate and blow off some steam.

"Dare," I said hesitantly.

Last year, you wouldn't have caught me playing truth or dare, never mind choosing dare.

The girls whispered between each other.

"We dare you to run from our doorstep to your doorstep ten times."

"I can do that. Easy." I was naive to think that was the entire dare.

The girls looked at each other and spoke in harmony. "Naked."

"You're joking, right?" I couldn't even picture such a thing. The girls installed a little crazy in me each time I saw them, but I'd never done anything like that before. I couldn't. I'd be seen and laughed at by other students.

"Nope. Not joking one bit. If I had to go next-door asking for batteries for my sex toy, you are absolutely running across the street naked." Amelia had a point. That had been a genius dare, something I could only half take credit for. I'd just told her to go next door and ask for something; the girls had turned it dirty.

"Fine." I began to strip off down to my boxers.

The girls wolf whistled at me like builders on a construction site, and the crazy drunk person in me did a little dance.

Once the girls had finished and I got to the front door, I kicked off my underwear concealing my private area with both hands, leaving my arse on full view.

One.

I ran across the street that was nearly as dark as when the blackout happened, with only the streetlights leaving an orange glow on my bare skin.

Two.

Nobody was around, not yet anyway.

Three.

I could already feel myself getting out of breath. Damn asthma.

Four.

The girls continued to laugh as I ran as fast as I could.

Five.

Wait, was that someone taking a picture? I swear I saw a flash.

Six.

Bloody Amelia and that camera of hers.

Seven.

A shadow of a man appeared at the top end of the

street. I knew I could finish the ten laps before he would get anywhere close to seeing me.

Eight.

Why was this humility not over yet?

Nine.

The girls continued to chant through the numbers with me.

Shit. Is that a police car?

I raced back over the road to the girls, somehow gaining more speed than I'd mustered during the entire dare. I launched towards them, jumping up onto the concrete step with one foot landing on it and the other slamming into it. My big toe took the brunt of the force as I collapsed to the floor, naked and in pain.

Ten.

"Are you ok?" the girls asked in-between laughter. They all thought it was pretty hilarious until they saw the state of my toe—my nail-bruising, tip-bleeding, wonky, broken toe.

"Absolutely fantastic." Over the past few months I'd become fluent in sarcasm—they'd taught me well. They considered it the native language of their house.

In between the agony and thumps of my aching toe, I couldn't help but feel a little proud of myself. Once again, I had been pushed out of my comfort zone, even if it was mostly down to alcohol and peer pressure. I'd heard that friendship meant your friends always carrying you back into your comfort zone, but for me it was the opposite. Real friendship was about pushing those close around you to becoming better versions of themselves.

October 2013

I'D BEEN IN my new room for nearly two months and it already looked like a bomb had hit it multiple times. Half-full spirit bottles, crushed cans, empty food packets and playing cards all spread out across the room. I was normally quite tidy , and so were the girls, but since Roxy had moved back home, the cleaning rota had gone out of the window.

The majority of the house had remained relatively clean, but my room had become the hub of all things social in the house. Everyone had gathered in Roxy's room before hand, and when it became mine, things just stayed the same.

I was thankful to have the biggest room in the house compared to my last box room across the road.

Amelia had wanted it, but I'd convinced her of the hassle it would be moving all her things.

Life was good and nothing could put a dampener on how I felt.

"Hey, so we've had an idea for our Halloween fancy dress costumes. We want to all match again when we go out," Amelia said, looking nervous.

"Awesome. Hit me," I said picking up broken crisps that were becoming entangled within the carpet.

"Okay well, we're dressing up as Peter Pan characters…"

"Great. I'll be Peter Pan then, or Captain Hook," I said not letting her finish.

"Well, Sophie is being Peter Pan. Apparently it's political. Hailey is being Captain Hook. She's already got a pirate costume. I'm gonna be Mr. Smee, so we thought it would be really fun if you were… Tinkerbell," she said with haste.

"Can I not be one of the lost boys? Or, I don't know, the crocodile? I'll be the bloody boat, I don't care, just not Tinkerbell," I pleaded. I knew I had no chance—I knew on Halloween I'd be walking out as a fairy.

"We've got you a green tutu, though. It's so cute."

"Have I ever told you that I hate you?" I said, grabbing the tutu off her in a strop.

"All the time."

Why in God's name am I wearing a green tutu and wings meant for a child?

Amelia, that's why.

To an untrained eye, Amelia seemed quiet and timid, but I'd figured out that she only spoke when she had something to say. She wouldn't let words trail from her mouth just for the sake of it, and boy did those words pack a punch of persuasion.

I was already feeling like my world was spinning after downing my drink as the taxi beeped whilst the girls spritzed their perfumes one last time.

We headed to the usual night club, by-passing all the bars on the way because we stayed home for pre-drinks. We were students after all; we couldn't afford both. The usual club had a variety of music depending on which storey you were on, with huge staircases joining the floors together. We went straight to the floor called Nostalgia, which played all those guilty pleasures that made up my Spotify playlists. Large martini glass fishbowls were filled with our favourite cocktails, and we all somehow managed to carry them to the dance floor and not spill them whilst dancing.

Not even half an hour into our dancing and Sophie was gasping for a cigarette, so we lugged ourselves up to the top floor. I wasn't keen on the smell, so I never understood why I put myself through it every time. Sophie was plastered and had Amelia and me holding her up straight each time a bouncer would pass.

"Okay, I'm done," Sophie slurred, flicking her cigarette on the floor as we made our way to the top of the stairs.

"Are we going back to Nostalgia?"

"Yeah," Amelia agreed.

We were just about to walk down the stairs when a group of people started to climb them. The stairs were narrow and so I tucked myself into the corner at the top. Crowds began to gather behind me, becoming impatient in their intoxicated state as I waited for them to pass. Not even a moment had passed when I heard…

"Come on, Ryan. Fly, Tinkerbell, fly!" Sophie screamed as I felt a push behind me. I tumbled down around 20 concrete steps, bashing all parts of my body.

Everyone gasped.

I heard Amelia shout, and I saw darkness—the same darkness that had filled Bromley Street the night of the blackout.

This time, though, the lights didn't seem like they'd come back on.

Years Later...

THE WORLD NEVER sat still. No matter how much I wanted it to amongst the mayhem of university, it was never going to happen. The years that had passed felt like decades, but my time with all the girls had flown by just like a flash of light.

It's funny how your life can change so quickly. People you think you'll love for the rest of your life can show you that you were wrong to. Things you thought were dead certain to remain the same can instantly be taken away from you.

It was hard leaving university, going from being surrounded by those I wanted to be close with to having barely anyone. I'd felt fine one minute and the next I'd have an ache in my chest. It only took seconds to grow but it felt like it stayed there for eternity.

Why haven't I seen these people for over a year? Why is nobody texting me back? Have I done something wrong?

I knew I'd done nothing wrong deep down, but that didn't make the aches go away. Instead, they just kept growing the more I thought about them.

There was not one second I'd thought I'd not be able to use my legs again, never mind be confined to a wheelchair for the rest of my life.

My parents blamed themselves for encouraging me to socialise, for trying to make me seem like a normal boy who had friends, but they didn't need to.

Life before university had been miserable, and then I'd met the most wonderful people and each day had seemed to get better and better.

Then I had the accident and lost the people I'd thought mattered.

Hailey had moved back home and never bothered to reach out, not to Amelia or me, and Sophie, although she spoke to Amelia on the odd occasion, she hadn't spoken to me since the accident. Not once had she replied to any of my messages and at the time, it consumed me. Amelia put it down to guilt.

The only person who truly mattered now was Amelia. She was the only constant in my life. It wasn't my shadow I couldn't get rid of, nor was it the shadow of my wheelchair that persistently followed me around. It was her.

Darkness defined a huge part of my life. For a long time, my social anxiety had kept me in the dark. It used to sit over me like a storm, and naturally I'd tried to hide from it. What I hadn't realised was that the more I hid away, the more it had grown. It had grown to the size of a category five storm, wind battering my face with enough rain to suffocate me.

Then came the Bromley Street blackout.

I remembered it not because of the obscenity of a power cut in the twenty-first century but because it was how I met Amelia, my greatest friend. I remembered the time I played drunken truth or dare and broke my toe. I could barely walk for six weeks after streaking across that damn road.

I couldn't escape the darkness, and I didn't want to. After night came day. After sadness came happiness. I reminded myself as I knew Amelia would. I'd learnt to live with the darkness because afterwards, light would always shine, and I'd always remember how my friendship with Amelia flourished in the light: walking down the street, talking about absolutely nothing of importance; comforting Amelia as she cried watching penguin documentaries; and the countless laughs we had while watching sitcoms.

I couldn't use my legs anymore, and each day that passed, I learnt to accept that. It was tough but had my life changed so dramatically? No, and Amelia made sure of that. We'd go to the theatre, we'd play games and we did everything we loved.

It didn't matter that I spoke to nobody else but her, because the friendship I had in her was worth more than a thousand people. With Amelia around, I never felt alone. In fact, it always felt as though I were wrapped in lights.

THE END

Always Been You

LIZZIE JAMES

Chapter One

Callie

SITTING IN THE airport, my leg was bouncing up and down. No matter how much I tried to calm it, I just seemed to get more anxious. Looking up at the screens with all the current arrivals and departures, I couldn't help the sigh that escaped me.

The flight from Germany had just landed, and the nerves had now quadrupled. It had been seven years since I had last seen Liam. We had been best friends since we were in kindergarten and all through high school. When we'd graduated, everyone always told us how much of an amazing couple we would make, but we both used to laugh off those comments.

I would often pretend they were ridiculous, but inside was a different story. Inside those comments stabbed me deeply because there was nothing that I wanted more than to be his—for his arms to be the only ones for me.

That wasn't the case though. We were friends, and only friends we would ever be.

On the day of my nineteenth birthday, Liam broke my heart. He had signed up to serve our country and he was leaving me behind. Seven years ago, I stood in this exact spot and watched him as he walked away from us. From me. From his family. From everything that he knew and loved.

I was proud of him and terrified for him in equal measure. The things he would have to see and do would forever change him, and I knew that if he did return, he would never be the same.

"Sweetheart." A warm hand took hold of mine. "It'll be okay."

I turned my head and smiled at her. Liam's mom had been such a huge support when he went away. I didn't think I could have got through the last few years if I hadn't had her by my side.

"I'm sure he has missed you just as much."

"He may have forgotten about me." I chuckled, trying to make light of the situation.

"I think it's time you find out." She looked over my shoulder towards the gateway he was expected to come through.

I took a deep breath before standing at her side. She takes my hand in a tight grip, squeezing my fingers reassuringly before releasing them.

"Deep breaths, sweetheart."

I nodded at her words and followed her advice, resolved to accept whatever fate had waiting for me. On the other side of that gateway was my destiny. I had two choices: I could either be patient and wait for him to wake up and see what we could be, or I could make him wake up.

Watching the passengers filter in through the gateway exit, I smiled when I felt the first fizzle of excitement shoot through me. Families and civilians began making their way through. My eyes scanned everyone, waiting impatiently.

I wasn't sure if he would be wearing his camouflage trousers and jacket or if he would be wearing normal clothes like everyone else at this airport was.

The fizzle of excitement that I had allowed to take over my body was slowly turning to impatience, and I was at the point where I was swaying from foot to foot. I turned toward Liam's mother and froze when I saw the expression on her face.

There was only one thing that could cause a mother to be filled with so much love.

He was here. Her boy was here.

Glancing back to the swarm of people, I gasped when I saw him. He broke through a gap in the crowd, and I could feel my eyes fill with tears when I saw the beaming smile on his face.

He still seemed the same as when he'd left only now he was a man. He was more muscly and had scruff on his face, but had never looked more beautiful.

I chuckled when he turned to the man next to him and threw his backpack at him. Seconds later, he was moving toward us, running through the crowd and across the lobby.

His mom took several steps forward and jogged the next few to reach her son. Seconds later, they impacted as Liam's arms wrapped around her and lifted her until her feet left the ground.

I couldn't stop the tears as they slid down my cheeks. As much as I had missed him, she had missed him ten times more.

He was her baby boy.

His beaming smile lit up the room as he settled her back on her feet. She reached up and took his face in between her hands.

"I'm so happy you're home." Her voice was full of emotion.

"So am I, Mom," he replied. His gaze flicked over the top of her head, and I couldn't help but smile at him.

He grinned before gazing back down at his mother.

"Go on." She nodded her head towards me. "She's been waiting for you."

He ducked his head and gave her a kiss on the cheek before he turned away from her.

As he took a step closer, I felt the nerves shoot through me. The butterflies fluttering in my stomach quickly turned into a swarm of bees, my hands were clammy and I wanted to shake my head at myself.

What the hell did I have to be so nervous about? It was only Liam.

Liam. My best friend. The one who used to share his pocket money with me. The one who made my skin tingle.

I giggled when I saw him run towards me, loving the idea that he wanted to be as near to me as fast as possible as I wanted him to be.

This day was finally here, and I couldn't have been more thankful that it was.

His arms reached for me at the same time as I reached for him, and seconds later, I was being lifted and spun around.

An excited squeal escaped me before I was placed back on my feet.

"You're finally home!" I stared up at him, hating the

tears that had escaped and now streaming embarrassingly down my cheeks.

He reached up, taking my face in his hands and wiped them away with his thumbs. "I'm sorry I took so long," he whispered, gazing into my eyes.

I shook my head and placed my hand over one of his. "You're here now."

Chapter Two

Liam

STARING DOWN INTO Callie's eyes, there was nowhere else I wanted to be. I never knew that enlisting would take me away from my family for so long. When I first joined up, I naively and stupidly thought that you'd go away for like ten months and then home for three.

Seven years was just six years too fucking long.

I was man enough to admit that I was a mummy's boy and that I'd missed her terribly, but when I think back to how much I missed the beautiful girl currently looking up at me as though I was her whole world, I'd been unprepared for how much I would miss her, how much I'd ache for her and how much I would need her.

Our entire lives we had been best friends, always there for each other. But only friends.

I had never looked at her or felt for her the way that I was currently.

I had never allowed myself to act on the way she would look at me. I'd always known since our teen years that it was more than friendship for her. I knew her feelings had changed for me, but I had never let myself go there.

This was Callie, my best friend. Not Callie, my fuck buddy. I had more than enough women for that—women who didn't have the sensitive nature that my Callie did.

It sounded like such an asshole thing to say, but those women meant nothing to me. I could use them and lose them, and I was free to move on. Moving and losing would never apply to Callie. She was too special for that—she was too special for me.

Before I could say anything to her, I was jolted from behind. Callie's eyes widened in surprise before a warm smile graced her lips.

"Aren't you going to introduce me to these beautiful ladies?" Parker asked from behind me.

I rolled my eyes at him before turning around and taking my backpack off him.

"This is my mother Lillian." I proudly introduced my mother before turning to Callie. "And this..." I smiled at her, loving the blush that stole over her beautiful cheeks. "This is Callie."

It was strange introducing her without a title. She wasn't a friend. She was more than that. It didn't sound right introducing her like that but it wasn't as if I could introduce her as something else and claim her as mine in some way.

She wasn't mine. Not yet at least.

She was just... Callie.

Before I could say anything else, Parker reached forward and took Callie's hand—the hand that belonged to me, the hand that I should have been holding—and lifted it to his lips. He kissed her knuckles before giving her his smirk. It was the smirk he had used to get countless other women before her to drop their panties.

"It is a pleasure to meet you, Callie." He then gave her a wink and released her hand.

Callie looked up at him, appearing dazed before she ducked her head and stared shyly at the floor.

"It's nice to meet you, too," she mumbled.

I have never wanted to punch Parker so hard before. He grinned at me cheekily, knowing full well the thoughts that were running through my head.

"So." He pushed past me and offered his arm to my mother. "How comfortable is your sofa?"

I rolled my eyes at him. I already knew he'd have my mother wrapped completely around his little finger by the time we got to the house. I turned back to Callie and froze when I saw she was staring up at me.

I smiled at her and reached my hand out to her. Extending it in the distance between us, I left the decision to her. I needed her to make this choice.

Being so far away from her for so long had left me with nothing but my memories to focus on over the last few years. I had done nothing but think back constantly on the way that we were with each other—more specifically, the way that she was with me.

But that was then.

This was now, and I needed her to lead me. I could never forgive myself if I was reading it wrong. This was me giving her the chance to decide what she wanted. As I held my hand out to her, I was offering her more than just my hand. I was offering her my heart, my time, my life. I was offering her myself—something I had never before offered another—and if I was honest with myself, something I could never offer another.

Only her. She was it for me. She was everything.

Just when it felt like I was about to blow, she slowly raised her hand and placed it in mine. Entwining our fingers, I pulled her gently towards me and led her towards the exit, trailing behind Mom and Parker.

As we got outside, Mom already had the car idling at the curb with Parker sitting in the passenger side. He grinned at us before pointing his thumb at the back seat, silently telling me where to park my ass.

I had no complaints. If this meant I didn't have to be separated from Callie, then I was all for it.

Climbing into the backseat, I tucked my backpack down at my feet and laid my arm across the back of the seat. I hoped she'd take the invite, but I was doubtful. Callie had always been shy around other boys, and I wasn't sure how much of that had changed.

In a way, we were strangers to each other.

Before I could wonder for too long, she scooted across the seat. As she tucked herself against my side, I let my muscles relax and enjoy the closeness that her body near mine provided.

I placed my arm around her and held her close to me. She lowered her head and rested it against my chest and allowed me to hold her, cocooning her body to mine.

"Let's get you boys home then, shall we?" my mother asked, filling the car with her thoughts. She sounded so calm and relaxed, but I knew that my time away from her had been anything but relaxed.

I lowered my head and pressed my nose against Callie's hairline, inhaling her sweet scent. I knew how she would smell because she always smelled the same, and I was glad that it hadn't changed.

Lavender.

"Yeah," I whispered before lowering my lips and pressing a soft kiss to her forehead. "Let's go home."

Chapter Three

Parker

AS THE CAR came to a stop outside Liam's house, I planned to escape the vehicle as quickly as possible. My boy needed some serious alone time with that girl. I was going to steal Mom away so he could do what he needed to do.

I had no doubt that his house would be full of relatives and friends who were bursting to see, but first he had to get sorted with Callie. A girl like that was only going to be unattached for so long.

Before I could say or do anything, Callie shot across to the other end of the backseat and was out the door. Liam and I both stared after her in confusion.

What the hell was her problem?

"What did I do?" Liam mumbled. His gaze flickered to me as we watched Callie quickly escape into the house.

"I don't know, dude," I answered. "But I think you need to fix it." I cocked an eyebrow at him before reaching for the door handle. "I'd do it sooner rather than later, if you catch my drift." He nodded and exited the car, waiting for me on the sidewalk.

"What do you mean?" He frowned at me, still looking kind of confused.

I rolled my eyes at him, not believing how dense he was being. "Dude!" I held my hand out to stop him from walking any further. "A girl like that"—I nodded my head towards the house—"isn't going to be single for long." I chuckled at the way his eyes widened. "If you think she still has feelings for you and you want to act on them now that you finally have your head out of your ass, then go for it. But if you're not..." I shrugged my shoulders, not sure what else to say.

"Then you need to step aside and let her find someone who is willing to give her everything that she wants."

I patted him on the shoulder before taking a few further steps closer to the door. "But first you need to get this over with," I said, gesturing to the house.

He sighed before stepping past me and opening the front door. Before we even got over the threshold, we froze in shock when a chorus of "WELCOME HOME" was shouted out through the room. Liam was swallowed by the crowd and was being pulled into hugs and kisses on the cheek. It was a happy scene to witness and one I never got to have. That's what had made enlisting so easy for me. When there was no family to leave behind, nobody missed you.

I froze when my eyes landed on Callie standing at the back of the room. Where everyone else appeared happy and excited to have Liam home, she just looked heartbroken— like her entire world had been taken from her.

I glanced back at Liam and realized exactly why she seemed distraught. He currently had a trio of sexy country girls around him, and by the expression on his face, he was eating up all of the attention.

I rolled my eyes at how much of an idiot he was and quickly made my way to where I last saw Callie. She was nowhere to be found, but I had an idea where she'd be.

I quickly grabbed two bottles of beer from the fridge and opened the back door.

"Want some company?" I glanced down at her sitting on the step staring out at the fading sunset.

"Sure." She nodded her head before giving me a small smile. She patted the step next to her and I quickly took the spot before passing her one of the bottles. "Thanks."

I tapped the neck of my bottle against hers and took a large gulp. My exhale of appreciation must have given away how much I had missed a nice cold bottle of beer.

She giggled before taking a sip of her own.

"Not one for parties?" I asked, cutting right to the chase.

She shook her head before biting down on her bottom lip. "You must think I'm such a horrible person," she mumbled. "Everyone is so happy inside, and here I am acting as though someone died." She shook her head, obviously feeling ashamed for how she was acting and feeling.

"Not at all." I wanted to alleviate whatever she was feeling.

The sad thing was that there was nothing I could say or do. Only Liam could fix this.

"You've missed him a lot."

She glanced away, avoiding my gaze.

"Hey." I reached over and grabbed her hand. "He's

missed you just as much."

She turned her head, looking at me doubtfully.

I grinned at her, loving the wicked thought that had just taken root. If these two were going to be difficult, I was more than happy to interfere.

"Now, how about we go inside and you give me a dance?"

She widened her eyes at me in surprise before the cutest smirk graced her face. Seconds later, she slipped her hand into mine and allowed me to pull her up. We entered the kitchen and placed our bottles on the side. Before I could lead her to the lounge, she spun around, stopping me by placing her hand on my chest.

"Why are you doing this?" she asked, looking up at me curiously.

"Doing what?" I could play aloof when I wanted. "It's only a dance." I reached down and took her hand in mine before pulling her behind me. I was aware it may end badly, but if we waited for these two to get their act together, we'd be waiting a while.

Chapter Four

Callie

I WASN'T SURE what wicked plot Parker had in mind, but judging from the evil smirk on his face, I was sure it would be creative. When Parker told me how much Liam had missed me, I tried to ignore it—to block out the words that would be my undoing—but no matter how hard I tried, I just couldn't.

I wanted him to miss me, to ache for me in the way that I ached for him.

Parker slowly led me to the dance floor. There were other couples on there, but Liam was not a partner in any of them. As I looked further in the room, I was disappointed when I saw him talking to one of the girls that worked down at the bar. I had worked there for the last few months and I knew just how good they were at securing a male's attention. It looked like Liam was next.

Parker may have thought that Liam's feelings for me

were more than friendship, but I knew better. I knew that friendship was all that Liam and I would ever have.

"Hey." Parker placed his finger beneath my chin before lifting my head to gaze at him. "Don't worry about that. Just look right here."

I nodded my head and allowed him to pull me closer to him. Parker was tall, handsome, cheeky, sexy and obviously had a sense of humor. As I stared up at him, I wanted to feel something. If I could feel something for him, I could finally move forward from being hung up on a best friend that was never going to return my feelings. I willed myself to feel something as he slid his arm around my waist but I only felt...

Comfort. Friendship. Nothing that suggested I was sexually attracted to him at all.

He rocked us from side to side to the slow beat and I slid my arms up and around his neck, allowing myself to feel the music.

"Damn, you are beautiful." He smiled down at me. "You know, if Liam ever messes up, you are welcome to use me if needed."

I laughed, leaning my head back. His arm tightened around my waist before his fingers reached up to play with a loose strand.

"In fact, if he ever messes things up, I may just give him an ass–kicking myself." He winked at me, increasing his rating of sexiness.

"I think you may be mistaken regarding Liam and me." We may have been apart for seven years but that didn't mean I had forgotten about our past. I may have cared for him as more than a friend, but that didn't mean that everything had suddenly changed. Absence would never make the heart grow fonder in our case.

"You sure about that?" His eyes flicked over my head before he lifted my hand in the air and twirled me in a circle.

I giggled as I spun but froze when I collided with a hard chest. Looking up, I knew who it would be. I'd know him anywhere.

"Can I have this dance?" He reached up and tucked a loose curl behind my ear.

I looked behind me to ask Parker, but he was gone.

"Sure." I nodded and took his hand in mine, allowing him to pull me closer. Shivers slowly traveled up my arm from where he touched me. I tried to act as if they didn't, but it was obvious. I had given up trying to pretend he didn't affect me a long time ago.

I leaned my head forward and rested it on his chest, closing my eyes as I listened to the 'thump thump' of his heart. I loved the sound. It had always calmed me and today was no different.

It was just that today, I was more resigned to the fact his heart would never be mine.

"Don't do that." He placed his fingers beneath my chin and tilted my head up. "Don't think that."

"You don't even know what I was thinking," I replied.

"But I know you. I know how you are—how your mind works." He frowned down at me, gazing into my eyes. "I know that you always think the worst. I was hoping you'd have outgrown that."

I stared up at him, hating that his words hurt me. I also hated what I was about to say to him because I knew they would hurt him also.

"You don't know me anymore." I don't know why I said it. Instead of pulling him closer, those words would only serve to push him away, but maybe pushing him away was for the best. That way I couldn't get hurt.

That way I couldn't be left behind again.

"I don't, don't I?" He stared down at me. "Just like I don't know that you cry at movie trailers. Or the way you *have* to have jelly on peanut butter. Or how obsessed you are with your books and how you can't read them if they are signed by an author."

I smiled up at him, trying to keep my emotions in check.

He lifted his hand and rubbed his thumb across my cheek.

"I love the way that you always give everything to someone and never ask for anything back."

I stared up at him, surprised. Not surprised by the things he was saying—the things he was saying were things that he should know, things that any best friend should know about the other. What surprised me most was the way that he was looking at me.

He was looking at me in a way that he had never looked at me before.

He was looking at me in what I imagined was the exact same way that I always looked at him.

Like I was his own world. The center of everything.

I wanted so badly to be the one for him, but I was scared: scared that he was forcing himself to feel a certain way for me.

What I felt for Liam wasn't forced, it was natural, and I wanted so badly for it to be the same for him.

"Please don't." I shook my head and took his hand that was still resting against my cheek in mine. "Please don't think that you have to look at me like that. In that way." I couldn't bear it.

"Like what?" he asked.

"Like you finally want everything with me that I have

wanted with you. I have loved you for so long, Liam." I hated that my lip wobbled. I hated that I was being so emotional, but it had to be said. "But I think it's time."

I slowly moved our arms until they were hang at our sides with only our fingertips touching.

"Time for what?" he asked, gazing down at me.

I took a deep breath before uttering the words. "It's time for me to let you go."

Chapter Five

Liam

THIS WAS NOT how tonight was supposed to go. I was supposed to sweep her off her feet, not send her running in the opposite direction.

I finally pulled my head out of my ass and realized everything that I had left behind was still here waiting for me, and she responded by basically telling me to go away.

I shook my head and quickly made my way towards the front door, avoiding all hugs and handshakes. By the time I made it outside, she was already in the front seat of her jeep, pulling out of the drive.

"For fuck's sake," I muttered. I turned around, feeling completely dejected. What the hell was I supposed to do now?

"Where's Callie?"

My head shot up at the sound of my mother's voice. She had taken Callie in from day one as one of her own children, and over the years, I had come to love the bond between them. You'd mistake them for mother and daughter. That's how close they were.

Callie's mother had died when she was only eleven years old from breast cancer. For a month straight, she wouldn't cry or even speak to anyone. Including me. She'd just slipped into her own little bubble where no one could reach her.

Until my mother.

We'd gone to Callie's one day after school, and she'd disappeared straight upstairs, leaving me trailing after her with Callie's father. My mom had walked into her bedroom and sat down next to her on the bed, wrapping her in the tightest hug I think she had ever given anyone.

In the seconds that followed, my heart had splintered into a thousand pieces, hearing the deep, gut–wrenching sobs that came from her. My mom was the only one who could reach her in her dark place, and I was thankful every day to her when little bits of Callie came back to us.

I thought I had lost my best friend until my mom brought her back.

"She's gone home." I take a seat on the steps and stared down the street that took her away. Mom sat next to me and stared at me with her eyebrow raised, waiting for more.

"She may have also told me to leave her alone. To let her go."

Mom smirked, confusing me even more. "And instead of going after her, here you are sitting, feeling sorry for yourself."

"But she said…"

"Sweetheart," she interrupted me. "That girl has missed you more than anyone. For the first few months after your deployment, I don't think she stopped crying. Every time I saw her, her eyes were always puffy. Whenever she saw me, she would ask if I had heard from you."

Now I felt like more of an asshole. I knew she'd missed me, but imagining her crying into her pillow at night fucking killed me. I opened my mouth to say... I don't know. What could I say?

"She loves you." She reached over to take my hand, and instead of her warm skin, the cold feel of metal landed in my palm. Looking down, I saw they were the keys to my motorbike.

"It's parked in the garage. Now you have to go and get that girl."

"What if I mess it up?" I asked, voicing my fear. If I screwed it up with Callie, I would lose her.

"What if you don't?" she asked. She folded my fingers around the keys before reaching over and giving me a quick kiss on the cheek.

I grinned at her. "Thanks, Mom."

I ran to the garage, like my ass was on fire, and climbed on, not even bothering to appreciate how stunning my bike still looked. As the bike came to life, I gave the handlebars a gentle rev and sped out of the garage.

It was only a short drive to Callie's. I parked next to her jeep and took a deep breath before stopping in front of her door. After three knocks, I waited patiently, cringing at the thought that she may not open it, especially due to her having a peephole front and center.

I tensed when I heard her door being unlocked, still not having a clue what to say to her.

I wanted Parker here so he could give me an ass–kicking.

The door slowly opened. Her eyes were puffy and her

cheeks were wet from her tears. She looked so lost, and I hated that I was the one who had made her feel like that—the one who had made her cry yet again.

I shot forward and took her face in my hands before kicking the door shut with my foot and stared down at her. I expected to see anger in her beautiful eyes, but all I saw was her love for me.

That's all that I ever saw when I looked at her. She was it for me. She was all I wanted and needed and that was never going to change.

She was the one.

I slammed my lips down on hers, sucking her bottom lip into my mouth, and she gasped in surprise at my actions. She held onto my wrists as I stumbled forward trying not to shove her against the door and dry hump her.

My Callie deserved better than that.

"What are you doing?" she whispered, pulling away from me a little.

"I'm sorry," I replied in a quiet tone. I rested my forehead against hers.

"What are you sorry for?"

"For everything." I shook my head, at a loss of what to say. "For leaving. For not seeing what I had. For not appreciating that everything I ever needed or wanted was right here in front of me."

She closed her eyes, and I wasn't sure if it was to block me out or...

"Please don't close your eyes."

She slowly opened them and stared up at me. "I don't know what you want, Liam."

"I don't want anything," I quickly replied.

She continued to stare up at me, refusing to back down.

"I only want one chance. One chance to show you."

"To show me what?"

"That I'm the one for you. I'll be the first one you see in the morning and the last one you see at night." I pressed my lips to hers quickly, giving her a gentle kiss. "Give me one chance to show you just how much I can love you. One chance to have forever with you."

"One chance?" she asked. Her grip on my wrists tightened, and I knew right then that forever would never be long enough for us.

"One chance and I'll…"

"Shut up and kiss me," she whispered before pushing up on her toes and pressing her lips to mine. I chuckled against them and did just that. I trailed my hands down her sides and lifted her up, groaning as she wrapped her legs around my waist.

"Take me to the bedroom," she whispered.

I pulled back, surprised at her words. She had to know that wasn't the reason I came here. I would wait forever for her.

"We don't have to…" I said. "That's not…"

"I know." She reached up and smoothed my hair back and off my forehead. "I've waited so long for you. I don't want to wait any longer."

I dipped my head, taking her lips in a gentle kiss and carried her into the bedroom. As I laid her in the center of her bed, I smiled down at her, loving the way that she looked up at me.

She was so beautiful.

"Make love to me," she whispered, placing her hand on my shoulder and pulling me down to her.

"I'll never stop, Callie." I pressed my lips to hers and gave myself over to her, surrendering all that I was. "I'll never stop."

THE END

Until Next Time

K. L. JESSOP

Chapter One

IVY

AS I EXIT my car, I shield my eyes with my hand to block out the low evening sun, scanning the view before me. Satisfaction fills my veins and warmth covers my heart. I've longed for this for twelve months, and now that the school term has broken and I'm finally back, a smile grows across my face.

Ever since I was a child, the Cotswolds sunflower field has captured my heart—be it the glorious smells, the river of vibrant yellow or the fact it's just a fond family memory that has always stayed with me. Back then, I had been just a young girl enjoying life, school holidays being the fuel that had kept me going for the rest of the year. Now, at the age of twenty, the holidays are much-needed breaks to help me recover from the workload. Teacher training and studies can be exhausting, and I honestly don't think I would have got through it at times if it weren't for

Dad.

Family holidays to the Cotswolds provide the relaxation everyone needs from living in a busy city. The chaos of London is overwhelming, and the second we'd started the drive to Guiting Power to stay with my aunt, my soul had felt like it was returning home.

Looking around, I make sure no one is about before I head down to the gate that leads to the field. The low sun covers the ground like a spotlight, weaving its way through the tall sunflowers as I brush my fingers along the thick stems, heading further into the field like it's a secret garden.

As always, viewing times to the public are only on Sundays. They always have been for as long as I can remember, but that has never stopped me coming down out of hours and climbing the gates to walk amongst the six-foot giants alone.

My thoughts go to my mother and the times we'd walk the field together. She had been the biggest light in my life, my best friend, and was taken too soon when I was just fifteen years old.

Coming to a stop, I look up towards the sky and close my eyes, letting the sun cast a glow over me as I think of her. I miss her more than life itself, and these past few years without her have been an undeniable struggle at times. Cancer took Mum from us, but being here makes it feel like she never left and my heart feels full once more, even though it will be forever broken with her loss.

My emotions get the better of me, and the everlasting ache I have for Mum causes silent tears to fall although a smile remains on my face from the memory of her running through the field. I'm finally in my place of peace and pure bliss. That's until my sixth sense has me opening my eyes at the feeling of being watched. I lift my gaze to see a shirtless physique that makes my mouth water with a shotgun slung over a muscular shoulder.

However, it's the pair of intimidating blue eyes that has me frozen in place.

AIDEN

I'VE BEEN WATCHING her from the moment she jumped the gate of the field like she's the lifeline I've been longing for. My shitty day had somehow ceased to matter when I saw her basking in the sunlight like an angel, and it's like everything in the Cotswolds suddenly feels great again.

Usually, I'd be firing my shotgun into the air when it comes to trespassers wanting to walk the field, scaring them shitless and laughing under my breath when I see them run. But I haven't. I haven't even loaded it. Something inside my twisted heart had told me not to. Either way, I've followed her every move like her presence is a calling and it's brought me to stand a few feet away from her with my heart racing so hard I can barely breathe.

I take in her golden blonde hair, big green eyes and strawberry colour lips that I suddenly want to feel against mine. I've not felt like this in a long time—if ever—and it's shaken me up so much that I've lost my fucking words.

She stares back at me like a deer in the headlights, which is no doubt due to the gun slung over my shoulder. Her thin frame is curved perfectly in the right places, her tanned legs a temptation that extend from underneath a short floral skirt. Her yellow vest top matches the colour of the field.

When I clear my throat, she blinks hard before quickly wiping away fallen tears that I long to know the cause of.

"Oh, I'm sorry. I didn't think… I didn't think anyone else was here." Her soft voice causes my stomach to tighten as I try and work out what the hell is happening to me. Twelve months of no sex has turned me into a pussy.

"That's because no one should be here. The field is closed until Sunday. Says it on the main gate."

"So why are you here?" she asks, this time with a confidence that surprises me considering I'm standing here armed.

"Because it's my field and you are trespassing."

"Well, I am sorry. I didn't mean to cause any trouble." She points to me. "And you don't have to use that either. I'll go."

"Wait." The word comes out a little harder than I'd intended as she starts to back away, the desperation in me wanting her to stay. She halts, looking at me with uncertainty. "Why are you here anyway?"

And why were you crying?

It's none of my damn business, and besides, I need to get my head back in the fucking game as I've been distracted for too long by a stranger with no name.

"I…" She closes her eyes briefly and swallows before looking back at me—a look that seems all too familiar—holding my gaze. "I come here every year. Out of hours. It's the only time I can truly feel close to my mum and not be disturbed. I've done it ever since she died. This was her favourite place."

That low, gut-wrenching feeling of loss hits my stomach like a heavy weight, and I have to quickly compose myself: I don't wish for her to see the effect her words have had on me. I lost my brother twelve months ago, and it's almost fucking killed me.

"She liked sunflowers." It's an obvious statement given the fact we are in a field full of them.

"She did," she whispers. "I'm sorry. I didn't mean to—"

Without a second thought, I step towards her and the words fall from my mouth faster than I can stop them. "Would you like to walk with me?"

Her eyes widen as if my question is ridiculous before they latch onto the thick gun barrels. "That depends."

"On?"

"On if I'm likely to end up dead and buried in this very field if I do."

I chuckle. I like her. Taking the shotgun off my shoulder, I show her it's not even loaded. "I have no intention of shooting you. I'd just like to walk with you a little. If you're willing to do that with a stranger with a weapon that is?"

"Well, I'm all for the thrill and adventure, so it would be wrong of me to turn down such a proposal I guess."

I grin. Five minutes in her company and I feel like the weight I've carried for so long has been lifted. Holding out my hand, I introduce myself. "I'm Aiden. My family owns the farm up ahead, along with this field."

She places her hand in mine and it triggers a tingle to run my spine. "I'm Ivy. My Aunt owns the Guesthouse in Guiting Power Village."

I frown. "Lucinda?"

"That's her."

"Shit. If she knew I'd greeted you with a gun, she'd blow my head off."

"I don't doubt it." She laughs, and Jesus it sounds like heaven.

Chapter Two.

IVY

"YOU'RE A TEACHER?" Aiden asks, now thankfully with his T-shirt on, stopping my eyes from wandering as we continue to walk the sunflower field. His manner is completely different from the persona I was first greeted with. His tall, confident physique had screamed power and intimidation as he'd kept me captive with his eyes. Somehow, they'd been more frightening than the shotgun, holding a depth to them that told me he's troubled. However, in the short time I've been with him, he's dropped his guard giving way to an easiness between us. I feel like I've known him for a lifetime when it's barely been five minutes.

"Not fully qualified yet. I have one year of studies left, including my final teaching practise."

"Wow. That's impressive. I take it you've always wanted to be a teacher?"

"I follow in the footsteps of my parents. Mum was an English teacher, and Dad works with Maths."

"So, I take it that as it's summer, you are here on holiday?"

"Yes. Each year we leave London and visit Aunt Lucinda for a month. She is my mum's sister, and even with Mum gone, the rest of the family didn't want the tradition to change, and neither did I. The only thing I long for more than the others is the impact this field has on my heart. Everywhere Mum went still feels like home to, but this place somehow becomes more."

He nods, now looking a little more solemn than moments ago. "That's understandable. Sometimes we need to do things to make those we've lost remain close. Or keep their spirit alive for the sake of others."

"That sounds like the words of someone with experience." I smile, unsure whether to push him on it as I sense there is more but also know it's none of my business.

"I lost my brother a year ago. Farming accident. Joey was five years older than me and the best friend and brother anyone could ask for. The loss of him has had a massive impact on our family for many reasons. Since his death, I've been head down with working the farm. Meanwhile, my mother doesn't seem to give two shits about my heart and what I want."

"It may come across like that, but maybe deep down it's just her way of dealing with it all."

He shakes his head. "Trust me it's not."

Never has a man made me feel all kinds of emotions like Aiden has in the short space of time I've known him. Neither has my body wanted to be close to a person so strongly as it does now. We have a connection, granted its completely different circumstances, but grief is the same

141

regardless.

Like it has a mind of its own, I reach out and place my hand on his arm. His blue eyes are now dark and poignant. "I'm sorry, Aiden," I whisper. "I didn't mean to pry."

"You didn't. I chose to talk, which believe me is a first."

I watch him as he walks off in front of me. I can't imagine how hard it must be trying to support his mum while he, too, is feeling the loss. Thankfully, Dad coped considerably well with Mum's death. Somehow knowing she was terminal prepared us for the worst. Regardless of her absence being unbearable, it hadn't been a shock when her final day came.

"Have you left me already?" I hear Aiden shout out of view.

I follow in the direction he's just gone and come to an opening in the field that is sectioned off with wire fencing and a gate. The large space is Sunflower-free and Aiden is lying among grass, the soft glow of the remaining sunlight casting over his golden skin, highlighting his facial features more. His eyes are closed, and his dark hair and the scruff of his jaw look like a masterpiece.

God, he's gorgeous.

Around the space he lies are a few rocks and the remainders of a campfire. I've never seen this part of the field before, and I question how far we have walked.

"I never knew this was here."

He opens one eye and peers at me. "It's new. Somehow the flowers just stopped growing here, so with it being at the bottom of the field, I took it upon myself to make it my own, so I could come here to think. Fencing it off soon made people realise it was out of bounds."

"But now that I know what it's used for, it's not your

142

own."

"I know."

I don't want him to think I'm intruding in his space, and in any other circumstances I'd walk away. But I don't want to.

He sits up and pats the ground. "Which is why this is now your space, too. You can come here whenever you want to be close to your mum."

My heart does a little dance at how thoughtful he is, but then my mind wanders to the possibility of something else. "And would that mean seeing more of you, too?"

His eyes flash to mine causing my heart to race as a smile tugs his lips. "I will be here waiting if you'd want me to be."

"I think the question is more, do *you* want to be?" I raise a brow, a smile slowly spreading across my face.

He looks away from me for a moment, and I want to know what he is thinking, but his reply is one that takes me by surprise. "You're here for the summer, right?"

"Four weeks of it, yes."

"Okay." He clears his throat, and those blue eyes hold me captive once again. "How about you spend your time here with me? We can hang out, have fun."

A buzz of excitement hit's my core. "Hmm, that depends."

"On?"

"On whether guns are involved. Because I'm still not convinced that you didn't come here with the intention of killing me."

He raises a brow. "And yet for someone who is still unsure, here you are."

"Fair point."

"So, what do you say? Wanna spend time with the

local farm boy?"

Everything inside of me is screaming yes. What better way to spend my time here than with a hot guy with killer eyes and a body I'd climb without a second thought.

"You'd do that?"

"I just offered, didn't I?"

I hold his gaze, wondering if this is a good idea or if it's the best idea I've heard in a long time. After all, we only live once. "Okay. You're on." I smile, feeling my cheeks flush before I take a seat on the grass beside him.

"Awesome. Welcome to Guiting Power."

I laugh. "You do know I've been here many times before, right?"

"Yeah. But you've never spent a summer with me."

AIDEN

"WOW. YOU DO not get to experience this in the city," Ivy breathes.

We are laid on our backs, looking up at the night sky and the canvas of bright stars, the full moon glowing down on us like a spotlight. After making a call to her dad to say that she was okay and that she'd be back at the guesthouse a little later, we've just talked like we've known each other for years. I now know she is single, has just turned twenty, has a phobia of spiders, hates mushrooms and has an obsession with Tom Hardy. Despite her pain from losing her mother, she has great expectations of life and an enthusiasm that I envy. Because while she is like a breath of fresh air with her goals set for the future, I'm laid here at the age of twenty-five, a few months off inheriting a farm I don't want and have no intention of running. I want to be a mechanic by trade. Grease and tools are my passion, not livestock and barns. It's not that I don't like anything to do with farming—truth is I secretly love it which in itself is a contradiction—but I stopped wanting this life before Joey died, and when he was taken, everything I wanted outside of the farmhouse walls came to a halt.

"It's quite something, right?" I turn on my side, now wanting to look at Ivy because I've seen the stars many times and will continue to for years on out. This summer may be the only time I get with her, and I intend to spend as much time with her as I can if she'll let me.

"It's breathtaking."

"It sure is," I whisper.

She tilts her head to the side to face me, and when she catches me watching her, I don't miss the halt of her breathing and I swear her cheeks are flushed. She is beautiful.

"You're staring."

"I am."

"Why?"

I want to say that it's because she is mesmerising. I want to say that from the moment I saw her, I've wanted her lips against mine. But I don't. Instead, I say the one thing that's been on my mind from the very second we started talking.

"Do you believe in fate?"

"Wow, you've gone deep on us fast. Next you'll be asking for my hand in marriage." She jokes, causing me to grin.

"Well, do you?"

"I've never really thought about it. Why do you ask?"

"Because from the moment I saw you, everything seems to have fallen into place—like I've known you for years, yet I hardly know you at all; like I was meant to walk the field this afternoon, even though I never needed to."

"You see. Real deep."

I laugh.

This time she turns her body to face me, mirroring my position. "I must admit, I've never felt more relaxed than I do now in a long time. There is something about you, Aiden Hope, that makes me chilled. Even seeing you with a shotgun over your shoulder never truly bothered me."

"Your eyes said otherwise."

"It's called acting."

"I guess I need to work on being more intimidating then."

"You can try, but it won't wash with me now. I know you have a secret love for little lambs that hop around the field and even had one sleeping in your bed as a child. And I'm not afraid to voice it should I need to."

"I told you that in confidence."

"And I never said I *would* expose your secret. Just that I'll use it should I need to."

I frown. "I don't see a difference."

"Nah, neither do I really, but it sounded good."

I hold her gaze before we both burst out laughing, loving the feeling she's granted me. For too long, I've been lost in a world I couldn't find a way out of.

"Thank you, Ivy," I find myself saying.

"For what?"

"Making me smile. I feel like spending time with you will make everything feel right again."

Compassion clouds her eyes, and for a moment, she looks away from me, focusing on the chain around my neck. "I'm only here for the summer, Aiden," she whispers, and I'm unsure if she is reminding me of that fact or telling herself.

Not able to hold back any longer, I reach out and take her hand in mine. Her eyes flash back up to me and I hold her stare, murmuring the words that are true to my heart. "Then I want to make it one of your best. I'm glad you said yes to my crazy, on the spot request because if I'm honest, Ivy, I don't think I can watch you walk around Guiting Power and not be a part of your time spent here this summer."

She smiles. "My mum always told me to go with my gut, and from the moment you asked me to walk with you, I knew it was the right choice to make. I can't think of anything better than to spend my summer with you."

I grin, fighting the urge to kiss her. Who would have thought a girl amongst the sunflowers would have me all as knotted up as Ivy has. Either way, I'm going to make this summer one to remember because I sure as hell know it's one I'm never going to forget.

Chapter Three.

IVY

"HE'S TAKING YOU shooting?" my dad asks with horror in his eyes from the other side of Aunt Lucinda's breakfast table. I've spent three weeks in the company of Aiden and I've never laughed so much. From water fights to riding his quad bike, to pub lunches and exploring his farm, I've enjoyed every second so far, and the ache in my heart with not having Mum here has eased more that it has done in all the years since her passing.

"Clay pigeon shooting, Dad. Not actual shooting."

"It still involves a gun, sweetie. And you've only known him a few weeks."

"Aiden Hope is one of the nicest men I know," Aunt Lucinda adds as she places another plate of toast down on the table. "A little troubled, I have to admit, but honestly, Neil, there's nothing to worry about. And she's spent time with him already."

"See." I raise a brow at Dad and try and ease his anxiety as he looks at me with uncertainty. Honestly, you wouldn't think I'm an adult when my dad is around. In his eyes, I'm still his little girl who needs to follow him around. "There is nothing to worry about."

"I don't agree."

Taking the butter knife that now has a dollop of strawberry jam on it, I spread it over my toast. "Dad, you and Mum always told me to live my life. So, I am. Because let's face it, I could get run down and killed by a bus tomorrow."

"Ivy," he warns.

Meanwhile, Lucinda just snorts at my matter-of-fact comment. "Let her go, Neil. What else is she going to do around here other than help me make beds for the guests and man the phones? The girl is on holiday."

I've not required Dad's permission since I turned eighteen, but that doesn't mean I don't respect his opinion or wishes at times. But Lucinda is right: I haven't come here to be making beds and work.

Then, like my prayers have been answered, the honk of Aiden's quad bike blasts from outside and I'm out of my seat.

"That will be him." I grab my phone and my toast and lean over to kiss Dad on the cheek. "I promise you, I will be fine."

"Just keep me updated with what you're doing."

"Will do." I head out, shouting to them both over my shoulder that I love them just before Aiden's smile greets me.

It's another glorious day, and what we have in store fills me with excitement.

"Your carriage awaits. Please try not to get crumbs all

over the quad," he jokes.

"I'll try not to," I say with a mouthful of toast. "Have you eaten?"

"Ivy, I live and work on a farm. I had breakfast like five hours ago."

"Awesome. It will soon be lunchtime then. You're buying the burgers today."

"I'm aware. You've not stopped reminding me since I mentioned it."

I grin, finishing my toast, taking the helmet he's offering and place it on my head.

"Right. I'm ready."

"Alright. Let's go do some shooting."

"I'm so excited." I jump up and down with a happy dance, and he looks at me like I'm crazy.

"I've never known a girl to be so excited about shooting shit."

"First, I'm a woman, and second, when you live in the city and all you see is people and traffic, you forget that there's a bigger life outside of it. Humour me on this please."

He chuckles. "You are something else. Hop on; let's get out of here."

Jumping on the quad, I secure my helmet before wrapping my arms around his waist and breathing in the woody and spicey scent that I can't get enough of as my heart rate picks up from having him so close.

AIDEN

"PULL!" I SHOUT to Ivy before a pink clay target flies through the air. I pull the trigger of the shotgun and instantly pink dust bursts into thousands of pieces right before Ivy screams with excitement behind me. I grin every time I hear her.

"That was amazing. You are so good."

I've not missed one yet as I've been showing her what to do. Joey and I used to do it every Sunday, take some time out from studies or feeding the herd and just shoot shit. Be it rusty old cans or wooden targets, we'd fuck about for hours.

"You wanna turn now?" I ask, noticing she has taken her defenders off yet loving the joy in her face as she sits on the bark of the old oak tree.

"Can I?"

"Well, that is what we're here for. Put your ear defenders back on, we don't want the sound of the shots fired damaging your ears."

"Damaging my ears? Trust me, you haven't been in a class full of eight-year-olds."

"Either way, keep them on and get over here."

I reload the shotgun and Ivy comes to stand next to me, her proximity causing my skin to heat as her strawberry shampoo wraps around me like a new form of air. I glance at her as a smile tugs my lips.

"Have you ever killed with it?"

I laugh. "Jesus, Ivy, you make me sound like a murderer."

"I mean animals. Have you killed any?"

"Only when I've had to."

"Like what?"

"Rabbits. Birds. Cattle if there's nothing more we can do for them due to injury or diseases." I click the chamber once I've loaded the new rounds ready for her. "And no, I get no fun out of that before you ask."

151

"I wasn't going to."

I look at her and grin when I see a devilish look in her eye. "But you were thinking about it."

Her face lights up. "You know me so well, Mr Hope."

"I'm getting there. Now, come stand on the spot."

She stands in front of me facing the open field, confidence in her frame as I hand her the gun. She studies it and the thrill of seeing her in possession of it chases through me.

"You ever held a gun before?"

"No. But now the confidence in me has suddenly gone."

"Here." I stand close behind her and position her hands where they should be on the gun. "Hold it steady. The key is to be in control of it, not let it control you. And ensure you have power in your stance." I place my hands on her hips and my fingertips make contact with the bare skin of her waist. I don't miss the hitch in her breath from my touch, and it only heightens my desires for her more knowing that I have this effect on her. The connection between us has been growing since the first time I saw her, and I'd give anything to explore it further.

When she turns her head to the side, our eyes lock. Her cheeks flush and I press my fingers a little harder against her waist. Her gaze drops to my mouth and her tongue darts out to wet her lips, sending a jolt of desire straight to my cock. I clear my throat, regaining my composure as desire runs through my veins. It's clear she knows damn well what she's doing to me when she turns back towards the field with a grin on her face.

"Okay, aim it into the air, and when you're ready, shout. But don't worry if you miss the target. It's your first time."

"Okay." She blows out a breath, and I head back to the hut ready to release the clay target from the trap. "Remember: you control it. And breathe."

She nods, and I wait for her call, my smile wide as shit because no woman I've been with has ever wanted to try this before.

"Pull!"

I release the trap and like a fucking professional, or just pure fluke, Ivy smashes her first target on the first hit.

"Yes! I did it! I did it!" she screams, spinning around in excitement and forgetting she is holding a loaded gun.

I duck, covering my head with my hands. "Whoa, Ivy. That fucker is loaded," I yell, laughing as her hysteria bellows out.

Placing the shotgun down and throwing her defenders on the ground, she skips over to me still on cloud nine with her achievement. The joy in her features fills me with pleasure.

"How is that for fucking control!" She beams, catching me off guard as she jumps on me, causing us to fall to the ground laughing as she straddles me.

As our hysteria subsides, the mood between us instantly shifts and we hold each other's gaze. My dick twitches with the feel of her around me, my heart pounding with her being so close and the thought of kissing her has never been so great.

"Did you see me?" she whispers, her breath now raspy as her eyes flicker between my gaze and my mouth.

"I did." Reaching up, I tuck the hair behind her ear before holding the nape of her neck as my other hand snakes up her thigh. "I did see you. I do see you."

Lifting my head, I pull her towards me, meeting her halfway before our mouths crash and I kiss her senseless.

153

Chapter Four

AIDEN

"YOU PLANNING ON doing any work today?" My uncle grunts as he throws the morning newspapers down on the kitchen table, knocking my coffee cup for it to spill everywhere.

"I haven't decided."

"Since that girl turned up, you've let things slip. Again."

I swallow down my irritation for the sake of my mum, who is making bread, but I'd love nothing more to pin him up against the fucking wall.

I look up, hating the fury that is now racing through my veins due to his presence. "I've been up since four and finished fixing the top field fence with Scott before heading down to the sunflower field to check up on things there. What the hell have you done other than go and get a paper you don't even fucking read?" I growl.

His jaw tightens, anger now in his eyes. "You can't run a business with no farm, Aiden."

That's rich coming from him seeing as though he does fuck all around here yet still gets the glory.

I stand, hearing enough of this shit. "And I can't run the farm with only one farmhand. So why don't you pull your fucking weight."

Saying bye to Mum, I grab my phone and head out of the house, finding Ivy's number to call to see what her plans are today, hoping she can take my mind off things once again.

A part of me hates the fact my uncle is right: I've not done as much work on the farm since Ivy showed up, but why the fuck is it all on me? It may soon be my farm, but I'm still keeping a roof over his head when I don't even need to.

"Come save me," I say to Ivy when she answers, and her soft chuckle is like music to my ears.

"Bad day?"

"Yes. That and the fact it's been more than twelve hours since I saw you."

And kissed you.

Ever since our first kiss, we haven't stopped. She tastes so sweet and her lips are so soft. Fuck, I want to kiss her more before she leaves. "Time is short. Our days left together are numbered." We are into our final week and I hate the fact it's gone so fast. I want to make the most of our last four days together.

"Well, in that case I'm on my way. What's the adventure today?"

"The pleasure of my company."

"That's it?"

"Or you can muck out the stable."

"Such a gentleman. I'll take option one. I'll see you in a bit."

"Can't wait." I cut the call, grinning to myself as I prepare for another day in the best company I've found in ages.

***

"Are you going to the village fete on Friday?" Ivy asks as she takes a bite of a strawberry.

I inwardly curse at her question. I've not been to the local fete in years—too many people and not enough home brew beer—but something tells me from the big green eyes that stare back at me that she's hoping I'll say yes.

"I've not been to the village fete since my dad died when I was a teen. It doesn't interest me anymore."

She nods slowly, popping another strawberry into her mouth before moving to lay on her front to face me. My mood from this morning hasn't fully shifted.

"Will it interest you if I said I was going?"

I grin. I somehow knew a question like that was coming. "Well, I guess I can make an exception just this once."

"Correct answer, farm boy."

We are having a small picnic in the main field up on the hill that overlooks the Village. A contrast of greens and yellows from the sunflowers fill the space below us, but it's the woman beside me that is the brightest light of my day. When we kiss, she takes me under with a feeling I can't comprehend while her body moulds against mine like she was made just for me.

Then, out of nowhere, a feeling of uncertainty washes

over me, reminding me that she's only here for a few more days before she goes about her life, living her dream, while I'm stuck here hating mine.

We lay silently for a moment, the only sound around being the birds in the trees. I could get used to this. The silence. The comfort.

"Is that one of your farmhands?"

I tilt my head back and follow her line of sight, making eye contact with the enemy of the Hope family as my jaw tightens.

"That's my Uncle."

"Does he live on the farm, too?"

"Unfortunately."

"Oh. You don't get on?"

"No."

"Why not?"

I've not gone into too much detail about him with Ivy. Purely because he's not worth my time. "He doesn't like the fact I have authority."

"Has that been worse since your dad died?"

I suddenly feel like I'm being interrogated. "Can we not talk about my uncle?"

"I'm sorry."

Laying back on the ground, silence falls between us, and I know that my sudden change in attitude has made her feel uncomfortable. For that, I need to explain because she's told me everything about her life and family.

Curling my fingers around hers, I stroke my thumb over the back of her hand. With a heavy sigh, I let out the story that has become our family's worst nightmare.

"Long story short, the eldest son inherits the farm. It's been in our family for years. Dad died when Joey was only nineteen making him a young owner with a massive responsibility. Now with Joey gone—"

"You get the farm."

I nod. "Once the paperwork is drawn up and signed."

"And you're happy with that?"

I stare up at the blue sky and think about all the things I want to do with my life that is beyond the country fields of the Cotswolds. The adventures, the opportunities. But as long as my mother is alive, they're ones I'll never get the chance to take. I may not want the farm, but I will never abandon her or leave her homeless. "I don't have much choice. Any chance of being what I want to be or seeing what is beyond Gulting Power was ripped away when my brother died."

She smiles flatly. "So how does your uncle fit into all of this?"

"Ray's pissed because he never had the chance to take over. Being the second youngest in his family and having a wife who didn't want to stick around to give him kids, he wants revenge on anyone he can get it from."

"You being the number one target."

I tilt my head towards her. "You got it. He hates me, and he certainly doesn't like being told what to do, so this morning's little spat won't have gone down well."

"Why, what happened this morning?"

I never told her. I never told her because I don't wish to talk about my life when we're together. I want to talk about everything else and nothing at all—to make her laugh because her smile and laughter are infectious, and the thought of not having that when she leaves forms a heavy weight in my chest.

Four weeks with a beautiful woman had been the plan. However, the longer I've been with her, the more she has weaved her way into my heart more than I'd ever expected her to.

"This morning, he told me that I've not been pulling my weight the past couple weeks."

Her eyes widen. "Oh. And that's because of me."

"Yes," I admit. "But I wouldn't have had it any other way."

"That still makes me feel shitty because I'm the cause of your rift with him."

Leaning up on one elbow, I reach out and cup her jaw, speaking with honesty. "The rift with him was strong long before you came here, Ivy. I don't care what he thinks. I don't care what anyone thinks. I wanted to spend the summer with you. Work can come after. I don't feel guilty for holding back on my job, and you shouldn't feel responsible that I'm doing that either."

She holds my stare for a moment. "You know, for a man with a harsh scowl at times, you sure are the sweetest."

I grin. "Shut up and kiss me."

Her lips make contact with mine and she welcomes my invasion. Our tongues entwine, and I try hard to ignore the feeling that is creeping up my body. It's more than desire. It's a feeling I can't explain but know it's one I don't think I'll experience with any other.

"So, I have a question," she grins.

"Go on."

"Is this classed as a summer romance?"

"I guess so. You've sure reeled me in that's for sure. But Christ, don't tell anyone. I wear my harsh scowl with pride, and I don't want to be known as a pussy."

Chapter Five

IVY

"IVY, SWEETIE. YOU look lovely." Aunt Lucinda beams from one of the tents wearing a straw hat and carrying a glass of gin. The village fete is in full swing with numerous tents and even more coloured flags decorating the field. "I'm so glad you're here with us."

Guilt grips my stomach. It's no lie that I've spent the majority of my time with Aiden this holiday than I have with my own family. A part of me hates myself for that because family has always been important to me, but at the same time, there is something about Aiden Hope that draws me in. He's intoxicating, and the more I've got to know him, the less appealing the thought of leaving him becomes. His touch alone makes my skin tingle. Add that to his incredible kisses and he's got me on my knees and my stomach in knots. The adventures we've shared may not seem all that exhilarating to others, but to us, they have been enough, and I've experienced things that I never had before.

I know in my heart that Aiden hasn't experienced the freedom or the laughter that he has had before my visit—not in the way he should have. He has a spirit that he keeps guarded against others but one I've managed to reveal.

And what I've uncovered is beautiful.

Coming here to meet someone was never my intention, but I can't stand here and say that I'm not going to miss him, nor that my heart will be okay with saying goodbye. I know I will be back, and this is not forever, but the thought of leaving makes me feel sick.

Scanning my eyes around the villagers who gather in the field, I search for him desperately, wanting to spend as much time with him as possible as we leave the day after tomorrow.

"Have you seen Aiden?" I ask Aunt Lucinda. Only her response is a wicked grin as she nods behind me.

"He's over there talking to your dad."

Turning, I find both men over at the beer tent, talking in-depth. Aiden's eyes latch on mine and a smile tugs at his lips—a smile that has me walking towards them both. I'm pleased he's here considering this is not his thing.

"Hey, guys."

"Ivy, darling. You look lovely."

"Thanks, Dad." I'm dressed in a black and white checked dress, my hair down and loosely curled. "I see you're enjoying the beer?"

"Aiden has introduced me to some of the finest."

"Your dad thought he'd found the perfect brewed beer until I told him to try my favourite. Would you like one?"

I screw my nose up, not a beer fan. "I'd rather have a

161

wine."

"Coming right up."

"So, what do you two have planned for the rest of the day?" Dad asks.

"I'm planning on thrashing Aiden on the pineapple bowling."

"Oh, are you now?" Aiden says handing me a glass of wine with a wicked grin on his face.

"Yep. My throw is as good as my shots."

"That shot was a fluke."

"You'll see."

"I will. Lead the way then, Miss Confidence." He turns to dad. "Nice talking with you, Neil."

We head down through the crowds of villagers and wait our turn at the bowling game. My skin heats when I feel Aiden's fingertips dance over the small of my back and the desire that I have for him grows stronger. I need it to stop because this is not forever, but the more he touches me, the more I crave him.

I turn to look at him when it's our go, only to find his eyes already on me, causing my breath to catch. "You ready to lose, Mr Hope."

"Bring it on, Ms Taylor."

We play five rounds and where Aiden thinks he is off to a winning streak with the first two, I come along and win the last three. I jump with excitement whilst he stands there protesting for a rematch.

"So, what do you want to play now?" I ask, finishing off my popcorn.

He stops walking and wraps his arm around my waist, looking at me with those blue eyes. "Can we go to the sunflower field?"

I frown. "Yeah. Everything alright?"

"I just want to spend as much time with you as I can. And I don't want it to be here. Besides, I want to kiss you."

I grin. "Well, in that case, lead the way."

***

"This is nice," I say, sitting on the grass at the bottom of the sunflower field. Aiden has lit the small campfire after stopping off at the farm to get us some wine and blankets. It's dusk, and there's a low hum of music in the distance coming from the village fete.

"It sure is." He sits down beside me, his legs brushing against mine, awakening the yearning inside that's been burning since our first kiss. "I thought it would only be right that we spend our last night together back where it all started."

My stomach drops at the thought of leaving the day after tomorrow. Like always, our last night in Guiting Power always ends with a family meal and Aunt Lucinda telling dad and me how much she loves and misses us. And although I know I need to be with my family tomorrow evening, I can't help but want Aiden to be there with us, too.

"It seems like a lifetime ago that I was fearing for my life in this field," I joke.

"Oh really? I had no idea fear came in the form of agreeing to spend time with a stranger."

"Me neither," I chuckle.

His eyes find mine. "Do you regret it?"

How could I? I could never regret my time with him. Ever. "Not one bit," I whisper.

I hold his stare, and my heart pounds when he reaches out and tucks my hair behind my ears. "Same."

He grasps my chin, bringing me closer before his lips

cover mine. Our tongues dance and I lose myself in him, needing him places he's yet to touch—needing to get closer. I straddle him and the feel of his erection against me sends electricity through my veins.

His mouth trails down my neck, his hands dangerously close to my sex, as he teases my thighs, driving me crazy.

"Aiden…"

"Ivy, is this what you want?"

Yes.

Even though I know that one night with him is going to ruin me in every way and make my heart more knotted up with the feelings I already have for him, I still want this.

"Yes. I want you."

He pulls his shirt off over his head before his mouth is back on me, decorating me with kisses. He deepens the kiss, lifting my dress up and off my body. His large, callused hand spans the soft skin of my back, his other pulls down my bra, cupping my breast before he takes my nipple into his mouth.

I release a moan.

He turns us, placing me on the blanket and removing my underwear before covering me with his body. The flicker of the fire catches the thick desire in his eyes as he looks at me.

"So beautiful."

My back arches and I moan when he sinks his fingers into my heat, pushing me to my limit as my body starts to come undone.

Finding the buttons on his jeans, I pop them open, pushing the denim down, needing to feel him. The unearthly groan that leaves the back of his throat when I wrap my hands around his hard length only makes me ache for him more.

"Jesus, yes."

"Aiden, please. I need you."

Reaching for his jeans, he takes out his wallet, latching his eyes on me once again as he takes out a condom. I've never been so consumed by anyone like I have Aiden. And if that was his intension all along then it's worked. I can't get enough, which only makes this harder.

When he pushes inside me, he wastes no time, thrusting over and over as my name falls from his lips. I fist the blanket, loving the intensity of him as my body burns from head to toe with the orgasm that builds fast. When his thumb circles my clit, I'm tipped over the edge and cry out his name as I crash around him.

"Fuck, Ivy." He groans with his own release, right before his mouth collides with mine and he kisses me like never before.

***

"So, I think it confirms it," Aiden murmurs, tracing his fingertips over my shoulder as I lay against his chest, the blanket still covering us both.

"What?"

"That with the kissing and the sex, this is most definitely a summer romance."

I snort. "Always wanted one of those."

"Well, in that case, you're welcome."

I shift myself to face him, wanting to know why he's not taken already. "You know, I've never asked why you don't have a girlfriend."

"You ask me that after I've just made you orgasm.

165

Poor timing, Ms Taylor. What if she's back home waiting for me?"

"Well, we both know she's not."

"Ouch." He grins, but his features soon change, and a heavy exhale leaves him. "There was someone, but she much preferred the sexual company of my best friend."

"I'm sorry. Why didn't you say sooner?"

"I don't talk much about the shit parts of my past, Ivy. I don't want people's pity; I don't want their advice. I just want to move on as best as I can, even though sometimes that is easier said than done. Everything happened all at once, and in the space of a few months I lost the girl I thought I'd spend the rest of my life with along with my brother. Life has just been one big shitshow and I wish to forget it."

I think about everything he's told me over time and how much pain he has suffered; how much he tries to keep the farm running regardless of the challenges he faces or the dreams he's wanting to follow but doesn't know how to because of his loyalty to his mum; and how he's put his life on hold since Joey and now seems stuck.

I don't want that for him. He deserves more than what he believes. Reaching up to cup his jaw, I turn him to face me. "Promise me something, Aiden."

"What?"

"That despite all the hurt you are feeling now, you'll find a way to move on—do what *you* want in life not what others expect you to."

"Kinda hard when you have a farm to run."

"But no one is saying you have to stay to run it."

"It's been in the family for years."

"It doesn't have to remain that way. People change, all the time. Life moves on. Why stay and make yourself more unhappy when you can be the person who's fighting to get out from inside of you. Go live your dreams while you're still young. Do the job you're wanting to do. And if you feel you can't give up the farm, get someone in to keep it going while you're gone."

He sighs. "My uncle would love that."

"Fuck what he thinks. Give it to him if it means you get the life you truly want. Just promise me you'll think of your options and opportunities before getting more weighed down than you already are."

He tucks the hair behind my ear and studies me for a moment. "It's so unfair how I have only just found you and soon you'll be leaving."

My stomach dips. I've thought this myself so many times, but I bury the feeling that creeps over me, not wanting to let my emotions take over because this isn't about me. I feel in all of this that the journey we've both shared has never been about me, and deep down I believe he knows this.

"No one said that this is all we have. We can stay in touch. FaceTime, or write letters."

He raises a brow. "Have you not heard of a text message."

"But letters will be more memorable. It'll be part of our history."

"Jesus, you sound like such a teacher right now."

I laugh, poking him in the ribs. "I'll be back before you know it, and should you not be here because you are off living the life you want, I'll enjoy it with you by staying in contact."

"I like the sound of that," he whispers.

"Good. You've gained a friend for life in me, Aiden Hope."

"I'm honoured."

I grin. "You should be."

Needing to hide the sudden ball of emotions that has hit my chest, I reach up, kissing him softly, and fall into his embrace one more time, loving the feeling of him against me and knowing that it's going to be incredibly hard to leave him.

I didn't come here looking for any kind of connection with another, other than wanting to absorb the lasting memory of my mum. However, finding Aiden and building the whirlwind friendship that we have, he's weaved his way into my heart in so many ways. I respect him as a man, I adore him as a friend and I know in my heart that regardless of where we are or the distance between us, the memories of this summer with him will stay with me forever.

Chapter Six

AIDEN

"THANK YOU FOR everything, Lucinda. Loved seeing you again."

"Oh, I'm going to miss you like crazy. You know you're welcome here anytime."

Ivy hugs her aunt as her dad places the last suitcase in the boot of the car and heads towards me. We are outside the guesthouse in the village, and today seems to have come around faster than I'd have liked.

My time having this feeling of easiness inside me is now coming to an end as I'm moments away from saying goodbye to a woman who has blown my mind in all the right ways, making me realise that there is good in the world after all. She's made me enjoy life once more when I thought it had ended when Joey left us. She's made me realise so many things and feel a whole lot more than I ever expected to feel when I first asked to spend more time with her. And as much as I know that she has to go back to London and carry on with her studies, I can't stand here and say I'm okay with that.

I'm going to miss her more than I thought I would, and the only thing that is keeping me from crumbling is the fact that not only have I gained a true friend in Ivy, but there is also no doubt in my mind that this won't be our last time spent together.

"Aiden." Ivy's dad holds his hand out and I place mine in his grip.

"Mr Taylor."

"It was good to get to know you. I must admit, I was a little apprehensive when Ivy said she was spending time with you this summer."

"It's completely understandable. You have a great daughter."

He smiles. "I sure do. Thank you for taking care of her and filling her days with laughter. I hope the two of you keep in touch."

"You bet. I've got a friend for life in Ivy now."

"Take care, Aiden." He taps me on the shoulder before turning back towards his family.

I lock eyes with Ivy and a soft smile graces her face as she takes slow, hesitant steps towards me. I swallow hard, knowing that neither of us is going to find this next part easy. She looks as beautiful as ever in her white summer's dress, and I mentally capture the moment so I'll remember it forever.

"You look beautiful, Ivy."

Her cheeks blush. "Thank you."

"So… this is it," I say, shoving my hands into the pocket of my jeans when what I really want to do is pull her towards me and hold her for a little longer.

"I'm going to miss you, Aiden."

My chest tightens. She doesn't just speak for herself: she's speaking the truth for me too.

How the hell am I going to wait another year?

A part of me has even questioned asking her to stay, but I can't expect her to up sticks and move from a busy city and a dream job she is training for to possibly stay with me. Our friendship will remain no matter what via social media, FaceTime or Ivy's request with handwritten letters—which I'm less impressed with—but wherever life takes us from here, I'll be forever grateful for the love I have for her as my friend.

So, for the sake of her heart, I silence my words, knowing that her dreams are more important than my own.

"There is nothing to miss, beautiful girl." I reach out, tucking the strands of her hair behind her ear. "I'll always be at the end of the phone, remember?"

"Or a letter."

I roll my eyes. "Or a letter."

I wrap my arms around her tightly and hold her, praying that the feeling she's stirred up inside me doesn't disappear too quickly.

Reaching into my shirt pocket, I pull out the little present I got made for her by one of the handcrafters in the village. Taking her hand in mine, I look at her.

"I got you this." I place the pendant in her hand, and she gasps. "I had one of the sunflower petals turned into resin. I thought that when you're missing your mum and want to be here, *here* will always be with you, no matter where you are."

"Aiden…"

"You can have it however you want. Be it a necklace, bracelet or turned into a key ring."

She looks up at me, this time with tears in her eyes. "It's beautiful. Thank you so much."

"I didn't know what to expect at the start of the summer, but it wasn't to find a friend as pure as you, Ivy Taylor. This has been the best four weeks of my life. Thank you for making it full of fun and adventure."

She places a soft kiss on my lips and my guard falls, wanting to taste her one final time. I slip my tongue into her mouth and consume her, memorising her taste, her touch. As a soft moan escapes her, I pull back before she truly pulls me under.

A single tear falls down her cheek as her lip quivers.

My heart is heavy at the thought of saying goodbye as my own emotions start to take over.

"I didn't expect it to be this hard leaving your scowl." She smiles through tears.

I chuckle. "I want photo's every week of what you have done. And I'll FaceTime you from the sunflower field, from our spot."

"You promise?"

"Yes." I cup her cheeks, wiping her tears away and smile. "Life was pretty dull before you rocked up between the sunflowers. You've made me smile again, and I'll be forever thankful for that. This goodbye is not forever, Ivy." I place a lingering kiss on her lips and swallow the thick lump in my throat and whisper. "It's goodbye until next time."

She nods, biting her bottom lip to try and control the tears.

Her dad's soft call breaks our farewell, and I walk her down to the car. My chest is tight with so many feelings. Wrapping my arms around her once more, I kiss the top of her head before she steps back to look at me, placing her hand on my cheek.

"Goodbye until next time, Aiden Hope. Long may your scowl live."

I grin. "Go be the incredible teacher I know you can be."

After she climbs into the car, she blows me a kiss that I pretend to catch before they head off down the road, Ivy waving like crazy. I have to fight to keep it together, still completely mind blown after all this time that she has had this effect on me and knowing that tomorrow I'll only see or hear her via a phone.

"I'm no professional, but I'd say you changed that girl's life," Lucinda says at the side of me.

Continuing to look ahead, I watch the car turn and head out of the village as I think about what her aunt just said, the memories of mine and Ivy's time together playing in my mind: her smile; her laugh; the way we've connected like we have; and the ability she's had to get me talking when I've been shut off for so long. If it weren't for her, I'd still be in that world. Things happen for a reason, and I believe that the blonde beauty amongst the sunflowers is the reason I'm now looking at things a completely different way.

No matter what the future brings, Ivy Taylor will always be a part of my life and for that, I can't wait until next time.

"No," I smile. "She's changed mine."

THE END… *for now.*

173

House From Hell

JAMES KEITH

HIGH UP ON Widow's Hill lays a house—a grand, old mansion that has been devoured by the endless wrath of time. The house sits on a winding estate, which in the past was beautifully maintained, now reclaimed by the waves of nature with over-growing bushes, weeds, and old elder tree, the roots of which dig deep and crack through pathways. The once pristine and elegant building is now ramshackle, with rotting, wooden boards and cracked stone, overgrown with vine and moss.

The aptly named Widow's Manor is well-known in the community of Shadow Grove, a small town in the middle of nowhere where not much really goes on. The only big news story to ever hit the town beyond the odd, freak weather incident is the well-known, triple murder-suicide that happened around forty years ago in the manor. Legend says that if you get close enough to the haunted building, you can even see bloodstains still marking the windows on the second floor. This is where one of the victims took a shotgun and pressed it to the roof of their mouth before releasing a final round into their own skull.

For the past forty years, the old murder house has become a place that young adults go to test their bravery, common challenges being to knock three times on the front door, once for every soul lost within the house. They often then run back in fear, claiming their own bravery, but nobody has been inside of the house since it closed after the investigation—the only claimant of the house wanting nothing to do with the misery it caused.

However, in the year 2020, a small group of young adults in their twenties who are on a road trip hear about the mansion and the horror that lays claim inside of it. They want to be the first ones to spend the night since the suicides all those years ago, so on October the 8th, on a cold, biting night, for the first time in over forty years the front door is opened.

The trio is dressed in T-shirts and jeans, ready to set up camp and gear in the house to try to find the ghosts. They are on a year off of university together, and upon discovering Ethan has rented a camper van, have decided to travel the continent searching for the spooky and supernatural.

Upon passing through the town on a road stop, they learn about the old Widow's Manor from some locals and decide that this will be the perfect spot to stay for the night. Despite having easily enough money for motel rooms, the trio grab the sleeping bags they keep in the back of the camper and head up the hill in the van. It takes a little while for this nerdy trio to get the courage to even enter the house, and surprisingly it ends up being Oliver with the bolt cutters who strips away the chain that has kept front door locked up before pushing it open.

Oliver Smith is the first one in through the doorway, slowly pushing open the once-chained shut door with a low, echoing creak. The man is tall, around six feet, one inch with a wiry frame and fairly pale skin. Green eyes flicker around the darkened room as a few mice and rats scurry away from the beams of warm, afternoon light that filter in through the new crack in the door. He turns to the pair behind him, nodding that it is safe to enter.

Oliver is a typical, young adult man with ebony black hair that lays about in a messy mop, making his pale green eyes stand out. As he surveys the room before him, his thin lips press in a line.

Swiftly after him, almost hugging his back out of anxiety and excitement, is Akira Row, a sweet girl of Asian American descent with a height of five feet, six, soft brown eyes, and freshly dyed, dark purple hair held back in a ponytail. She has one hand fisted in Oliver's shirt she had barely managed to be convinced into this shit show. She isn't a fan of the idea of interrupting the last resting place of so many tortured souls—well, three, but still! This place is more haunted than the other stupid tourist ghost spots that Ethan's dragged her to over the last few weeks, and she can feel it.

The last through the door is the ghost hunter himself, Ethan Brack—or as he is known to his friends, Ethan, the spook machine. He is shorter than Oliver, barely pushing past five , ten with dark caramel skin, smoky brown eyes, and hair dyed a mixture of green and red, which he thinks looks, "totally cool".

Now, all three stand in the foyer, looking around the room. The silence is suffocating, like an invisible, toxic fog.

Ethan breaks the silence, exclaiming how cool this

place seems then slowly begins walking the room, taking pictures here and there.

Akira clings to Oliver's arm, a little nervous when she whispers, "Do we really have to stay here, Oli?" Using the childhood nickname she gave him long ago shows how nervous she really is.

Smiling, he assures her that they will no doubt end up in a motel or the van soon because Ethan has the attention span of a goldfish and will get bored soon.

Slowly, they begin to get deeper into the house, taking pictures of what might be bloodstains, but also anything from wine to coffee to mould, looking into the different now-empty rooms and searching around to see what they can find.

Despite the lack of care, and obvious signs of weathering with age, the house is fairly well-kept. Spiderwebs cling in the corner of rooms, but it's suspiciously lacking any signs of graffiti or tagging, which shows they truly might be the first people inside since it was locked away so long ago.

Eventually, the trio find their way to a large, open room which seems to be thick with a layer of old dust. Ethan proudly explains that this is the room that the final death occurred, pointing to the window, which, yes, does appear to have an old stain splattering part of the wall by the window.

"This room is perfect to start hunting for ghosts and spirits! I can feel the energy here," Ethan proclaims to the group before he dumps down his backpack, which has in it the few things they will be using.

Akira looks up to Oliver, who gives her a warm smile, patting her shoulder and reminding her this won't be all night, just 'til he gets tired of it all. Sighing, she nods before she sits down on the worn, wooden boards, flinching when she tries to avoid a century-old splinter from pricking her soft skin.

Ethan takes out his phone and begins taking pictures of the room and rushing about excitedly.

Meanwhile, Oliver stands with his back against the wall, watching them do what they please. Ethan turns to the group, muttering something fanatically about this being the right room for it. Aki lets out a yelp as she watches a rat scurry through the room and out of a small hole in the rotting, wooden door.

"Ethan, this place is a damn safety hazard. Can we just get started with the communion to finish this quickly? I'd rather sleep in a stinky motel than this trash heap!" Akira's voice echoes through the silence of the room, breaking Ethan from his mutterings.

Oliver chuckles at the attitude the tiny girl shows: she is small but fiery and that's one of the things that attracts him to her the most. They are old friends, but in recent months, he has started to fall for her. Nothing has changed yet, but now he is seeing her in a totally new light, and it is wondrous.

He breaks out of his stupor, watching Aki pull the bag that clings to her side—a worn satchel she'd made herself back in high school and has used pretty much every day of her life since. She pulls out a strange wooden box decorated with curls and engravings with a seal across the top. The Ouija board is an old relic in her family; it's why Aki even came since she refuses to let the boys touch it without her. She places down a strip of black cloth on the ground to protect the board and then puts it on top of it before looking at them.

"Sit your asses down, and remember what I told you

last time. Do not take your hands off the board 'til the spirit—if we even get one this time—tells us we can go. If things start to get weird or scary, just hold onto it and let me handle the questions. Ethan, do not try anything this time, or I will book my ass on a coach and go home. Got it?"

For such a short girl, she truly has a commanding tone. After all, she may not be a ghost hunter fanatic like Ethan, but she is a believer in spirits. Ethan sighs, nodding as he sits down on one side of her and Oliver on the other. She slowly removes the lid, revealing the board and planchette beneath. The board is hand-painted with runic symbols whose meaning none of the trio really understand. It is painted with letters in order, and then a few phrases such as: good, bad, yes, no, hello, and good-bye—small things to make communication run smoother.

After taking out some simple, white pillar candles, she places them around the board between herself and the boys. She takes great pride in the preparations for her ceremonies, her grandmother having showed her how to do them when she was just a little girl.

Focusing, she softly whispers, thanking the gods for guiding her hand and for keeping them safe whilst they conduct their communication with the spirits.

Her eyes flutter over the pair of boys. Ethan is smirking, looking at the board like it's a glittering jewel and he is a damn dragon, greedy for the coming ceremony. On the other hand, when she peers over at Oliver in his dark green sweater, her eyes meet his. She pauses and gives him a glowing smile; it warms her heart to know his eyes are on her. She needs to impress him.

Removing some dark, oak incense sticks, she begins to burn them with sage in hopes of creating some sense of a safe space here. She sighs when Ethan starts to complain.

"You're going to scare all the ghosts off with your witchy stuff. Come on, Akira, let's go. I want to see if the victims are ready to chat!"

Sighing, she moves to begin the communication with the spirits. Ethan and Oliver place their hands on the board, and that's when the first mistake is made. Akira speaks words she instantly regrets: she's always been told never to ask this, but in Ethan's hurrying she forgot the warning.

Never leave the invitation open.

"Anybody out there who would like to speak to us?"

The house seems to shake for a moment, causing the group to tense up and look around. Probably just...the wind, right? The planchette begins to move, slowly crawling across the board, causing Akira to gasp. She isn't even touching it yet! It drifts over to 'yes'. Then it moves again to 'hello'.

"Holy shit! Holy shit, Aki, you fucking did it!" Ethan gasps, moving to look around the room worrying if a drifting visage will be standing there, hovering over them.

Akira can't help but look in shock. Usually, she moves it a little to tease them, but this is all real. She coughs and keeps going, unable to keep a shake from her voice.

"Al-Alright. Okay. So, what is your name?"

Once more, the carved wooden planchette begins to move. S. H. A. D. O. W.

Wait. What? She looks to Ethan, who seems rather confused.

"Um ... none of the victims were named Shadow. Ethan gasps, eyes wide, and peers down at the board.

Akira curses him, he was meant to let her lead this. She knows the story a bit, that there was supposedly a killer who caused the whole horrid event and was never found.

The planchette begins to move again, but as it does, things begin to change. It flits across the board at light speed, jumping from one answer to another. It says, 'yes, no, yes, no'.

Okay, this is going wrong. Akira needs to finish this now, but Ethan—stupid Ethan—won't stop.

"No, and yes? So, you didn't kill them directly, but you influenced it, right?"

Akira tries to hush him, but Ethan is so focused: this is what he has always dreamed of. Direct contact to not only a ghost but a serial killer's ghost.

The planchette moves over another phrase.

Yes.

Ethan gasps loudly and moves, causing the next stupid mistake: he lifts his hands from the planchette.

Akira shrieks at him, the entire house seems to shake and shudder, light filtering in from the windows appearing to grow dark and dim. Freezing, Ethan looks to Akira this is when he realises what he's done.

"Ethan, for fuck's sake! We need to finish this now. Whatever this shadow is, it's dangerous and now your hands are off the damn board there's only me and Oliver holding it back!" Her voice is harsh but full of nerves. This doesn't seem to be an ordinary ghost or spirit. It's rather fearsome and powerful from the way its mere presence shakes the floorboards and causes the glass on the windows to shudder and shake. The board between them seems to twitch as if it is in pain, and Oliver and Akira do their best to hold on.

Akira tries to take control, calling out, "Shadow, we are sorry. We didn't mean to wake you up or upset you! Please, let us go, and we will leave your home!" She attempts to appease the creature, begging for release…but it isn't done with them yet. It hasn't even started to play.

The planchette moves rapidly across the board at the same time as Akira reads out what it says.

"I don't think so; I want to play a game." The entire house began to shake once more, and Akira whimpers, glancing at Oliver who appears to be equally terrified.

"Look, we don't want any trouble, friend. Let's just stop this, and we will go and never come back. We don't want to play your games," Oliver speaks up for the first time, his deep, echoing voice clearer than Akira's. He tries to take control of the situation. The desire to protect her from the way she feels is strong.

At this point, Ethan backs away from the board and his gaze bounces nervously around the room. "G-Guys, th-the shadows. The walls!" Ethan whimpers while taking pictures.

Oliver and Aki look up in horror as their own shadows have become distorted and elongated. Their necks were snapping back and forth like an unseen force is breaking them over and over again. Limbs seem to flail and writhe as they feel their own bodies twitch with sharp pains. The spot on the window with the dark marking became alight suddenly; now, it is very clearly a splatter of blood, this time they can see so much more. A shadow of a lifeless corpse appeared slumped against the wall as if appearing out of nowhere.

Akira shrieks bloody murder when the shadowy form twitches, mimicking the way their own casted shadows move. The stagnant, irony scent of blood reaches in the air, and finally another breaks when Akira shoves back from the board, terrified by the sudden visage, leaving Oliver to be the last one holding the creature back.

The house is alive, there is a howling, hissing noise

that echoes throughout the room. The planchette moves once more, and Oliver looks down, reading it as Akira runs to the doorway. Unfortunately, she finds it has slammed shut, locking them in. She pulls at the door and is about to cry out about how they are trapped, but Oliver's voice cuts through and he reads Shadow's message.

"It's been so long since I had new toys—new toys to play with, new prey to break. Let's see which of you will snap first, shall I? Snap when they snapped me. Break as I was broken. Twist and snap and bend and bow. Which one will be the first to go?" His voice cuts off when the planchette suddenly pulls itself off the board and through the window.

Finally, Oliver lets go before the board itself splits in two, and he is thrown against the wall with a dull, sickening crack that makes Aki fear for the worst. She sighs, seeing him shift and groan when he tries to stand up. The door suddenly flings open, and all three stare at the now open portal to the rest of the house.

Ethan is the first to move as he turns to the other three, stating the most obvious and urgent fact. "This house is fucking haunted and not by anything I want to question. Let's get the hell out of here."

All three rushed toward the door to head for the front of the house, but as they pass through the doorway, they all find their worlds going black.

Ethan is the first to awaken. His head is blurry, like it is full of spiderwebs, slowly his eyes began to open. He is in a room they passed by earlier—it seems to be the kitchen. Old, stained, what were once white countertops frame the room.

He slowly pushes himself to his feet, looking around the room, feeling his breathing rising to a panicked state.

He's alone. Akira and Oliver nowhere to be seen. His eyes dart around the room, landing on the door leading out to the hallway. He slowly walks over, keeping his eyes trained on everything around him as he wonders how he got here, and where his friends are.

What is this strange creature named Shadow that they have somehow awoken?

He reaches a hand out for the doorknob, grasping it between his fingertips, and moves to turn it when he feels a sharp, searing, red-hot pain. Screaming, he pulls his hand back, fingertips burning from the heat the metal doorknob gives off. He stumbles back with a start and a whimper when the door suddenly bursts into a wall of fire. Within seconds, the door seems to just flake away into dust, but instead of an empty doorway, all that is there is a damn brick wall, sealing him into this tomb. Ethan falls onto his ass stunned he looks around the room. It's internal, so no windows and no other doors. He is trapped.

He does the only logical thing: he begins to scream.

"Hello! Akira, Oliver, where are you? Are you out there? I'm stuck and I can't get out. Please, somebody help me. I don't want to be trapped in here!" His voice rings out but isn't answered. All he hears is the steady, quiet drip, drip, drip of the tap on the far side of the wall. He slowly pushes himself onto his feet and moves to where the door is. Reaching out, he presses his fingertips to cold almost damp stone. There is no trace of the fire that once licked up the door frame, no trace of even a door frame. It is like it never even existed. He begins to bang on the wall, trying to see if it is thin or even there, wailing he cries out once more.

"Let me out! Please, I'm sorry. I didn't mean it. I'm sorry." What he's sorry about he doesn't really know…sorry he even came here?

Suddenly, the dripping sound of water from the tap begins to get louder. It had been just droplets, but now it seems almost deafening. He puts his hands over his ears it is the only sound he can hear besides his own voice. And it hurts. The sound gets louder and louder, forcing him onto his knees, and he can feel blood beginning to leak from his ears. Looking down at his shaking hands, he sees red staining his skin. However, he also sees water, rising around his ankles. He scrambles to try and get to the tap to turn it off, but his hands are so slick with blood he can't do a thing. He can only cower atop the rusted, stained countertops as the water begins to rise.

He calls out again, his voice panicked with terror and anxiety. "Please! Please, I don't want to drown. Oh god! Please, Shadow, please let me out. I-I'm sorry!" He sobs, his chest shaking when the water rises past the countertops, the tap still just letting out a faint drip, drip, drip. The water continues to rise, somehow dyed a deep red from his own blood that trails down his ears, down his neck, staining the water. He gasps due to the freezing cold liquid creeping up to his neck, and the last thing he sees before he is swallowed whole by the bite of the cold water is the stark white ceiling above him. The last thing he hears is the cry of an animal that appears to be treading the water trying to escape its own watery grave.

Akira is next. She awakens with a start, her wrists bound behind her back, ankles tied together as she sits upright on a chair. Shaking in terror and fear, she looks around her. She gasps, the air is stale and dry, and almost hurts her lungs to breathe in. She flinches when she tries to sit up straight and gazes at her surroundings. The room is dark and cold, bare of any kind of furniture besides what must have once been a furnace. She can see a glint of silvery metal off to the side—a collar—small enough to belong to a cat or a dog just tossed beside the furnace. She can see a strange kind of white ash inside of the furnace, but she can't move to inspect it any further. Suddenly, she feels a sharp blast of pain against her back, white-hot and searing her. She lets out a shout of pain which quickly fades, and she stares, trying to see what caused it. But she is alone. So like Ethan before her, she cries out to the open air.

"H-Hello? Spirit? Shadow? Please, whatever you are, we beg your forgiveness…I beg your forgiveness. We did not know this is your domain. We are so sorry. Please just let us go, and we will never bother you or your home again. I—" Stopping, she shrieks in pain. She feels the bindings around her legs and ankles grow tighter, the room grows hotter.

The furnace door slams open, and the fire roars like a wild beast has taken control. She opens her mouth to scream but feels a cord wrap around it, gagging her before even more than a squeak can escape past her lips. Her eyes widen in horror as a beast seems to crawl out of the fire— a beast made of crumbling bone and licking flames with eyes like dark smoke. It is not one beast but many, and suddenly they surround her. Creatures of fractured limbs and extended, elongated forms all crackling with flames. They hiss and spit and roar. Their bodies seem distorted and shifting, as if the flames are burning them alive, but yet they are part of themselves.

Akira shifts, trying to move, and she whimpers when the flames lick at her skin, burning the edges of her clothing. Sobbing, she twists in her bindings.

Wait, when did the cloth that had curled around her wrists and ankles turn into biting metal chains?

189

A voice like smoke begins to echo out from some of the strange flame creatures.

"Revenge! Burn her. Turn her to ash. Make her feel the same. Burn her. Burn her. Turn her to flame. Feed her to fire; feed her to the shadows." Then they begin to fling themselves at her, creatures of liquid flame covering her mortal form asshe writhes and turns, screaming in pure agony. The scent of smoke, burning flesh, and fur fill the room. Her body burns alive. She howls in pain, her voice more beast than human.

Two down…

Oliver, the last one holding the board, watches it all happen. He saw the shadow-like smoke that had come from the now-shattered wood and how it curled around him, forcing him to hold still in its unbreakable grip. It squeezes harder every time he moves, and so he is forced to sit and watch the true reality. He see's both Akira and Ethan writhe on the ground in pure agony, their minds tortured by scenes not truly happening. They scream out for each other or for him, begging for help. He tries to call out to them, tell them it isn't real and to fight it, but they seem to not be able to hear him. He cries out, shaking as he watches Ethan's life fade before him—how the blood pools onto the ground from his ears, and the blue tint of his lips when he suffocates in the smoke that surrounds them, the same smoke that came out from the board. No, not smoke. Shadow.

Then it is Akira, the girl he's adored for so long. He stares as the shadow cut at her, how it seems to glow brighter, causing her form to burn in front of him. She is alight with the darkest of shadows. Her body twitches and crackles as if on fire. He cries her name and how sorry he is. He wants to help her so much, but he can't even move.

He is forced to watch. Now his two best friends lay before him, dead and their forms twisted.

"Why…why did you do this? W-We did nothing…"

"Why?" the shadow's voice echoes in a slow drawl. "Why? Revenge. Humans brought the creatures who lived here nothing but misery. You burnt us alive, drowned us in water, tortured us and our young. We simply want what is owed. Blood for blood." The voice is like liquid shadows, echoing in his mind when it curls around his throat. He can see the form from the corner of his eyes. It's catlike, with a long, thick tail, sharp, pointed ears, and eyes that burn like coals. "Now it's your turn, and I like to chase. So run, little human. Let's see if you can escape."

The shadow suddenly releases him, letting his form go, and he takes one last look at Akira's burnt corpse before bolting down the hall, to the stairs. He can hear thundering footsteps behind him as the beast gives chase. This is a shadow, right? So, if he can get outside and into the daylight, he can escape it!

He runs and runs, trying to outwit and outsmart the creature, but the house seems to aid it as smaller creatures born of shadow reach out at him with fang and claw, trying to trip him up. Rats, small dogs, birds. There has been so much death here, so much that it has sunk into the house and created this shadow creature who seeks human blood in return for the animal blood that was spilled.

He sees it ahead of him; he is so close. The front door is open and light is streaming in.

They never closed it properly.

Hope fills him when he reaches out, feeling the warm, afternoon light dance against his fingertips. He will return, come back with light and never let the shadow return He will make sure that he collects Akira's body and Ethan's so he can put them to rest. He will escape and be free. All this rushes through his mind before he feels claws digging into his back and he falls to the floor.

Slowly turning his head, he sees the same cat now a shadow, now huge and grinning with a tooth-filled maw.

The final words he will ever hear are, "Don't you know, silly boy, shadows only grow stronger in the presence of light."

The door slams shut, sounds of screaming echoing through the now darkened hall of the Widow's Manor. Three new human souls are claimed to avenge all the beasts killed by the past tenants of the manor—new souls to torment and feed the starved beasts whose spirits still lingered there.

The shadow only grows that evening as it purrs contentedly after playing with its prey.

THE END

Undercover Vogue

C.N. MARIE

Chapter One

EVER HAVE A dream, an infatuation, in your childhood? Ambitions are just that: perfect picture portraits that forge in the mind's eye that you strive to accomplish; images that could stem around one true focus and ambition. I came to understand that nothing else in life would matter, that other factors would be trivial in comparison. I believed that I had found my fascination, and nothing could discourage me away. Ideas and wonders, though, were a blurred representation of the true reality that lay ahead.

If I, Keren Berkley, could have talked to myself all those years ago, I hope I would have made her see the reality of the world of fashion, not the manufactured, fake opinion that had been shown to me.

Fashion, glamour and the catwalk had been my callings, except the real nature of the world was the polar opposite of my expectations. Bitchiness came into play, and a dog-eat-dog attitude. It was a constant battle to be the best and produce the next showstopper before being laid out with the trash: either play with the top of the industry or crash and burn trying, two options that needed to be weighed up and ones that

didn't allow a woman like me much influence otherwise.
I vividly recall the phone call that changed everything.

3 MONTHS AGO

FASHION SCHOOL HAD always been tough.

I flew into the room with my ideas for my latest review, ten minutes before the deadline. A brainwave had hit me in the early hours, and it made me rethink the whole design idea. It was my prerogative after all. That design, though, was my calling card to the big time, but I didn't realise that at first—well not until the call that came later on in the day.

Glamique fashion guru, Guy Simons, was on the phone, offering the contract of a lifetime—the opportunity to play with the big boys and girls in the fashion world and complete my studies all in one motion. I should have been a girl who was able to take chances at face value, but nothing was ever as good as it seemed. A flash new apartment and investment into my image to convey the company status they wanted. Everything seemed too picture perfect. I had to let the inkling of doubt sit in my stomach and hope that the gossip was just that: gossip. I knew this business could be dirty. The rumours of his cutthroat business etiquette and tough remarks in the media were evidence of that. I understood I would be required to toughen up if I expected to hit the big time, despite the apprehension I felt.

I knew I couldn't change the opinions made about Guy Simons, and in truth, his opinion mattered little to me—everyone had one though. It was a power that designers in the business held over us, the ability to crush dreams or make them soar all with whispered words in the correct ears. The only difference was that I was being offered a chance of a lifetime, and I would be a fool to decline it.

A meeting was set, and plans were put in motion. They knew I was my own person, that I had goals I wanted to aspire to and that my own style was something I would always push at every given opportunity. I had to agree to the decisions to fit their set model, but my style wasn't negotiable on my terms—a sticking point to begin with, but my designs overturned the original decision and proved I was capable of performing to the level required.

Irina Tenix, Guy's personal assistant, gave me the final tour of the building and gave me the documents required for me to take the next steps. A start date, time to adjust and the launch event were all imminent, and I knew a lot had to be done.

I couldn't quite believe Guy Simons had found me and that three outfits on a catwalk launch would all be mine, but I had to find a way to accept he had the belief in me to pull this off. The designs and models would all be led by my judgment. I just had to get through the introduction launch event first and find my feet.

Chapter Two

THE LAUNCH EVENT soon came around, especially as I spent so much time being pampered. I wasn't used to all this, but according to them, it was essential.

With a new look—a sharp change from my previous blond locks to now jet-black shoulder length bob with side fringe—it had taken a while to recognise my own appearance. I couldn't fault the way it suited me, but the stark change played havoc with my mind. The nails that had been picked accented the black of my hair and the red tones of the event. Each piece fell magically into place.

The brief from Irina was detailed and to the point. I was told red was the colour for the night and to dress appropriately, except my originality had struck and wanted to come into play.

After hours of endless graft, I was excited to finally dress the part and ultimately meet the vast team. I slipped the fabric loose from its bag and hanger and admired the beautiful fabric as it ran through my fingers. I pulled the red knee-length dress over my head as I smoothed it along my curves and checked the way it clung to me like a fitted glove. There was a split on the side that travelled up my thigh with a large lavallière to the right-hand side of the neckline giving the sexy result I had planned. I wanted to be the centre of attention and have all eyes focused on me. My brainwave of having shades that were slightly varied had paid off and the pussy bow being in a velour fabric reinforced the details. The variety of shades exhibited individual creativity, an imaginative streak I hoped would impress.

I pulled up to the swanky hotel that I wasn't allowed to know the location of until the last minute due to the risk of uninvited guests showing up. That riled me up straight away, but I put a brave face on, looking at the logistics they had stated. Once I had given my details at the door, I was directed to the ballroom where everyone was beginning to congregate.

The room was beautiful, elegant, and pure sophistication with lots of crystal and mirrors to reflect every angle possible—a clever thoughtful design. I could see why these people were top of their game.

"Remember your etiquette since you obviously couldn't follow the brief I sent." Irina honed in on me the moment I stepped through the door with the need to reprimand me.

I paid no attention to her lecture: my style was my own, and I wasn't going to compromise who I was for anyone or apologise for wanting to be an individual force. Maybe not following the brief wasn't the smartest course of action given that I was still new, but I had told them what to expect from the start. It wasn't my fault that they hadn't listened to my intentions. A detail I would have to pick up with Guy at a more convenient time.

The man of the hour appeared and the women in the room moved out of his way. I wasn't sure if that was because of who he was or due to the power he exuded. I could tell he was making a beeline straight for me with a hot, sexy man in tow. My mind screamed, wondering which direction to run as I was stuck to the spot, unsure of who or what may be thrown at me. I was certain Guy's companion wasn't one of the high-flyers as his engagements with other people seemed to show an air of mystery. An unknown breath of fresh air to the current cliental. This man was something else, and it seemed I was about to find out just who he was. I felt my mouth dry up and my palms began to sweat as I stood in front of the stranger. I was about to look like a bumbling idiot and was unsure if I could have stopped it.

"Luca, this is Keren, our new addition to the team, who I've been briefing you all about." Guy's approach had unsettled the calm manner from the room and there were hushed whispers as the eyes of people that surrounded us focused their attention on the three of us. I tried to shake a feeling of dread that was beginning to grow deep within me, hoping it wasn't anything to worry about.

Luca greeted me with a kiss to both cheeks.

"Hello, it's lovely to meet you," he said as I attempted to control my mouth and the provoking images of his smooth hands running over every inch of my body in my head. I could feel the heat in my face, and I hoped the extravagant make up I was wearing would cover the instant blush that I assumed had appeared on my face. I was suddenly very hot as a shiver ran down the bare skin across my arms causing me to shudder and my stomach somersaulted with nerves. This guy was hot as fuck and my body tingled with the anticipation of wanting his touch on me again. My obsession with Italians was a weakness, and it wasn't helped by having such a fine specimen before my eyes.

"Keren, Luca is your new assistant. You will make a fantastic team together as 'new designers'," Guy stated with air quotes. "It's important to embrace and learn from one another's skills. Luca has a completely different skill set, which—if used to its full potential—will make you an unstoppable team." With the decorum I had promised, I held my head high as I realised Guy had, yet again, wormed his way exactly where he wanted to be.

Apparently, Luca had an artistic, creative flair that complimented my style impeccably and would give an edge to my pieces. I was intrigued about where else this skill set laid, as filthy, hot, ravishing thoughts filled my mind, and I hadn't even touched the good stuff yet.

I couldn't believe that Guy was so sure I would accept his proposal that he managed to find this so-called 'amazing entrepreneur' and get him to agree to work with me and fly to this event tonight. I called bullshit. If Guy was so impressed with my style, then why was he hiring someone to work so closely alongside me? Did he think I was just going to go falling flat on my arse just because I hadn't worked my way up all the ranks like a traditional designer? Surely not or he wouldn't have hired me in the first place.

Guy's curled lip said it all as he could probably sense my change in demeanour and the fucking reason for it. I was starting to realise I should have listened to my gut and that maybe this contract wasn't such a good idea.

Luca had certainly been thrust onto the floorshow just like me. He didn't deserve any of my animosity because of the prick beside him. It certainly helped to be good on the eye; I would use him to enhance my repertoire in whatever means possible. An extra pair of hands meant at least the ability to manage my time easier. Except, all I could think of was how those hands could be used to explore my body. I excused myself to introduce Luca to the team I had already met. Drinks in hand, the party could really get started now.

After finally bypassing another colleague, I smirked. "Luca, why have you come to work for Glamique or was it the offer of me?" I wasn't shy in the slightest. Maybe flirting wasn't the best idea, but I had no other idea how to keep his attention focused on me rather than the other women who kept watching the pair of us off his radar.

I knew I had affected him, but his bottled words couldn't be hidden away as the fire ignited within his eyes whilst he placed his hands in his trousers pockets, accessing the people around him, before allowing his eyes to return to me. Luca was smooth, he knew how to work the room and me. I would give him that.

Alcohol is my nemesis: my inhibitions had run wild.

I recall my spectacular show of embarrassment, running through my thoughts that the juices from another part of his body were as tasty as Luca's creative juices.

Oh, the shame.

I remember each revelation, of how I described his devilish looks and smooth sexy voice. How can I ever live down leaving the toilets and jumping him like a sex-starved slut whilst he never even flinched, just took it within his stride.

I turned into a lioness and prowled my way over to him as if in heat, wrapping my legs around his waist and tucking my head into the curve of his neck. Anything to get as close as possible to that masculine aroma that I wished I could bottle up to decant at my own intervals—the scent that managed to create endless flutters in my pussy that throbbed with the desire to be relieved.

Other guests, though, maybe weren't as understanding to my actions and I'm sure my name already had red marks against it. Guy and Irina had already left, but I knew word would travel fast to them—that was the way in the industry. I expected Guy was going to come down on me hard because of the linked association to himself. I couldn't blame him if he did and would take the warning in my stride.

Misconstrued visions of the evening allow me to remember Luca coming to my rescue, especially of him calling me Bellezza. Those Italian words had made me weak at the knees.

I rambled on and divulged every emotion that ran through my head, but he remained the perfect gentlemen and never left me alone. Surprisingly, he even managed to get me home prior to me passing out.

Nothing happened between us both, but fuck I wish it had. After all, I still had needs that hot Italian could certainly fix.

Chapter Three

I ATTEMPTED TO flatten my bed-roused hair and the pounding headache in my temples with coffee and some toast. The clock had to be wrong, but if it wasn't, I needed to hurry up to make it to the studio in time. I took two paracetamol and rushed to attempt to look somewhat decent, hopeful the pressure would reduce as my mind drifted to the people I had to confront today. Although, the only one I was concerned about was Luca. This man… I was done for. How had he got under my skin already?

Only slightly late—I had forgotten how much of a bitch central London traffic could be early in the morning—I rushed through to the main studio without an ounce of elegance to be greeted by a room of eyes all focused on me.

"Glad you could make it. I'm sure you are fine with a reduced lunch and extended day today. I will talk to you later on." As Guy went back to address the whole room, my eyes connect with Luca's and the slight nod of his head grasped my attention. I couldn't give a shit about being called out by Guy: embarrassment should have been present, but my only concern was the person at the other end of the room. I knew I had to remain stoic, but he looked like a meal good enough to eat. The worst thing was he knew the effect he had inflicted upon me. My heart pounded in anticipation as my skin became aroused in goosebumps, wondering if Luca had the guts to bring up the events from last night. My fucking traitorous mouth certainly knew how to lead me astray after I'd consumed all that alcohol. Damn.

A diversion was always best; he was obviously a kind natured individual. In this world, you couldn't have favouritism, and if I showed him any, what would others think? I appreciated that may have made me sound like a bitch, but I knew I was already up shit creek without a paddle after last night's escapades. I couldn't afford anything else to cause Guy more concern.

Dismissed like a naughty school child, I set to work with my plans with my delegated team. At least last night dealt with the pleasantry of introductions. Three teams of two were set with detailed outlines already plotted out. The first task I had given was to pick one aspect in the garment they felt required an extra lift. In fashion, we always focused on a specific area of a piece to add our imaginative input. Guy wanted the team to add to the creative aspect, so this helped to meet the brief.

Power pumped through my veins as they set to work, glad of a challenge to get stuck into. Even though each team member understood I was the lead designer, we all worked between our boundaries; I wasn't about to dismiss anyone else's opinions. I don't know why but this seemed such a huge morale boost between everyone. The togetherness created through the team building talk seemed a fantastic concept, I just hoped it projected through in the collection produced.

Each pair took their own separate room, and as I was about to start booking models, my hand was grasped, and I was led quickly to a different studio away from prying eyes. I didn't need to glance up to see who it was: the heat of his touch was burned into my skin after last night. The tingles started to radiate up my arm and I knew the desire had been kindled between us both. It didn't matter about the copious amounts of alcohol I'd drunk: nothing would make me forget Luca and how he overwhelmed my senses as electricity jolted through my body.

"The minutes have felt like hours as I've waited for us to be alone," Luca whispered into the crook of my neck as he spun me around to pin me against the edge of the cutting table.

"What are you doing, Luca? Anyone could walk in at any moment." I tried to hide the spiked, aroused tone in my voice as my chest rose heavily. The slight touch of my body as he inched past me and my nipples grazed against his hard, formed muscles of his chest had me wanting to reach out to grab him, but I needed to know this wasn't just an act—a crazy game in which I was the central attraction. My heart skipped a beat with the sudden behaviour change from the previous night. I wished I could have seen what was flying around inside his head as the building force of being so close screamed at me to take action.

"Keren, I want to do exactly what you said last night. I want to fuck that tight little pussy of yours and make you scream all that frustration away. It was the hardest thing being the perfect gentleman because all I wanted to do was to take what I knew we both wanted. I was fucking glad one of us had the sense to say it." He closed the distance between us to a hair's whisper. The moment the words left his mouth, the heat between my apex increased, the wetness intensifying, and I was lost to him.

"Less talk and more action, I say." My words were muffled together, his mouth crashing onto mine as I spoke, intoxicating every fibre alive within. I had a primal appetite that required unleashing and only one thing could satisfy me. Jolted sparks ignited the butterflies within my stomach. I knew I had everything I desired before me.

Our mouths danced as one, and his tongue pushed for entrance against the seam of my lips, begging for more. As the intensity increased, so did the passion. Forget that we were in a public work area, I needed to escape the trapped, enclosed restraints I currently felt—feel and allow everything else to melt away. I wanted fire, pure and unadulterated, to ignite the missing link he currently held. I was lost to the sensation created and he knew it. I was so glad I'd opted for the last-minute change of attire before I left the flat this morning as I hitched my skirt up to my waist. Needing oxygen, we pulled apart from another, just to allow the time to communicate our next steps. Mind reading could be a new calling for us both and from the twinkle in his eye, I knew he was hoping to blow my mind.

"Trousers?" I made quick work of unbuckling his belt and buttons, the metal clashing, sliding them down off his hips just enough to gain access to what I needed. Controlled movements were gone. I was a woman on a mission. His smooth, sexy voice had provoked my frenzy to have him. Fuck his dirty talk. He had made me obsessed with just one thing: his cock and how fast he could fill me. My body craved a release, and I was sure he could give me that pleasure.

Quick and fast, Luca ran his fingers along my clit and sucked them clean. "All for me? You dirty girl." He sheathed his cock with a condom he had torn open in one fluid motion. "Bellezza guardami." He grabbed my chin with his thumb and forefinger to direct my gaze straight to him. I was glad of the bench behind me to stop my knees collapsing from his sensual Italian words.

With a quick surge forwards, his lips met mine as his cock filled me to the hilt. My breath was laboured as our kiss bound us, a connection that neither of us sought to untether. Luca ran one hand through my hair as his other gripped my waist, allowing me the time to adjust to his large girth.

"Fuck me, Luca, now."

That was all the confirmation he needed as he surged forwards, fast and hard, deep inside me. My body played his tune like a violin until it wanted to scream with delight, but he somehow managed to push me to another level. His fingers trailed to my breasts and pinched my nipples hard. My orgasm was about to take hold when I noticed movement in the corner of my vision.

Unable to stop the shockwaves as they travelled through my body, Luca pumped his thick cock into me twice more as my walls tightened hard around him. We both came together, as my eyes connected with the one person, I wish they hadn't. His disappearance was as quick as his appearance, but that was a dilemma to contend with later. Guy Simons, for fuck sake.

Thankful Luca hadn't noticed him and with no time to bask in our afterglow, we decided to split direction for a while, lessening the risk of suspicion

Chapter Four

I TOOK A few minutes breather, to hopefully align my thoughts and rid myself of that freshly fucked look and compose myself to a dignified level. Flustered wasn't a good appearance for anyone, let alone when trying to make a good impression, and at the moment, I felt mine was right at the bottom of the garbage pile.

Luca had taken his leave, not without a promise of a kiss first—whatever that meant. I wasn't about to explore it and waste any more valuable time, especially when Guy's warpath of terror could reign at any given moment. Obviously, I would take the flack for what he had witnessed. I was the designer, Luca only an assistant. Hopefully, leniency would be an option. If not, at least I could say Luca was a god damn good fuck. Worth risking my career for, though? It would depend on where we went. A discussion for a later time.

Head high, shoulders pulled back, I took the first steps towards the exit that led to the linked rooms I was heading to when a figure approached and stopped me in my tracks.

"Do you enjoy mocking me? That smart mouth of yours always retaliating against my every move, Keren?" Guy put his right hand around my throat and trailed his left down my cheek, edging closer towards my breasts. He walked me backwards into the room until my back hit a hard surface, my voice silent, my breathing short and sharp full of panic watching his pensive eyes.

His touch made my skin crawl, and I wanted to scream, but no one was there to help, that I could tell. The position of his hand would make it a fruitless endeavour even if I wanted to. My heart thudded as if it were attempting to escape its confinements, the fear evident as a sheen of sweat. I could only imagine the morphed features plastered on my face as his smirk curled at the edges like he was enjoying every moment. Guy had the timing perfect: Luca had made his way to clean up and complete his briefing with one team, so it wasn't as if he would have returned to help me. I knew I should have listened to my gut. I'd been waiting for Guy to make his next move, praying he would leave me alone.

"Did you enjoy him fucking you hard while I watched, wishing it was me touching your body and pretty pussy? Or are you more adventurous, Keren?" Guy let one of his greasy hands start to trail down to my hip, keeping the other pushed on my windpipe. I reacted by squeezing my legs together. I gulped hard as my eyes flitted. My body moved at his touch, trying to avoid his hands, and dread rose in the pit of my stomach.

"Answer me, you bitch—you normally like to." His snide remark burned through the air. Bile rose in my throat and I wanted to escape, scream anything to be away from this man.

"No, I only want Luca." Pushing the words through gritted teeth, I struggled against the pressure. I had to fight and not let him know he could win. It took every ounce of strength for me not to resist the fear within. I bottled my emotions up, praying he would realise the stupid mistake, but why was my gut screaming that this was more the type of *power* he wanted?

"Are you sure? The way I saw it was your orgasm connected with me and my cock. I just wish I could have thrust *this* down your sexy mouth and shut you up for a while." Guy grabbed his dick and squeezed it hard to show me what he meant. "Come on, relieve me. Let me shoot my cum in lines across those breasts of yours and mark you as mine. You would love that." As he let go of my throat with his remaining hand, I gasped for gulps of air to regulate my breathing back to some normality. Guy forced my hand down to his crotch to reinforce his message. If I could have seen my eyes, I knew I couldn't have hidden the disgust within them, but my fight instinct had kicked truly in.

"Never would I go near a controlling, self-centered arsehole like you." I grabbed and twisted his bollocks leaving him scrunched in a pile on the floor, an etched look of pain on his face. As my retribution shone, I knew I couldn't celebrate. The bile still felt heavy, and I had to be clear. My heart raced.

The walk towards the door seemed to take forever. I felt an overwhelming desire to run away from the chauvinistic pig as he attempted to stand. Guy's words sent shivers down my spine and couldn't be mistaken.

"Miss Berkley, you have just committed career suicide."

Irina made her way past me, asking if I had seen Guy,

and I directed her with a pointed finger. There was a look of concern plastered all over her face when she saw him, but he dismissed her worries, putting it all down to a silly accident.

Fuck the others: I needed to be alone. I knew no one would believe a word I said, but I couldn't be around Guy alone anymore. He was a psycho, sick and twisted. The implication of sleeping my way to the top with him as my only way of progressing through the ranks was insulting, and I would rather be stuck where I was. Getting out as fast as I could, would be my only option moving forward, and that was my sole intention.

Luca and I became more creative with our sexual exploration, and soon our relationship became laden with more meaning. An attachment of a title between us happened naturally, but I knew Guy had a plan in place. When he would enact that only time would tell.

Violated was the easiest way to feel, but I wasn't the type of person to be pushed away from a situation. Karma would catch up to Guy one day, and then I would bask in the glory of it. As it stood, I spent as much time as possible surrounded by other colleagues and became a proper team player—only having to be in contact with Guy when it was a team meeting or review period.

Guy had been ecstatic during the review process with praise for the combined team but couldn't help giving the odd dig of refinement when it came to management style and structure. Glares between the pair of us hadn't gone unnoticed, but I hadn't dared to challenge a word he said. It was positive feedback, and each person deserved that respect. I wasn't going to cause an uproar. Luca's quick squeeze of my arse soon shifted my thoughts to a better place.

Models had been cast, hair and design support booked with trials undertaken and tested. Tomorrow would see my name in lights or flopped to the ground. I just knew that I had a clause in my contract after the show to leave. If I stayed, that would be a bonus; if not, I'd go back to my old life. At least I knew I'd tried. But leaving Glamique would leave a discussion to be had with Luca.

All the mannequins were prepped with each garment laid out in exact precision, shoes and accessories surrounding the area. I felt a hand trail along the curve of my waist, and I was spun around into Luca's chest. He peppered kisses along my cheek, trailing down my neck to my collar bone.

"Bellezza, shall we go? It's getting late now." He looked to the window at the darkness falling in the sky to grab my attention; I hadn't realised where the hours had gone.

"Hmm, of course. Let's go to mine. I need feeding, too." Luca was causing my mind to jumble with his magic mouth. If he carried on the way he was going, I couldn't be blamed for my actions.

"Pasta? Then my cock. Will that suffice for dessert?" Luca questioned as he pulled back. I knew he was unsure of stepping on unfamiliar territory with cooking for me, it seemed logical for me though, trying his heritage food together, learning more about one another. His cock for dessert was the perfect complement, I thought, if we were able to hold out to eat in that order. It remained to be seen. Starters may work better.

Luca's mind seemed to be filled with endless questions tonight—jittery and nervousness—even though it was the first time cooking for another it felt like our relationship had transported a few levels. I wasn't sure if his demeanour had changed because of the situation or something else was at work. Not long after Luca and I had our sexual escapade, a brand-new camera system was installed. It was as if Guy was power starved, desperate to watch every movement and pounce when desire took hold. Guy was privy to our relationship within these walls, but I tried to keep as much for our own domain as possible. You never knew what information could be held against you, and I wasn't willing to find out after Guy's threats.

Arms linked we made our way out of the door to get home.

Chapter Five

LUCA WAS TRUE to his word. The moment we stepped into the flat, I was ordered to the bathroom immediately to unwind and relax in the tub while he prepared a quick homemade carbonara. Relaxing wasn't in my nature, especially when the desire to see him working over the hot stove in the kitchen was too high on the list. Being comfortable in my loungewear was top of the agenda. I knew Luca saw the person within, and not just the body it was in, so I wasn't worried about him seeing me in it.

Dinner was orgasmic, as were the multiple dessert sessions we engaged in after. Who knew food could cause such a sexual awakening? The bedroom seemed too far away; the kitchen table was a much better substitute. We lost control and my velour trousers dropped to the floor. Glad of the chance to bathe first, I allowed Luca to eat my pussy before the delight of his own cock pounded hard inside of me. Next time, my body would apparently be the dining plate.

With tension relieved in the both of us, I needed to sit down and discuss what my plan was moving forward with Glamique whilst being as vague as possible. The more ambiguous the details were for Luca, the better. At least he couldn't be held accountable for anything in the process.

"Luca, after tomorrow, I'm going to use the 'get out' clause stipulated in my contract at Glamique. The fashion industry isn't what I expected, and I just can't work somewhere without the support I need." The faster I spoke, the easier the words rolled off my tongue.

"What about Guy?" Luca cautiously watched my reaction with great interest as he fidgeted with his fingernails.

"I just don't have that connection with him." My attempt to put the mask in place and be nonchalant with the man my heart was starting to care deeply for was proving harder than I thought.

"I see the way you avoid him, Bellezza. Do you trust me?" The fact he could see right through me and daren't call me out on my actions showed me his true character.

"Of course, I do." Without hesitation, my heart leapt in my chest as the words rose from my stomach and spilt out of my mouth.

"Then don't do anything until the last model has walked tomorrow." He pleaded with me, and his eyes drove into the back of mine, looking for the confirmed acceptance from me.

"Why?"

Luca's mouth crashed down onto mine, silencing me in a kiss to stop any more questions leaving my mouth.

He broke away to ensure he had the final word in the matter, a confirmation shared between us. "It will become a clear picture in the end." A glint appeared in his eyes as

216

his thumb caressed my cheek. "Keren, I will do anything to protect you; I just need you to trust me when I ask you to for a few hours of time. Now, let's go to bed. Tomorrow is a big day." Our hands slide into each other's as he pulled me gently up from the sofa to his side, guiding me into the bedroom.

The word 'protect' repeated in my head. Why had Luca said it? Was it silly for me to think he knew anything about why I may want to leave the company? I couldn't seem to shift the edge of doubt that had settled in the forefront of my head. An inkling had been placed, but if it was watered, I was sure it would grow. With no evidence, what could I do? It wasn't as if I could outright ask him the question, was it?

Luca had never asked anything of me. It was true I trusted him. He had asked me for time and a few extra hours. It wouldn't matter in terms of the agreement, as long as I took the next step by the end of the day. For him, I would do it, but I was interested to know the reason behind his pleading.

An early rise after a restless sleep proved a challenge at the best of times, but today was one that caused a lot of change. The various circumstances spun around like a tornado, and I couldn't seem to correlate anything into order.

Luca calmed my nerves normally, but this morning he rushed off with a quick kiss. "Promise me. I will meet you there." If I wasn't already panicked, then I was now.

"Of course," I replied softly, feeling deflated as he rushed out of the door without a second glance back at me. It was out of character, and I didn't have time to try to solve that mystery today. I made my way to Glamique to face the day ahead, knowing that at least everything else would be ready.

The event had been organised as a showcase on the theme of seasonal love, set up as a launch of the new lower ground extension at Glamique—a place for the designers to showcase the new exclusives. The platform span in a circle, looking at the indoor and outdoor elements. The team had thought of everything with a raised canopy erected to keep the outer stage dry, which was decorated with spring and summer silk flowers; the detail was immaculate.

The autumn area was my favourite by far, especially as one of my designs seemed to resonate with the brief so well: fresh and vibrant with a twist of originality, the perfect combination of design from the whole team. It brought the piece to a new level, one I hoped would be appreciated.

With the setting all prepared, I knew I needed to head to where all the action was taking place upstairs and attempt to ensure composure remained within my whole team, models included. I was in charge with my bag of tricks, pins and tit tape—anything could be sorted. The lift door opened the opposite way to how I'd expected it to, complete chaos and people flying straight towards my direction.

Irina grabbed my elbow with a pointed stare and dragged me straight to the nearest vacated room, away from the growing noise surrounding us. "Keren, where have you been and why haven't you been answering your phone?"

With the edge of my tongue laced with excitement, I replied. "I've been downstairs, looking over the production. Isn't it beautiful?"

"Enough, shit, Keren. Why did you not answer your phone?" Irina goes to close the door and shouts out into the room we walked through. "Back to it. I will sort this mess out." Her sternness makes everyone take notice as the noise starts to dissipate.

For the life of me, I couldn't find where I had placed my phone as I dug into the depths of my bag and patted my coat pockets. I finally found it lurking in my blazer. The screen lit up when I pressed the button and I noticed eight missed calls; I had missed a critical piece of information. Worse still, whatever it was, I wasn't going to like it.

"It must have been on silent, last night. I'm sorry."

Irina's face was thunderous, I had never seen her this angry before. "Keren. I tell you now. Guy is missing. Luca is missing. No one could contact you. All your designs have vanished, and the show starts in two hours." She looked at her watch. "We have every top name at this event, people flying in especially, and the main pieces are gone."

My eyes widened and tears began to form. "Gone, what do you mean? I left them laid out ready for today. Irina, where the fuck are my garments?" Anger permeated through each vein as my hands clenched together. I tried to breathe deeply and find a sense of inner calmness, except everyone who could help give me any reasonable answers seemed to be missing.

"I hoped you may have them with you—maybe a last-minute adjustment had to be fixed or something. I know it's against policy, but with your streak of retaliation, I thought it was a possibility."

Flabbergasted at her audacity—I knew the importance of the pieces—I challenged her gaze.

"I would never do that. Where could they be? There are other designs, aren't there?" My attempts to find an alternative plan struck me as I wondered what options I possibly had at such short notice.

"Yes, of course. But Autumn Kisses has started a

bidding war. It was meant to be a surprise tonight. Of course, the designers want to see the goods beforehand. This is the perfect opportunity for them."

A ball of dread started to rise in my stomach, and I felt like I was going to be sick. "What are we going to do?" As I looked at Irina, I prayed she had a plan in place or at least an idea.

"Put our masks in place, pretend everything is fine and pray to god that those outfits show up in time. If not, I don't know." I knew the people outside were counting on the both of us. We had to at least make others believe the charade for the interim at least.

"Oh, Irina what about Guy and Luca?" I questioned.

"We will just keep trying them; someone has to keep the show going. Looks like it's our situation to contend with." The look of defeat she tried to bypass me was slightly too obvious as a sigh struggled to be hidden from her lips.

The strength in unity between us ascertained the power we had. Colleagues listened and accepted our excuses. Time had been bought. All that remained was to instruct everyone as if we were still continuing the original schedule.

I was distracted by worries of where Luca had rushed to. Guy wanted to grind me down, with worry of his whereabouts it seemed but it was the last thing I needed on top of everything else. Especially if Irina was to discover that nugget of information too. I had to pretend I wasn't fazed by their actions. The long game was always the best idea: holding those cards tight to the chest and not revealing your hand to anyone. Avoidance and bluffing the situation was the only technique I had left to use.

Designers headed down to the backstage area and briefed me with times. Luckily, due to the nature of my pieces, we were to be the final garments to grace the stage. With twenty minutes to showtime, the monotonous clock's seconds dangerously ticked down as the start time verged closer.

Models prepped, dressing gowns worn, all accessories and underwear in place… The only items missing were the garments. With everything on the line, I would be the person admitting all to the world. That honour always lay with the designer at hand. Irina may have been a major part of the company, but it was my name in association with the designs that were missing.

As the designer and trio of models of the showcase before mine walked off the stage, I realised I had run out of time.

Chapter Six

BRIGHT LIGHTS WERE my only focus the moment I stepped foot onto the catwalk. Everyone must have thought I was the start of the next collection. The interval between shows had been announced at the start. Designers were to be met at the end of the collection when we each returned with our models—a way to get additional exposure of the pieces.

The volume of the voices in the audience began to increase and the questions of confusion rose. The microphone that wardrobe had attached earlier to my clothes had been activated. As I tapped the speaker with my forefinger, the room fell quiet.

"Hello everyone, I just wanted to say a few words if I may? I know, a slightly unorthodox way of starting my collection and different to the stated running order. My name is Keren Berkley, and I know many of you are excited to see Autumn Kisses but…" I didn't get to finish my sentence before the door opened and Luca stormed in dressed in a uniform. He was with Guy, who was wearing handcuffs and was being escorted by two officers, one either side of him. I raised my eyebrows, wondering what was going on.

Heads flipped round and eyes bulged, mine included. Words faltered in my mouth at what was happening as Irina brought my models out on the stage for all to admire. In my head, I thought everyone couldn't give a damn about the outfits and wanted to know what the fuck was going on with the influential Guy Simons.

As the screen behind began to play divulging information no one expected to hear, I was glad Guy wasn't here as I expect the clientele inside could turn nasty. The whispered voices of others drew my attention to the rumoured sexual misconduct of Guy and him not being such an innocent party and him now being held in police custody made me want to collapse to the ground.

We had the outfits back, and it looked like officers had collected some evidence. How had this happened? My mind was confused by the events unravelling before my eyes.

It seemed Guy was as shady as they came. He had got rich by guaranteeing he was always at the top no matter the consequence. They say greed is a disease, in his case, it was multiplying, taking over his body, like cancer. Fashion and money linked to power for him, without that combination he was a nobody, something that Guy couldn't allow to ever happen.

The other designers were unaware the designs weren't his. A gentleman's word was always gospel, and his high standing meant he was never questioned, even when the style was a different quality. Guy had built people up in their careers and knocked them down slowly brick by brick;

he'd stolen my dreams to keep his passion alive.

With Irina's bossy exterior back, she directed and excused everyone. Enough speculation had been elicited for front page gossip, and we didn't want any more scandals. Guy's predicament aside, another situation needed handling, one closer to home, and I felt my demeanour had remained rather calm and intact as it stood at the moment. I didn't know if it would be the same once I knew more.

My attention wavered as my mouth drooled: he was sexy before, but in uniform, he was even sexier. I wasn't ashamed to admit to being hot under the collar. The bright lights in the room certainly weren't helping the situation. The desire to persist in ogling him in the tight skin fitted pieces did nothing but cause crazy wild thoughts in my imagination. I wanted to tear each layer of his clothes off with my teeth, or even better, a strip show would get me really hot and bothered. I knew in my heart, though, I should be feeling confusion and potential anger, except I didn't know if I did.

His hand grasped mine as he gazed into my eyes and spoke softly. "Keren, I'm sorry. My name is Luca Giovanni, and I am an undercover police officer. Irina is my partner."

"Partner?" My voice raised an octave as I dropped his hand and took a step back with the need to create space between us.

"No, at work. It's always been you." Luca kept his eyes trained on me as he cautiously stepped forward.

"Oh, I'm sorry. It's just a lot to take in." His comfort was required as I allowed my feet to move me forwards, taking solace by his side.

"I know. Irina has been trying to take Guy down for years. She has got close before but has never been able to secure that full arrest." Luca kissed the top of my head and wrapped his arm around me.

Through gritted teeth Luca confessed, "We needed an alternative angle and that lay with me. I wanted to tear him apart the moment he laid a finger on you, but I knew I would blow everything. I knew that I had to increase surveillance—anything to secure his demise."

Tears bubbled as I struggled to hold them back. "Oh Luca, I'm sorry." As the words left my lips, the tears fell from my eyes.

"Don't be. I just didn't expect that I would fall in love with the woman who's boss I had to take down." He swiped away one of the tears with the pad of his thumb, kissing the place where it had been. Luca's mouth trailed to my lips as he gave me a sweet kiss.

"Love? Luca, you love me?" There was shock in my voice, and a need to touch my lips to know he was there— to know that the tingle he left behind wasn't a figment of my imagination. He had conveyed such meaningful words to me, and my heart felt it was about to explode with realisation that the man in front of me had confessed his love for me.

"I do. Always and forever. If you will have me. My bellezza." He kissed my knuckles, which sent the shivers down my spine.

I realised love wasn't about what you wore or how you wore it. Design could show it of course, but that could be through many medias, not one fixed type. Guy was addicted to the wrong type. Fashion was a bitch and one of mistaken identity. The fashion show today was supposed to showcase the beauty within, but it obviously wasn't meant to be. Guy ruined his chance, and Glamique stood strong: it showed who really ruled in the end.

Love and devotion could come in many forms. For me, it was a hot Italian officer. There was only one way Luca knew how to show his love for me: fucking me where it all began.

THE END

The Sweet Taste of Revenge

TRACIE PODGER

Chapter One

REVENGE WAS THE dumbest name I'd heard for a girl, but that's exactly what it was; Revenge Carlotti, daughter of one of the most horrific mob bosses in modern history. I'd known her when I was younger and rumour had it, Revenge was the product of an affair, and duly named by her mother who had subsequently paid for her infidelity; for the past twenty-five years she had been resting at the bottom of a deep lake in the grounds of her own home.

I had been contracted to *find* Revenge, paid half a million dollars to take her home to her father. I'd accepted that fee, of course, but little had her father, or Revenge herself, known, she was currently sitting in a secure location within my estate; a cave with metal fencing across the entrance, and a gate that only two people had a key for. She wasn't meant to be there. It had been a monumental fuck up on Revenge and her lover's part, but here we were. So not only was I tasked to find Revenge, I also had to return her without her knowing where she was and who was involved.

I strolled across the garden, close to the cliff top and breathed in the scent of the Mediterranean Sea below me. My house was perched near the edge in my beloved Sicily, private and secure.

The clatter of a metal chains echoed through the cave as I undid the padlock.

"Enrico?" I heard bounce back. Revenge was calling for her lover, my nephew, who had panicked and dumped her on me.

I pulled a hood over my head exposing just my eyes. Slipped gloves on my hands, not because I didn't want to leave fingerprints, but because I had a distinctive tattoo that would easily identify me.

"No, not Enrico," I said quietly although my voice boomed, amplified by the cavern and stone walls.

I heard her sob before I got to the inner chamber that was her temporary home. A second metal fence and gate secured her within a small area that housed a bed, a bucket for her needs, an old-fashioned washstand with a jug of clean water, and candles. It wasn't ideal but I wasn't acting as the conscientious host.

"What have you done with him?" she asked, her voice broken, as was her spirit.

Revenge had surprised me: she'd fought for a few days and cursed like a sailor. I sported some rather impressive bruises before I'd been able to subdue her. It hadn't been my intention to keep her, or to have her look so sad. I simply couldn't just return her without it looking at least like I'd taken some time to find her.

"He's gone, Revenge. He isn't the hero you believe him to be." I wanted to be honest, although I wasn't sure why. I didn't owe her anything, least of all the truth.

"You lie," she shouted, spitting the words as she stood and walked towards the gate. "Who are you?" Her voice quietened a little.

"I wasn't the one who took you, but as soon as your father pays, you'll be returned." She visibly blanched at my words. "Don't worry, Revenge, you won't be harmed." I added a little menace to my voice, a hint that I might be lying.

"I can't go back," she said in barely a whisper. She stepped aside and it was then that I noticed her hands shaking. "You can't take me back."

If she could have seen my face, she would have noticed my brow furrow in confusion.

Revenge had arrived at my door passed out in the back of my nephew's car after being drugged. He'd spluttered through an explanation that he'd spiked her drink but thought he'd killed her and didn't know what to do. Carlo, my right-hand man had helped him bring Revenge to the cave, somewhere we often kept people when information was needed from them. I wasn't just contracted to find *people*, but information as well.

"What do you know about Enrico?" I asked, genuinely wanting to know the answer.

"He loves me," she said, squaring her shoulders as if making herself believe.

"He dumped you here and was on the first boat out of Sicily," I said.

"I don't believe you."

"I don't care whether you do or not. Where is he, Revenge?" I said, waving my arms around. "Why are you here alone?"

She sat heavily on the bed. "What are you going to do to me?" Her voice was little more than a squeak.

"I haven't decided. Who knows, maybe I'll kill you."

Her voice became steely. "Then why not show yourself? What would it matter if I knew who my murderer was?"

It was a good question, but I wasn't going to answer. If I did, I'd simply say, "I want to collect the half million dollars first."

Her father thought a rival family held her. An 'eye for an eye' crusade after Carlotti murdered a son. He'd murdered the boy because it was rumoured he was someone with an unhealthy interest in women; particularly, he liked to drug and rape them. He was better out of the community, not that the family would agree. Carlotti had asked me to rescue his daughter and I had to somehow make both parties believe she was being held by a rival family, and I was going to *rescue* and deliver her back. Her words earlier, however, worried me.

"Why can't you go back?" I asked.

Revenge folded her hands into her lap and bowed her head. I wasn't sure if she was playing a game or not. However, when I saw a tear splash to her palm my curiosity was piqued further.

"I just can't."

She didn't speak any more, and I turned and left. She'd be given some food and coffee shortly, slid through a small hatch from a second antechamber. I wanted her kept healthy while I investigated further. I'd believed her when she'd said she didn't want to go back, I just wanted to know why.

Chapter Two

"ENRICO, YOU NEED to return my calls. If you ignore me further, let me assure you that when I catch up with you, you won't ever be able to hold a fucking phone let alone answer it!" I slammed my mobile down on my desk.

"Do you want me to go find him, Boss?"

I looked up to see my greatest friend, Carlo, standing at my office door with two cups of coffee in his hands. I waved him in.

"Why doesn't she want to go home?" I said to myself reaching out to take the coffee from him. Carlo wouldn't have the faintest idea, I imagined.

Carlo shook his head as he sat. He acted as my *negotiator*. He was the only person that anyone spoke to, and on rare occasions met, when they contracted me to either find people or extract information. The man had endured many hours of torture once and yet he had never broken a confidence. I'd lay my life down that he'd never betray me. He had been my father's confidant before my father was gunned down in front of my mother, my sister, and myself. My mother went to her grave haunted by that image and Carlo was the only person I had to rely on. He'd become my surrogate father, uncle, protector, and best friend.

I sighed with exasperation. "There has to be a reason. I don't believe for one minute she thought the imbecile, Enrico, loved her."

Revenge was an intelligent woman. Enrico was not much better than the village idiot at times. His mother, my sister, had given up on him years earlier, something I detested. No matter how dumb the kid was, he was her only child. My sister and I hadn't spoken in six years because of it. He enraged me on a regular basis, but he was blood. I sent him a text message, a slightly softer request for him to call me, stating the urgency. I had no doubt he'd be drunk, drugged, and holed up with some whore somewhere, that was his way. He'd surface in a couple of days, come crawling back like a kicked dog with his tail between his legs. That didn't help me immediately, however.

"We know Carlotti killed his wife, perhaps his daughter has never forgiven him for that," Carlo said.

"Or maybe he torments her because he knows, or believes, she isn't his?" I added.

It wasn't widely known that he hadn't fathered her. In fact, my father knew and I often wondered if that's why he was murdered. I was also curious if his wife's adultery was all he saw when he looked at Revenge, spoke her name, even.

"I wonder why he never changed her name?" I mused, quietly to myself. Carlo didn't answer; it wasn't a question anyone could.

"Do you think she'll tell you why she doesn't want to return?" Carlo asked.

I gently shook my head. "I don't think so. Right now, I have no idea what to do with her. Collect the money and deposit her home, or... There was a tone of wretchedness to her voice when she said she couldn't go home. I can't ignore that."

What I hadn't told Carlo was that her words had pulled at my heart, reverberated through my chest. I'd felt a pang of empathy for her. I wasn't sure why. I didn't like her. I had, when I was younger, but she was bitter. Or was she?

"I'll take her some food and see if she'll speak to me," Carlo said, and I nodded my approval. Like me, Carlo had a manner about him that made people want to open up to him.

***

I flicked through some paperwork, my mind was not on figures and import taxes for my legitimate business of producing olive oil, but on Revenge instead. I growled out my frustration and slammed the paperwork back on the desk. Profit and loss accounts would have to wait. I stood and paced, eventually coming to a halt at a full height glass window. I watched the stillness of the sea, the azure blues that normally comforted me. A boat, one of mine, was moored just a small way off; it would often patrol the cliff to make sure my privacy was kept just as I wanted it. It wasn't unusual for a tourist or novice sailor to moor up on my private beach at the base of the cliff.

I trolled through my memory trying to remember any conversation I'd overheard or had about Carlotti that might help me understand. My mind hadn't been focussed on him over the years, but he was never that far away.

"Nothing, not a word," I heard Carlo say behind me.

235

I turned to see him walk back into my office. "Not even a thank you for the meal." He chuckled.

"She's consistently rude then," I replied, smirking at him.

Carlo left to make some calls, report our *findings* back to Carlotti, and I returned to my paperwork. Revenge would wait. However, as before, I couldn't concentrate.

"Fuck's sake," I said, slamming my clenched hand on my desk.

There was nothing for it; I had to see if I could get more information from Revenge. I grabbed my gloves and hood and left the office, careful to lock the door behind me. Carlo had a key, but after catching a previous housekeeper snooping, my office was off limits to any staff.

I walked through French doors and the sun blazed through the canopy of trees that generally kept the rear of the house cool in the summer months. I raised my face and closed my eyes, catching some of those rays on my skin. *I could do with a dose of Vitamin D*, I thought. I was becoming reclusive, a night owl since most of my *work* involved being out in the evenings.

I slipped on the gloves as I walked and pulled the hood over my head, leaving my face exposed for a moment. Revenge didn't call for her lover at the sound of the padlock and chain rattling this time. Although I could hear her gentle sobs. I rolled down the mask and stood by the second gate.

She looked up at me. "Please let me go," she whispered.

"I will, soon. I need to know why you can't be returned to your father," I said, keeping my voice soft.

Revenge simply shook her head. "If you know my father, you'll know he isn't a nice man. I dread to think what he will do to you." A fiery tone was creeping back into her voice and I smiled.

"I highly doubt he knows where you are."

"He'll have people looking for me."

"Then perhaps we need to get you back sooner."

Her previous fire was snuffed out. "He hates me. He has always hated me. He tells me constantly how awful my mother was, that he killed her. And I hate him in return. Enrico was going to save me. We were going to leave and…"

"And?"

She shook her head, and I wondered if she regretted that she might have said too much.

"And you were going to collect a ransom to live off?" I added, gently. Without looking up, she nodded. "What are we going to do with you?" I wondered if she knew there was no ransom.

Revenge stood and walked to the gate. Her hands wrapped around the bars and her eyes widened. "I can give you half of it," she said, eagerly.

I laughed. "There is no ransom."

"What about your fee then?"

"Revenge, do you think your father will give you the money to hand over to me? Or will he deposit the money in a bank account of my choosing? This isn't the Wild West. Is that what you thought would happen?"

I wanted to laugh at the absurdity of it all. Had she really known Enrico, she would have probably discovered that he'd have high-tailed it with the cash long before she even made it through her front door.

Whereas her knuckles had been white as she'd gripped the bars, the pink returned to her skin as she lessened her hold.

She visibly shrunk as reality sunk in. "I thought Enrico would be the ideal person to help me even though he was so much younger than me. I know what I'm about to say is wrong, but he isn't the most intelligent and that's why I chose him," she said.

I laughed out loud. "He spiked your drink, brought you here because he thought he'd killed you," I confessed.

"And you thought you'd cash in on me?" she asked. Her tone of voice had softened as if she genuinely wanted to know the answer rather than to accuse.

"No, Revenge. Before I could get any answers as to why he had you unconscious in his car, he was off."

"So here I am, really captive," she said. She chuckled with a bitter tone.

"I can always return you," I goaded.

She let go of the bars and turned, walking towards the bed. "No, I'd rather stay, although I'd like to get out for fresh air every day if I could."

"You're not staying here. I don't like people," I said.

"Maybe you need a housekeeper…"

"I have one of those."

"How about a nanny?"

"I don't have children."

"Oh, yes, you don't like people," she teased, but for the first time, I saw a brief smile.

"You'll have your freedom, Revenge, as soon as some things are wrapped up."

I had an answer of sorts as to why she didn't want to return home, but I wasn't convinced by it. She wasn't a child, she wasn't held under lock and key in her own home, so I had my doubts she was being truthful.

Chapter Three

CARLO RECALLED HIS conversation with Carlotti. He'd told him that I had located his daughter, and she would be returned to him soon. His gushing appreciation and thanks was nauseating, according to Carlo.

All the while I was with Carlo I had no need to visit Revenge but when alone, I felt a tug, a pull to talk to her. I constantly had to remind myself why I didn't like her.

I'd declared my love once, as a silly teenager with raging hormones. She'd laughed at me. I had nothing to offer her, so she'd said. There was a small, irrational, part of my mind that wanted to *out* myself. She would know how successful I'd become over the years and I wondered if her attitude would be different.

Revenge – so aptly named, she certainly encouraged people to want to seek theirs.

She was sleeping when I crept to the hatch in the antechamber and peered through the gap. One arm was thrown above her head; her long dark hair was knotted and fanned out around her. The lower buttons of her once white shirt were open and showed a tanned and toned stomach. A glint of silver caught my eye. I wondered what her father thought of that navel piercing, I highly doubted he would approve. Perhaps that was her small act of rebellion.

She mumbled in her sleep, not coherently enough for me to understand, however. When she rolled to her side, she rested one hand on the waistband of her jeans, her fingertips just underneath the material. I felt my cock harden as I watched her. I didn't want to be aroused, but there was, had always been, something *siren* about her. She'd bring any man to his knees, I was sure.

I wondered what expressions she made when she pleasured herself, what noises left her lips as she came. My hardness became painful and begged for some relief. I imagined running my tongue over her toned stomach, sucking that silver ring into my mouth, tugging at it with my teeth. As if my thoughts had been transmitted, she mewled gently.

The sound of wind howling and groaning outside the cave entrance echoed to the inner chambers, it startled her. She bolted upright and swung her legs from the bed. She tiptoed to the gate and waited, listening, I imagined. When she identified the sound, her shoulders slumped. I heard her sigh. Even that was arousing.

I needed her gone. She was fucking with my mind and I didn't like that.

I walked back to find Carlo in the kitchen discussing menus with the housekeeper. She nodded her head to me and left.

"I want her gone, Carlo," I said, reaching for a coffee cup.

"What's happened?" he asked.

"Nothing in particular, she's just…disrupting and I don't like it."

He softly chuckled. "What's your plan?"

"I'll hood her, and we'll move her out. We'll make it look like an interception."

Carlo nodded; it was a plan we'd used in the past when we'd played both kidnapper and rescuer. Anyone dumb enough to offer a good reward was worth the ploy. *Double bubble*, Carlo had called it once, a term he'd learned from a British friend that meant earning twice.

"When?"

"Tonight."

Although that didn't give us a lot of time, there wasn't any real planning to do. Carlo would move her, I'd *rescue* her. We'd fire some guns, shout a lot, cause confusion, have her scared enough that she would be distraught, and I'd swoop in like a knight in shining armour and carry her to my charger.

It should have been simple.

***

I checked myself in the mirror. I wore all black clothing, gloves, and my mask. I had a handgun in a holster at my shoulder loaded with blanks. We didn't want to run the risk of actually shooting ourselves, or her for that matter. Carlo was dressed similarly. It was he that headed down to the cave and returned a few minutes later with a hooded and bound, struggling Revenge. He shook his hand where she'd bitten him, and he screwed his eyes at me in annoyance when I smirked.

While I opened the boot of his car, she kicked out catching the lights and smashing the cover. Her muffled screams suggested he'd wedged something in her mouth, but she was still managing to make enough noise for me to worry.

Revenge was bundled into Carlo's boot and even after it was closed, she still kicked and made a racket.

"Take the back roads," I whispered, and he nodded. The last thing we needed was for the police to stop him for a broken rear light and find her in the boot.

I followed in my vehicle and the way Carlo drove a little too fast over the unmade road made me laugh. I was sure Revenge would have a banging headache.

He came to a screeching halt and our scene was played out. Shouts, gunfire, bashes to the panels of the car silenced Revenge.

I popped open the trunk and reached in for her. "Quick, come," I said, and I pulled off the hood and the handkerchief from her mouth.

"I…" She was clearly terrified.

I grabbed her wrist. "I'm not here to hurt you. Come, quick!" I laced my voice with a sense of urgency while pulling her from the boot. "Keep low," I said, tugging her and running to my vehicle.

Carlo lay on the floor, facing away from her as if shot. He groaned and I wanted to laugh. His acting skills were akin to a third-rate shoot 'em up movie, the kind where one shot had the victim spiralling and writhing for ages before playing dead.

"I need to see who that was," she said, trying to slow and turn.

"No, you don't." I had no intention of her looking anywhere other that my vehicle. I opened the rear door, making sure to take a quick glance that the child lock was in place. "Get in."

I threw her across the seat, slammed her door, and then climbed into the driver's seat. I hit the accelerator and wheelspun down the dirt road.

"Who are you?" she shouted above the engine noise.

"Someone sent to rescue you."

"I don't…" She didn't finish her sentence, but I had half an idea what she was about to say. I had to play dumb, however.

"Don't worry. I'll get you home soon." Although I still wore the mask, I smiled into the rear-view mirror.

Revenge righted herself and sat. She was still bound at her wrists. Her hair was a mess, more so after I'd whipped off her hood and seen tears tracking down her cheeks. For a moment, I felt awful that I'd caused those tears. Then I remembered how much of a bitch she could be, a great actress, and half a million dollars was about to hit my account.

"Please don't take me home," she whispered.

I stared at her in the mirror, pretending to be shocked at her words. I pulled the car over and turned in my seat.

"Please, I'm begging you," she said, her voice firmer.

"Your father has been searching for you," I said.

She huffed and shook her head. "I'm sure he has. I've been trying to get away for years."

"I don't understand," I lied.

"Please, whatever he's offering you, I can pay." I highly doubted that, but appreciated she needed to use whatever tactic she could. "Can I stretch my legs? I've been cramped up for ages."

I wanted to laugh. Revenge must have thought me an idiot, but I decided to play along. She wasn't strong or fast enough to get away from me. I slid from me seat and opened the rear door. I reached in to grab her elbow and help her from the car. I left her hands bound figuring that being unable to swing her arms would slow her down. She made a show of stretching and sighing, raising her face to the sun and gasping in.

"I've been kept in the dark for so long. They…" She sniffed, and I waited. "They *attacked* me," she said, giving a pretend sob at the same time.

"In what way?" I asked gently, obviously knowing it to be a lie.

I wanted to applaud her; her performance was worthy of an Oscar. She fell to her knees sobbed and wailed yet not one tear left her eyes. Under my mask I smiled, wanting to laugh out loud.

"I need some facts confirmed. The man who took you from the bar, who was he?" I knew, of course, but wanted to see what her *official* comment would be. Her father would demand this, of course.

"I don't know. I was with a girlfriend and the next thing I knew, I woke up in a cave of some kind. A man came to see me, he wore a similar hood to you," she said, staring up at me.

"Anyone can get these, Revenge. They sell them in the local clothes store." She squinted, frowned, and I continued, "You said 'they.' How many were there?"

"Oh, about five, I think. And a woman," she said, rambling.

I leaned down to help her up. It was my mistake. As I did, she kicked out, catching me in the balls. I wanted to double over in pain; I sucked in a deep breath to quell the nausea. Revenge started to crawl away. Unable to contain myself, I roared out in agony. I straightened and strode towards her, pushing aside the pain. I grabbed her under one arm and pulled her to her feet. She twisted and turned, grabbing at my mask and lifting it slightly. Not enough to expose my face, but my mouth. I grabbed her throat and pushed her against a tree. I needed her still so I could catch my breath.

"It was you, wasn't it?" she shouted.

"What was me?" I asked through gritted teeth.

"It was you in the cave."

"No, it fucking wasn't. I *was* here to rescue you. I've been watching, waiting for them to move you to a new location once they realised they had been found. Now, I've half a mind to fucking leave you here to be eaten by the wild animals."

"Do it, then." Her eyes were wide and full of fear, but her spirit was back. As much as I hated her, I admired that side of her. She had more backbone than the fool she'd tied herself to in her quest for freedom, that was for sure.

She let lose with a stream of profanities, calling me every son of a whore she could. She tried to kick out again, to swing her arms to punch, but she didn't have enough space.

I stepped closer and she stilled. Her breathing was rapid, coarse considering I held her throat tightly. I leaned down and crashed my lips on hers. At first, she tried to close her mouth. I forced my tongue inside, kissing her hard. It wasn't long before she relented. She opened her mouth further, returning my kiss with as much ferocity. When she gently moaned, I stepped back.

I laughed and then spat on the floor, wiping my mouth with the back of my gloved hand.

"What the…?"

"I just wanted to shut that ugly mouth of yours for a moment."

"You bastard," she said, her voice a low whisper.

"Revenge. Such a strange name, isn't it?"

"Apt if you know the history," she said.

"I do. I know about your mother. I also know that your father killed mine because he knew what your mother had done. Rumour has it, my father helped your mother meet with her lover."

Her eyes grew wide. "Then why are you insistent on helping him?"

"That's a good question. Obviously, he paid me a large fee to rescue you, but, and I'm taking a gamble here, you genuinely don't want to go back."

She shook her head. "I hate him. I lied to you earlier. Those men didn't mistreat me, I don't know who they were and there were only two of them. My *kidnap* was staged. My friend was meant to take me to a safe place, return me and collect the ransom, then we were to run away." She sighed heavily.

"Except, you chose the worst person to help you," I said, and she nodded.

She had at least confirmed what I believed and knew and hadn't contradicted any previous statements she'd made.

I pulled a knife from my pocket and she whimpered. I grabbed her wrists, and she closed her eyes. I sheared through the cable tie bind. Once loose she shook out her wrists, rubbed one where the cable tie had chafed her skin.

"Now what?" she asked.

"Now you run." I started to walk back to my car.

"Wait. You can't just leave me here."

"You had a plan to run away, yes? Execute that plan."

"What about the money?" I could hear her shuffle through the fallen leaves as she made her way back to the car.

246

"What money, Revenge?" I asked, turning to face her.

"The ransom?"

"There is no ransom. I..." I nearly added that I'd told her before there wasn't one but caught myself in time. "I was paid to find and liberate you. I've done both. My work is done."

"How do I get home?" she asked, her voice lowered to a near whisper.

"You don't want to go home, remember?"

She closed her eyes and sighed. "I don't have a fucking choice, do I? I can't be left here. I don't even know where I am."

"The little princess really didn't have a plan, did she?"

She frowned at me and shook her head gently. "I don't know what I've done to you, personally, but I'm sorry that you dislike me."

I took a step towards her. "You aren't much different to your father, Revenge. You step on people in your quest to climb to the top. You're rude, ruthless even. You don't care who you hurt."

"You don't know me at all," she said, squaring her shoulders.

It was time to give Revenge some facts. "When you were in school, do you remember Diana? The geeky girl that loved maths? You tormented her, locked her in a bathroom, and kissed her boyfriend even though you didn't want him. Remember bullying her? She slit her wrists. Or, how about Georgio? When you were in college you wanted to lose your virginity. You teased him, tempted him, and when he took your virginity, you told everyone he had assaulted you. He's dead. Or how about the time—"

"Stop! What are you doing?"

"I'm letting you see, Revenge, that for all your poor

choices, for all your jealousy of others because you had a poor childhood, there are repercussions. There are consequences. You have a choice. You're at a point in your life where you can change or you can carry on using people and becoming more bitter and miserable."

"Diana killed herself?" she asked after a moment of silence while my words sunk in.

"Yes. Her mother found her. Not only did you cause the death of Diana but her mother who died of a broken heart not long after. Death and destruction follow you, and you don't even see it, do you?"

For the first time, I saw the real Revenge. The one that had been abused by her father because of her mother's actions.

I saw the Revenge that was desperate for love but had no idea how to get it.

I saw the Revenge that had no idea how her actions had affected others.

"I loved you once, you spurned me. That's okay, I was older than you and I didn't expect any different. Not every woman falls at my feet." I chuckled at the thought. "But you didn't leave it there. You spent years laughing at me. I was the poor kid whose parents were dead. I was the one that you'd throw a jumper at in the middle of winter when I was cold. That jumper fell to the floor and you laughed as I bent down to pick it up, grateful for the meagre offering."

I slowly pulled the hood over my head and watched as her eyes widened.

"Angelo?" she asked, quietly.

"Yes, Angelo. I didn't want to take on the job your father offered, and it will be up to you if you tell him who he actually contracted. I ask you not to, of course. I'm banking, Revenge, that this experience might make you look at your life. I'm hoping that the ugliness in your heart starts to fade. Your mother was a wonderful woman, according to my father. Perhaps you need to remember her kindness and compassion. You're an adult, you can leave, but you don't because the money is more important than your freedom."

I turned and opened the rear door. She took a few paces and slid back into the car. I shut the door and climbed behind the steering wheel.

"Can you take me home?" she asked.

"I can."

I drove the rest of the way in silence. Occasionally, I'd glance at her in the rear-view mirror. Mostly she cried quietly while keeping her attention on the outside.

"Thank you, Angelo. I promise you, I didn't know about Diana. I didn't know about Georgio." She sighed deeply. "Can I get out here?" We had come close to the local cemetery. "I need some time before I confront my father."

I pulled the vehicle to a halt and said nothing as she opened the door and left the car. She paused just the once before she walked through the gates of the cemetery.

She looked over her shoulder. "I was wrong. So very wrong, especially about you, Angelo. I never believed I was good enough, I never believed anyone could love me, want me... I was wrong."

With that she walked away. I sat for a moment and reflected. I hoped I hadn't just witnessed Revenge the actress. I prayed that the experience had given her something to think about.

Now it was time to work on myself. To lose the hatred I'd harboured for her and her family. It was done; I had spent way too many years thinking about revenge. I laughed.

Revenge. A name so apt.

I started the car, turned around and drove home to the sanctuary of my cliff-top home.

Chapter Four

IT WAS SOME months later I discovered Revenge had finally left her father's clutches and found a trust fund her mother had set up for her that her father had hidden. It appeared that Revenge had set up a centre for children that were being bullied.

"Did you see this?" I asked Carlo, holding up a local newspaper.

He took it from me and read. "Well, maybe her experience did her some good," he said, verbalising my thoughts.

"I hope so."

I took the paper back and re-read the story. There was a photograph of her surrounded by young children. She was smiling and it changed her appearance. She wasn't sour looking, in fact, my stomach knotted at the sight. She looked happy, genuinely. I folded the paper and placed it to one side.

"There are a couple of contracts in discussion," he

said.

I shook my head. "I think I need a holiday for a couple of weeks."

Carlo laughed and nodded. "Okay, Boss," he said, and then left the office.

I picked up the paper again and stared at her. Her long dark hair hung in curls around her shoulders, her face was free of makeup, and her clothes weren't the tailored and designer brands she had favoured in the past. The Revenge I was looking at seemed the kind of woman I'd like to know. Pure, innocent, and kind.

Except I knew she wasn't that. Or at least she hadn't been.

A pang of loneliness hit me. I lived a very solitary life, for good reason, but I wasn't sure it was what I wanted anymore. I had my legitimate business that I called into, but it practically ran itself and Carlo generally dealt with any issues. Enrico, my nephew, came and went with abandon and right at that time, it was more 'went' than 'came.' That suited me. When he had returned after dumping Revenge he had been full of remorse and then anger when he realised she had used him. He had wanted to confront her until I told him that her father would likely assume him her kidnapper and kill him. I'd packed him off to the warehouse to sweep the floor or some such activity he couldn't fuck up.

I decided on a stroll to clear my thoughts. I wasn't a depressed person normally; I didn't reflect on what I didn't have. I only ever celebrated what I did, and I hoped a tour around my grounds might remind me of my fortunate life. At the end of the garden was a bench. I sat and stared out to sea. The salty air comforted me, and I breathed in deep. I closed my eyes and listened to the sound of waves breaking against the rocks below, to the occasional bird calling, and was then disturbed by the sound of a motorboat. I opened my eyes and shielded them. My security team were slowly patrolling the cove.

Perhaps a walk along the small beach, feeling the sand beneath my toes, might help settle my mind.

I walked into the coolness of the cave and past in the inner chamber that had held Revenge. The sight of it brought her back to my mind. I thought I could still smell her scent in the air. To the right of those inner chambers was another and a set of ancient steps carved into the rock. Legend had it they had been carved by priests as a means to escape. Or perhaps, and more likely, they used the steps to smuggle contraband up to the monastery that had once stood where my house did.

When I reached the bottom, the bright light blinded me for a moment. I waited until my vision adjusted and stepped onto the sand. I kicked off my shoes and walked barefoot to the water's edge. The hem of my jeans soaked up the warm water and held the sand as I stepped back to remove them. I pulled my T-shirt over my head and stood naked for a moment, allowing the sun to soak into my skin. I waded into the sea, diving under the waves when the depth allowed me to.

Swimming naked felt liberating and was something that I often did. I'd also cliff dive from great heights. The adrenalin rush was welcomed. That day, however, I wanted to submerge myself in the clear water that was chilled enough to invigorate. I swam underwater, unable to focus clearly but enough to follow the cliff line. When I could hold my breath no more, I emerged. I was some way off the coast and the speedboat, that appeared to have been following me, was to one side.

"Need a lift, boss?" I heard a voice say. I looked up to see Donny hung over the side of the boat with a cigarette in his mouth.

I treaded water for a while. "I think I'll make it back," I replied, giving him a wave. I swam slowly, knowing full well I'd reach the shore without becoming out of breath.

Donny was head of my security team, he was also a good friend. Carlo, Donny, and I would often sit and drink coffee or wine in the evenings. He lived on the estate in a small cottage with his wife, my housekeeper, Eleanor. It occurred to me in that moment that my friends were my employees and I struggled to remember which came first, I suspected the employee status.

***

By the time I had showered and dressed, I'd made a decision. I grabbed my car keys, waved off the offer of company from Carlo and headed into the village. I parked near the cemetery, and decided to visit my mother, something I hadn't done in a while. I was busy asking her forgiveness for not cleaning her plaque or laying flowers when I heard my name.

"I thought that was you. I'm sorry, I'm interrupting," Revenge said. She carried a small posy of flowers in her hand. "I was…well, I come here to lay flowers for my mum since she doesn't have an official resting place." I forgave the bitterness to her tone.

"Maybe you could erect something?" I offered as I stood.

Revenge shrugged her shoulders. "My nonna is here, and I like to think my mother's spirit knows I'm thinking of her." Revenge kissed her fingertips and transferred that kiss to a head stone.

"Do you want to get a coffee?" I asked. "I hear you've been doing some great work with the local kids."

She also stood and although she had her back to me, she nodded. "What you did, said, brought me up short, Angelo. I should have thanked you a while ago, and I've never told anyone it was you." She turned to face me. "I know it was you in the cave. You have a distinctive voice."

I didn't respond initially. When I'd gathered my thoughts, I repeated my offer of coffee. Revenge nodded again, and together we walked to the nearest coffee shop. I placed an order and we sat facing the square.

"Yes, it was me. Everything I told you then was the truth. Enrico dumped you in the cave, unconscious, he thought he'd killed you, and then he disappeared. In the meantime, I had been approached to find you. I won't apologise for deceiving you, although my motive was more to punish your father than you so, for that, I guess I ought to."

Revenge laughed. "That was about the most brilliant non-apology I think I've ever heard. I can't say I enjoyed my time with you, but I am thankful because it gave me the courage I needed."

"What happened?" I asked, curious to know what her father had said or done when she made it home.

"He demanded to know why you hadn't taken me to him. Someone reminded him that no one knows who you are, and that you wouldn't have shown yourself to him, or me. This is going to sound so wrong, but I loved the fact that I knew who you were. For once, I had something he didn't."

She picked up her coffee cup and sipped, and while we savoured the espresso, we sat in silence.

"He went from his normal pig-headed self to even

more nasty. I asked him why he'd paid you to find me if he disliked me so much. I think it was the first time I've questioned him. He got angry, one of his guys had to intervene and I walked out. I then found out I had a trust fund he'd been hiding from me, and it dawned on me, that was probably the only reason he kept me around. It's a substantial amount." She shook her head. Her normally bright eyes dulled as sadness clouded her features.

"I'm sorry," I said, and I genuinely was.

She turned to smile at me. "What's done is done. You did me a favour, Angelo. I'm now free. I didn't realise how horrible I'd been, how my misery had been taken out on others and I intend to change. I can't go back and apologise to Georgio or Diana, but I can make sure it doesn't happen again."

She held her hand flat on the table and I had an urge to take it in mine. Instead, I placed my hand in my lap, away from temptation. I asked her to tell me about her centre and she morphed into an excited and bright woman in front of me. She was enthusiastic about her future plans, detailing all that she wanted to do, telling me about an argument to secure a lower rent for the property she wanted to house her centre in. Although a fairly large village, there were surrounding villages where children were lonely, and she wanted to bring them all together. It wasn't just about the bullied, but about showing the local children their worth. It was something that wasn't done in Sicily, revolutionary, and probably common in other countries. I expected she'd receive some hesitation, but I hoped it took off for her.

"I'd like to donate. I'd also like to invite you to dinner so you can tell me more," I blurted out before I really thought it through.

"Oh…well, certainly yes to the first sentence."

"And the second?"

Although she hesitated, she then smiled. "Okay, why not?"

Instead of heading home until dinner, I asked to be shown the centre she had created. Perhaps I could help persuade the landlord to lower his rent. We finished our coffee and headed to my car. I opened the door for her, and she curtseyed in thanks, laughing as she slid across the leather and reached for her seat belt. I couldn't contain the broad smile that made my cheeks ache and I wondered how long it had been since I'd felt so happy.

Her centre appeared to be well equipped already. It had been open for a month despite her still negotiating her rent. I made a mental note of the landlord's details; I'd contact him later. Part of my donation could be a year's rent, I thought. Revenge was animated when she spoke. She was taking an online course to help work with the therapists she wanted to bring in. She wanted a 'youth club' feel to the place, games, toys, educational items to help bring some of the kids up to speed with their schoolwork. It sounded like something the village needed. It sounded like something that should be rolled out across Sicily.

Sicily wasn't a poor country but one still in the hold of the mafia. There were some very affluent areas, obviously, and some very poor. Those in the poorer areas suffered greatly, and those were the children, locally, that Revenge wanted to help. As she spoke, her passion was obvious. Her cheeks flamed and her loose hair spun around her head and she turned to show me things on walls or in corners. Her eyes were bright, and I found myself staring at her, not what she was pointing to.

"Are you listening to me?" she enquired, and I blinked a couple of times as if it would bring my mind back into focus.

"Sorry, yes, I was. I…you're so vibrant when you talk of this place. So different to what I remember. Beautiful."

Her cheeks flushed but more in embarrassment than animation.

"I'm sorry, that was very inappropriate," I added.

"No, it was a lovely thing to say. I haven't had many nice things said to me, or about me."

I reached out and pushed some hair over her shoulder. It was soft; her curls ran through my fingers. She sucked in a breath. I took a step towards her and watched as her lips parted slightly and her tongue ran over her lower one. I slid my hand to the back of her neck, my thumb gently gliding over her chin as I closed the gap. I couldn't have stopped myself even if I'd tried. I lowered my head and my lips gently brushed over hers. I felt her hot breath fan my face and my heart pounded in my chest.

I kissed her. She opened her mouth accepting my tongue as it tangled with hers. I wanted to taste her, to absorb her breath. My hand tightened on her neck and our kiss became more feverish. She wrapped her arms around my shoulders and stepped even closer, I could feel every inch of her body against mine. Her moan caught me off guard for a second. As did the grinding of her body against mine. I stepped her back against a table. She sat without breaking our kiss and parted her legs. I stepped between them. I had no intention of fucking her there, not that I didn't want to, but she deserved better.

It was with reluctance that I broke our kiss.

Her breathing was ragged. I took in some deep breaths to calm my racing heart.

"I'm…" she said, without finishing her sentence.

"You're?" I prompted.

"I was going to say, I'm sorry, but I'm not."

Her sureness was pleasant to see, and I smiled. "Neither am I."

She slid from the desk. "Perhaps we could…I don't know, pick this up after dinner?" She ran her hands over the lapels of my jacket.

"I'd like that."

"Oh, God, listen to me. I've never propositioned a man in my life. If I sound like a…a tramp, tell me!" She laughed nervously and looked to her feet.

I lifted her chin with my finger. "I've been propositioned many times, and you don't. Now listen to me, I sound like a lothario!"

"Only an educated man would know who Lothario was," she said, teasing.

"I've come a long way since my school days. I like to educate myself. Especially about you," I said, my voice lowering at the end of my sentence.

"My father won't be pleased," she said, raising her eyebrows and smirking.

"Then let me make love to you if only to piss off your father."

"I hope it might be because both you and I would like that."

I laughed. "First, we eat. I don't do well on an empty stomach."

She slapped my chest and placed her hand in the crook of my arm. "Lead the way, Angelo."

Dinner was enjoyable and it was a pleasant surprise to both of us to discover how much we had in common. The night was even more so. Especially since we also discovered we had a lot in common where our likes in the bedroom were concerned.

Revenge lay asleep beside me. I'd feasted on every part of her body, her pussy the most. I couldn't get enough of her. I smiled.

The sweet taste of Revenge lingered on my lips and I knew she wouldn't be leaving any time soon.

THE END

Sheltered Hearts

FINLEY SAWYER

Chapter One

I PULL UP to the curb outside my apartment and park behind Justine's car. I sigh, wishing I could have the apartment to myself tonight. I love my roommate, but today has been an extremely exhausting day with classes all morning, then working a long shift at the vet's office. Usually, I really enjoy work. I mean, who wouldn't love being surrounded by adorable animals all day long? Today, however, has been unusually tiring. We've had to put three dogs to sleep, and watching what the families go through— seeing their grief and knowing there's nothing you can do to take away that pain—it breaks your heart.

Gathering my things, I can't help but be glad there's only one day left until the weekend. It'll be nice to have a couple days to relax without having to worry about school or work. I climb down from my jeep and make my way to the front door of the house, taking the stairs up to our second-floor apartment. As soon as I enter, I hear Justine's voice coming from her room down the hall. It's loud and off key, her singing nearly drowning out the music that's playing.

I drop my stuff on the floor next to the couch and plop down. My cat, Bailey, wastes no time as he runs over to greet me. He jumps up and taps my thigh with his paw, something he always does to let me know he wants to be petted.

"Hey, buddy." I reach down and give a little scratch behind his ear. He settles down next to me, the front half of his body draped over my thigh while the back half rests on the couch. His eyes close, and I feel the vibration of his purrs as I pet him, his paws gently kneading to show his approval.

The singing stops, along with the music, and a few moments later Justine exits her room.

"Hey, Cassidy! I didn't hear you come in," she says as she rustles around in the kitchen behind me. "How was your day?"

"It was…long." I sigh.

"Everything okay? You sound sad." She knows me too well.

"Yeah, just a bit rough at work today. We had to euthanize three dogs and that's always a complete downer."

"Three? Wow, that's horrible." She rounds the couch and sits next to me, pulling me into a hug. "I'm sorry girl."

Bailey makes a loud half-meow, half-growl sound, obviously not happy with the disturbance, then jumps down and darts from the room. "Jeez, someone's a Mr. Cranky Pants." She laughs as she releases me and sits back.

I look at her and take in her appearance. Her dark brown hair is down and straightened, her makeup is done, and she is all dressed up. This can only mean one thing.

"Going out tonight?" I ask, hopeful that I'll have my

alone time after all.

"Yeah, Matt and I are meeting up with a few friends for a late dinner, then heading to the bar for a bit. Wanna come with us?"

"Nah. It's been a long day. I'm just going to stay in and relax. Read a book and get some sleep."

"Girl, you always stay in. I know he hurt you badly, but that was two years ago. You need to move on and live your life. Get out. Meet people. Have *fun*."

I flinch at the mention of my ex. She just *had* to bring him into this, didn't she? It's been her go-to lately to try to convince me to tag along with her and her boyfriend, Matt.

"I am living my life." I roll my eyes at her. "I'm just exhausted from today. And, for the record, this has nothing to do with Drew."

She flashes me a look that tells me she doesn't believe me.

"What? Seriously, it doesn't. I've moved past everything, but it doesn't mean I have any desire to date again. Not right now at least."

"You can't stay holed up forever you know. Eventually…"

Ring, ring.

My cell phone interrupts her, saving me from a talk I'm not in the mood to have anyway. The caller ID displays a number I don't recognize. Wanting to put an end to this conversation, I answer the call.

"Hello?"

"Ms. Knox?"

"Yes? Can I help you?"

"Hi there! This is Erin from Lone Paw Sanctuary," a cheery voice sounds from the other end of the line. "I'm sorry to call you so late. I see that you are scheduled for a tour of our Sanctuary in two weeks."

"Yes, I am."

Oh no, please don't tell me they are cancelling; I've been waiting six long months for this.

"Well, I'm calling because we had a last-minute cancellation for Saturday's tour. We wanted to see if you would be interested in taking the spot."

"This Saturday?"

Oh my God. No way!

"Yes. I know it's last minute, but we would love for you to come. Is there any chance you would be willing to switch?"

"Of course. I would love to!"

A car honks from outside and Justine signals to me she's leaving. "We'll talk later," she mouths, and I give her a little wave.

"Wonderful! We ask that you arrive by ten o'clock in the morning so that everyone has time to sign the waiver before the start of the tour. The tour will begin at ten fifteen, and should last around two hours."

"That's perfect. Thank you so much. I can't wait!"

"You're welcome. We look forward to seeing you. Have a good night Ms. Knox."

"You, too."

I end the call and let out a little squeal. I can't believe that after all this waiting, I'm finally getting to go. Ever since I was a little girl, I've had this fascination with wolves. They have always been my favorite animals, and now, I'll be able to see some in person. I couldn't ask for a better ending to a seriously shitty day.

Chapter Two

FRIDAY COMES AND goes in a blur, and before I know it, Saturday morning peeks its way through my curtains. I'm almost tempted to stay wrapped up in my blanket in the comfort of my bed—that is, until I remember what today is. Rolling over, my clock reads eight a.m., and I know I need to get up and ready. There's no way I am going to risk being late to the tour.

After showering, I quickly towel-dry my hair, thankful that it's naturally straight and I don't need to take the extra time to fuss over it. I pull on a pair of dark, blue skinny jeans with a pretty cream-colored floral top, then slip on my flats. I take my camera out of my nightstand and check that it has full battery before slipping it in my small purse.

The apartment is quiet as I make my way down the hall and into the kitchen. The silence has me wondering if Justine even came home last night, or if she ended up spending the night at Matt's place, like she often does after a night out. A peek out the window shows it's the latter. I send her a quick text letting her know what's going on and where I'll be for the next few hours. I love my best friend to pieces, but sometimes she can be worse than my mother with the worrying. She means well, that much I know, but ever since Drew decided to throw away our five-year relationship, she can be a little *too* worrisome.

By the time I finish breakfast, it's nine fifteen, so I grab my bag and head downstairs to my car. The drive should only take twenty minutes, but I figure it's better to have extra time incase of traffic.

***

The sign for Lone Paw is small and surrounded by overgrown bushes, causing me to almost miss the turn in from the street. Just as I'm about to pass by, I see it, and make a quick right onto the dirt road and through the open gate. Trees line both sides as I slowly make my way up the long winding road. After about a mile, the space around the road opens up and a wooden cabin comes into view. The sign reads: Welcome to Lone Paw Sanctuary. I pull into one of the open spaces that are marked with only a wooden beam lying in front of it, and park my jeep. My heart is racing with excitement as I walk up the small path and into the building.

Pictures of wolves in all colors decorate the walls. Some are of just the animals, while others have people hugging and cuddling with them. I stare in awe, trying to imagine what it must be like to be so close to the beautiful creatures with no barriers separating you. I walk slowly, taking my time to examine each one. Many of the people in the photographs are wearing T-shirts or sweatshirts with the sanctuary's logo. They must be the staff and volunteers.

"Well, hello there." A voice pulls me from my

thoughts and startles me. I turn to find a girl in her early twenties, around my age, sitting behind a desk that is off to the side. "Can I help you?"

"Oh, I'm sorry. I didn't see you there."

"It's quite alright." She smiles and pushes her glasses up her nose. "Are you here for the tour?"

"Yes, I am." I approach the desk. "I'm sorry, I know I'm a little early. I can wait in the car if you'd like."

"Don't be silly, there's no need for that. Let's get you signed in. What's your name?"

"Cassidy. Cassidy Knox."

"Cassidy… Cassidy… Oh! Here you are." She checks my name off on her paper, and hands me a clipboard. "If you could please just read this over, then sign and date the bottom."

"Of course." I glance over it before scribbling my name and handing it back.

"Perfect. You're all set. Your guide for today will be Liam. He should be in shortly. While we wait for the others to arrive, please feel free to take a look around. For the safety of you and our animals, we just ask that you please stay inside until the tour begins. Down the hall there are some information packets and whatnot. Feel free to take what you like."

"Thank you so much." I can't help the ear-to-ear grin that spreads across my face. I feel like a little kid in a candy store as I make my way from area to area, taking it all in.

Soon, the rest of the people for the tour arrive and get checked in. The girl from the desk stands, gathers us up, and leads us out back to an open area at the base of a rather large hill. From here, I see what looks to be some metal fencing at the top, that I already know sections off the area for the wolves. I squint, trying to make out any sort of movement.

I don't pay much mind as the girl introduces us to our guide. I stand at the far edge of the group with my back towards them. My focus is solely on the areas that we will be going to at any moment.

"Good morning everyone. My name is, Liam, and I will be your guide for today's tour. I'd like to welcome you all to the Lone Paw Sanctuary." The guide introduces himself; his deep voice flows through the air and seems to wrap itself around me like a cocoon. There's something about it that draws me in, and I find myself involuntarily turning toward the sound. My gaze lands upon him, and it's like the breath is knocked right out of my lungs. He's tall and handsome, and even with his loose-fitting T-shirt, I can tell he is well built and muscular. His hair is so dark brown it's nearly black, with the sides short and the top a little longer, falling messily onto his forehead.

"I'll be taking you to see some of our wolves and the areas they live in here. Unfortunately, I…" His words falter when he sees me and we make eye contact, holding each other's stare. For a few brief moments something passes through me, something almost electric, and it shocks me to my core. The last time I felt something like this was with… Drew. That thought alone is like a punch to the gut and snaps me back to reality. I quickly lower my eyes, breaking free from whatever it was that just happened.

"Excuse me." He clears his throat, but I don't dare look up again as he continues on. "Unfortunately, I cannot bring you into the areas with them, but you will be able to see the animals up close through the fence. You are welcome to take as many pictures as you'd like, and I assure you there will be plenty of photo opportunities. Is everyone ready to see our wolves?"

Around me, the others respond with their yeses and cheers of excitement, but I am unable to form any words. My own excitement has dwindled slightly, and I continue to wonder why my body reacted to him the way it did. The group begins to move, and I follow along at the tail end as we make our way up the hill.

The incline is greater than I expected, and when we reach the top where the ground flattens out, I am fairly winded. Metal fences line the path on both sides of us and stretch on for as far as I can see. We follow the path for a short distance before coming to a stop.

"This here is where one of our female wolves, Taya, lives. Taya, is a four-year-old red wolf who has been with us since she was a pup. She was brought to us along with her mother, and both were very ill at the time. Fortunately, we were able to nurse Taya back to health, but sadly her mother did not make it." Liam continues speaking about Taya, and providing information about this endangered species as I inch my way closer to the fence, trying to catch a glimpse of her.

"Where is she?" My eyes scan the enclosure, but all I see are trees, grass, and bushes. Moving further along the fence to get a different view, I huff to myself, disappointed that I am unable to see her anywhere.

"You see that cluster of trees back there?" A deep voice speaks softly next to my ear. My heart rate increases and goose bumps rise on my arms as a body brushes against my back. I don't need to see his face to know that it's Liam. His arm extends out in front of me, pointing to a specific spot, and my gaze follows. "If you look closely over there, you will see her laying on the ground, resting."

I squint, but still nothing.

"I don't see her." My shoulders sag and I turn, ready

to move on to the next area, but his body blocks my way.

"Keep looking."

"I really don't see the point when…" I go to step around him and he mirrors my movement.

"Just do it." He spins me back around, his chest pressing against my back, and points to the area once again.

"Someone's bossy," I mumble, but do as he says. Vibrations rumble against me as he chuckles.

"You see the spot I'm pointing to?"

I nod.

"Good. Now watch closely."

I can't help but roll my eyes as he, once again, commands me.

He pulls back slightly and shouts, "TAYA!"

Suddenly, a head pops up and looks our way, ears pointing straight up to the sky.

"I see her!" I gasp in excitement. "Right there, I see her!"

"Taya. Come here girl." He taps his palm against the fence, causing it to rattle.

Taya jumps to her feet and runs towards us. She's fast and, within seconds, she's closing in on us with no signs of slowing down. It looks as if she's going to come right through the fence. I leap back as she jumps up, her front paws slamming against the metal with such force. A shriek escapes me, and I turn, burying my face into Liam's chest.

My body shakes and it takes me a few moments to realize that it's not from fear, but rather Liam is causing the movement. He's laughing, and so are the others. Peeking over my shoulder, I see Taya standing on her hind legs with her front paws still up on the fence, and Liam is reaching forward, scratching the top of her head through the links. My face heats in embarrassment as I peel myself away from him and step to the side. He lets me go this time and continues talking to the group as if nothing happened.

Now that I don't feel like I'm am about to become Taya's lunch, I'm am able to see and appreciate just how beautiful she is. Her fur is a mix of brown and reddish-orange, with a few small white patches here and there. I've seen countless pictures of various wolves online, but nothing compares to what they look like in real life.

I look on in wonderment, watching the way she and Liam interact together. It's obvious they absolutely adore one another. When he stops petting her and pulls his hand back, she protests by pawing at the fence and rubbing her head against it. Without pause, his fingers thread through the links again and he gives a couple more scratches. Seemingly satisfied now, Taya lowers herself down so all four paws are on the ground. Liam feeds her a couple of treats, and I use the opportunity to take some pictures before we are led away and onto the next area.

***

The tour continues with us making stops at similar areas, housing various different wolves. I am so caught up in the wonder and amazement of watching these majestic creatures that I have almost forgotten about Liam and the reaction I had to his voice and close proximity earlier.

"And here we are at the last stop on our tour. You may notice this enclosure is much smaller than the others we have seen. The reason for this is when we have a female that gives birth to a litter, we like to allow them to have the freedom to roam around and explore the outdoors, but we also like to be able to keep a close eye on them to make sure they are healthy and developing properly. By having a smaller area like this, we are able to do both, and it seems to really help the pups thrive."

We stop in front of the fence and, immediately, three little pups come running over. They are the cutest things I have ever seen. Their fur is fluffy, colored in gray and white, and their mouths look as if they are smiling. They jump at the fence, falling over on top of one another, and it takes everything I have to not reach through and pet them.

Liam continues speaking, telling us about the birth eight weeks ago, and how the mother has cared for them. He tells of the milestones they have reached already, and the ones they will be reaching in the weeks and months to come. I soak up every bit of information he gives, wishing that I could bear witness to something as amazing as a birth like this.

On the far side of the enclosure, I see the mother wolf get up and cautiously make her way toward the front corner, away from the crowd of people watching her pups intently. She looks shy, scared almost, and I feel bad. I break away from everyone else and make my way to her. She backs away a couple steps, and I crouch down so I am closer to her height.

"Hello there, pretty girl."

She cocks her head slightly.

I half expect her to run away, but she doesn't.

"There's no reason to be shy. I'm not going to hurt you." I keep my voice low, not wanting to startle her or scare her off. I put my hands out in front of me, palms up, to show her I am not a threat. "You're beautiful. Do you know that?"

She continues to look at me, and after a few moments she takes a cautious step forward. I kneel and lower myself so I'm sitting on my legs that are tucked underneath me, gently tapping my palms on my knee to call her over. She takes another small step towards me.

"Atta girl. Come here. It's okay." I know they have rules for the tour—no one is supposed to touch the wolves, or the fence for that matter—but something about the timid way this one acts, makes me want to reach out and offer her comfort. I look to the left and see everyone is still occupied with the pups. Liam is speaking to the group, seemingly unaware that I have broken off. No one is paying me any mind. Turning back to the wolf, I notice she has come even closer all on her own. She is now only a few feet away.

Taking a deep breath, I slowly raise my hand, careful to not startle her. Her eyes show nervousness, yet she stands her ground and doesn't back away. I place my palm flat against the fence and just hold it there. She cranes her neck forward, nose in the air, and gives a couple sniffs. I hold my breath as she closes the remainder of the distance between us and proceeds to sniff my hand. Her nose is cold and wet as it brushes against my palm. Before I can react, she presses her body against the fence and begins licking my palm repeatedly. The roughness of her tongue tickles, and I can't help the giggle that comes from me.

"Wow. Looks like someone has taken a liking to you."

Startled at the voice, I pull my hand back and look up to see Liam standing next to me. Shit, I am going to be in so much trouble.

"I—I'm so sorry. I shouldn't have done that. I didn't mean to…" I go to stand, but he stops me and surprises me by lowering himself to the ground next to me.

"Don't be sorry. It's okay, really. No one saw it. Besides, your tour guide happens to be pretty damn cool, and he won't rat you out." He chuckles, and I let out a whoosh of air from my lungs. "You're Cassidy, right?"

"Yes." I'm shocked he's remembered my name from the quick introduction at the beginning.

"I'm Liam. But, I think you already knew that."

Looking around, I notice the group has gone. The only ones left are Liam and I, and that realization makes my stomach do little flips. What on earth is going on with me? "Where is everyone?"

"The tour's finished, so everyone's gone back down to the main building to check out and leave."

"Oh, I'm so sorry. I didn't hear you finish up. I guess I was a bit caught up in the moment. Thank you so much for such a wonderful tour, and the opportunity to see all these beautiful creatures. I better head down there as well."

"Don't!" He places his hand on my arm, effectively halting my attempt to get up. "I mean, you can stay for a little longer if you want to. It's okay."

I look down and my cheeks heat when I realize he still has his hand resting on my arm. Part of me wants to pull away, but the other part is enjoying the contact. My gaze slowly trails up his arm, coming to stop at the tattoo on his forearm. Although I can't see the whole thing because of the angle, I am still able to make out that it's of a wolf head. He must realize what I am looking at, because he turns his arm over allowing me to view the entire piece.

"Wow." My fingers move on their own, and softly run over the intricate ink. The picture is incredibly detailed, and so realistic looking. Every line, every shading, is done to perfection. From the corner of my eye, I see his body shiver ever so slightly, and he slowly pulls his arm back, placing it on the ground behind him and leaning back onto it for support.

"It seems Shyanne has really taken a liking to you." He nods, and I see she is still sitting pressed against the fence in front of us, small tufts of her hair pushing through the links. "She usually doesn't let people come near her, and never willing approaches someone on her own the way she did with you. Especially, a stranger."

"She just looked so timid and sad all by herself. I wanted to help calm her, but I never expected that she would actually come over to me."

"Yeah, she's always been a shy girl; that's why we named her Shyanne…Shy for short. You've managed to get closer to her than most of the workers here. It's pretty amazing." He reaches up and gives her head a little scratch, and she leans further into it.

"Well, she sure doesn't seem shy around you."

"I'm one of the few she'll come around. We haven't figured out why that is, but I'm not complaining. She's one of my favorites."

Looking at Liam, I could see the affection radiating from him. It's obvious how much he loves the wolves here.

"You want to pet her?"

"Really? I thought we weren't allowed."

"Well, seeing that you already broke that rule, I don't see any reason why not. I think it would be good for her to have the contact, since she seems to like you so much. Here…" He takes my wrist in his hand and opens my fingers so my palm is flat. "Let her smell you again first, and then reach your fingers through and give her a little scratch like I just did." He presses my palm to the fence, moves his hand from my wrist and gently covers my fingers with his.

Shyanne presses her nose against my palm, before turning her head and rubbing the top of it against the fence where my hand is. Without a word Liam curls his fingers over mine, causing them to go through the links and we scratch Shyanne's head together. Her fur is rough, yet soft, and she seems to be thoroughly enjoying the attention as she pushes even closer. There is no way for me to describe the joy that is flowing through me in this moment.

"Liam? Are you still out here?" a voice calls, and Liam quickly pulls back his hand and stands.

"Yeah, I'm still here. We're just getting ready to head down." He holds his hand out, and I take it as he pulls me to my feet.

"We? I thought you had finished with the tour." A woman rounds the corner and smiles at us. She seems to be in her late forties with deep reddish-brown hair and a smile that lights up her face. She's carrying a large bucket and places it down at her feet.

"I did. Cassidy just had a few questions, so I was answering them for her before she left."

"Oh, okay. When you are done, I could use your help with the feedings if you don't mind."

"Of course. I'm just going to walk her down, then I'll grab the other bucket and come back up."

"Thank you, dear." She turns to me and gives me a warm smile. "You must be Cassidy."

"I am."

She outstretches her hand, and I give it a shake. "I'm Erin. It's nice to meet you. Did you enjoy the tour?"

"I did, thank you. It was amazing, and Liam was a great guide. The sanctuary…the wolves…it's all so beautiful."

"Thank you. It's a lot of work, but nothing has ever been more rewarding than what we do here." She looks from me to Liam, and back to me again. Her smile grows even wider. "Well, I better get going. There are lots of hungry wolves waiting for their food. I do hope you will come back and see us again soon."

"Absolutely. As soon as I get home, I'm going to get on the waiting list again. This, honestly, has been one of the best days of my life. Something I have dreamed about since I was a little girl."

"Well, I'm glad we could help your dream come true." With that she bends and picks up the bucket she had been carrying. "Liam, I'll see you when you're finished."

"I'll only be a few minutes, Mom." Liam gives her a kiss on the cheek.

"Take your time sweetie. Don't rush." She gives a wink, and continues on her way.

Liam walks me down the hill and into the main building where I sign myself out. I turn to thank him and say goodbye, but he insists on walking me to my car. I agree, not quite ready for our time to be over.

I'm not sure what it is about him, but his presence makes me *feel*. That's something both exhilarating and terrifying.

We make our way to my car in silence, and I fish my keys from my bag before unlocking it. "Well, this is me." I pull the door open and turn to him. "Thank you so much…for everything."

"You're welcome." We stand there looking at each other. He seems as if he wants to say something else, but he doesn't. With a small wave he turns to leave, making his way back to the main building in front of me.

I climb into my car, close the door, and start it up. I sit for a minute, waiting for the air to cool. There is a slight ache in my chest when I think about how this is the first, and last time I will see Liam. I hadn't been aware until now just how much I'd wanted him to ask to see me again. This sudden realization hits me hard. Why now? After all this time, why is a stranger the one who makes me feel this way again?

A knock on my window makes me jump, and I let out a yelp. I had gotten so lost in my thoughts that I hadn't seen Liam approach the car again. He motions for me to roll down the window, so I do. What is he doing?

"Jesus, Liam, you scared the crap out of me!"

"I'm sorry. I called your name a few times, but you must not have heard me. I wanted to ask you something, and I didn't want you to leave before I'd gotten the chance." He sounds out of breath, like he has been running. Then I notice the bucket sitting by his feet on the ground. Just how long have I been sitting out here for?

"Um…okay. What's up?"

He looks nervous, something I wouldn't expect from him, seeing as though all throughout the tour he came off as an extremely confident guy.

"Well, I…" He clears his throat. "I'd really like to see you again and was wondering if I could take you out sometime. You know…like on a date?"

"Seriously?" Really Cassidy? That's how you respond? If my hands weren't clamped together so tightly in my lap, I would face palm my forehead.

"I'm sorry." His face falls in reaction to my response and he looks as if he's about to leave again. "I shouldn't have…"

"No!" I quickly cut him off. "Wait. Yes." I'm beginning to get flustered with myself, and my inability to get the words out properly. "I mean…" I take a deep breath. "I would love that."

"Yeah?" His face lights up and a big grin spreads across it. Like a switch has been flipped, the shy and uncertain Liam is gone, and is replaced with the happy and confident guy from earlier. "How about next Saturday? We close at four, so I could pick you up after I get off."

"Sounds good. What do you have in mind?"

"It's a surprise."

"Oh, no you don't. I hate surprises." I always have. Ever since I was little, they have made me uneasy. I'm not exactly sure why, though.

"You won't hate this one." He leans down and rests his arms on the door with his cell phone in hand. "What's your number?"

"Oh no. I'm not giving you my number until you promise me no surprises."

"I can't promise you that."

"Then I guess you aren't getting my number." I cross my arms over my chest and glare at him.

"Hey." His fingers brush along my arm ever so slightly, and there it is again—that electric current that races through me whenever we make contact. I gasp, and he smiles, a dimple forming on the left side of his face. "I can't promise you no surprises, but I *can* promise you it'll be something you'll love."

"And how do you know that? You only just met me; you don't know anything about me."

"I know enough. You are just going to have to trust me."

Trust. That word makes me want to run for the hills. The last time I gave my trust to someone, he took it and stomped all over it, which nearly ruined me. As I look into Liam's eyes, however, I see nothing but sincerity and determination, and I decide to do something I swore I would never do again: I take a leap of faith.

"Okay." Taking the phone from his hand, I quickly type in my name and number, press save, and hand it back to him before I can change my mind.

"Thank you." He takes a step backwards, slipping the phone into his pocket. "You won't regret it."

"See you Saturday." I put the car into reverse, back out of the spot, and begin down the dirt road that will take me out to the main street. I don't get more than fifty feet when my phone lights up with a text.

Looking forward to it.

Glancing into my rearview mirror, I see Liam standing there smiling as he watches me drive away.

Chapter Three

BETWEEN SCHOOL AND work, this week passes by quickly. Liam texts me daily, and that puts a smile on my face. My roommate, Justine, is absolutely thrilled when I tell her about my upcoming date, and her excitement is contagious.

By the time Friday evening comes around, my whole body is thrumming with anticipation for the next day. Taking the stairs two at a time up to my apartment, I get to the top, throw open the door, and bolt into my room. I begin rummaging through my closet and dresser in search of what I should wear for my date. A few minutes later, my bed is a mess, clothes strewn all over, and I am left utterly frustrated at the fact that I've come up empty handed. Why don't I remember it ever being this difficult in the past?

"Justine!" I cry out and plop myself down on the edge of the bed. "I need your help!"

"Coming!" she calls as she comes down the hallway. "Is everything okay…" Her voice trails off as she steps foot in my room and sees the disaster it has become. "What the hell happened in here?"

"I have nothing to wear." My shoulders slump.

"Oh my god, Cassidy. Seriously?" She begins to giggle. "All this"—she flicks her hand towards my bed— "is because you don't know what to wear tomorrow?"

"Yes! I need your help." I stand and begin rummaging through the pile on my bed again. Hoping the perfect outfit will magically appear.

"Okay, just relax." She places her hand on my arm and halts my search. "Have you been able to get Liam to tell you where he's taking you?"

"No." I huff. "He still insists on it being a surprise and won't tell me anything."

"Alright, well, if it was something you needed to dress up for, he would have at least told you that." She grabs the dresses from my bed and hangs them back in my closet. "It's not winter, so you don't need sweaters."

I start hanging my sweaters back up, and the pile on my bed gets smaller and smaller as we work through what *not* to wear. Sweatpants, baggy shirts, scrubs…they all get put away in their proper places. I pick up my black stretchy capris, and I'm about to put those away, too, when Justine stops me.

"Those! You *have* to wear those tomorrow! They hug you in all the right places. I have the perfect shirt for you to wear with them, too." She beams at me and I don't know whether to be thankful, or to be scared. "Why didn't I think of this sooner? Hang tight, I'll be right back." She rushes out of my room, and I hear her door swing open, hitting the wall behind it.

I'm folding the last pair of pants and putting them away, when my cell phone rings. With my mind preoccupied, I answer without giving it any thought.

"Hello?" I hear a sharp intake of breath, and then silence. "Hello?" When no one answers, I check the screen only to see it's an unknown caller. The silence continues on the other end, so I hang up and toss my cell on the bed.

Justine comes back with a huge grin on her face, looking as if she just won the lotto or something. In one hand she carries a plain, light gray, spaghetti strap tank top. "Here, put this on with the pants." She shoves it in my arms and gives a laugh when I just stand there staring at it.

"Umm…this is it? It isn't exactly what I had in mind "

"Trust me, okay? Just put them on."

Knowing she's not one to back down once she has an idea in her head, I strip my clothes off and pull on the black capris and the tank. My phone rings again, but when I reach for it Justine slaps my hand away.

"Leave it. They can leave a message. This is more important." She looks as if she is about to burst at the seams, and I, for the life of me, cannot figure out what has her so excited over this plain little tank top. "Okay. Now. Close your eyes and put your arms out."

"What for?"

"You'll see. Like I said, trust me."

I do as she says, after mumbling something about her being mighty bossy, and feel fabric brushing over my arms. When she tells me to lift my arms I do. She pulls the fabric over my head and lets it flow down my body. I let my arms fall to my side, and Justine squeals.

"Oh my god. It's perfect!" She gently guides me forward and turns my body. "Alright, take a look."

My eyes flutter open and I find myself staring at my reflection in the mirror on the back of my door. "Oh wow. It's…beautiful!"

The gray tank is now covered with a matching light gray lacy overlay, that has the most stunning design. The arms are loose and fall just below my elbow, and the holes in the fabric show just enough skin to make it look sexy, without being slutty. Justine is right. It *is* perfect.

"Liam is seriously going to drool when he sees you tomorrow. You look hot!"

"Thank you!" I pull her into a hug, squeezing her tight. "I love it. So much."

My phone sounds again. I walk to my bed and see unknown caller. I put the call to voicemail, and no sooner does it stop ringing, it starts up again.

"What the hell could be so important?" I grumble under my breath, annoyed at the interruption. Pressing accept, I bring the phone to my ear. "Hello?"

Breathing. That's all that comes from the other end of the line. I'm about to hang up when a shaky voice that's barely audible, speaks.

"Cassidy."

My body freezes the second the voice enters my ear. I break out into a sweat and my heart starts pounding in my chest. It can't be.

"Cassidy, baby. Say something. Please."

The phone slips from my hand and crashes to the floor. Time comes to a standstill, and I try and come to terms with what is happening. It's been so long—so long—since I have heard this voice directed at me. Memories come flooding back and I'm held prisoner in my body.

Everything from here on out happens in slow motion. I hear the muffled voice coming through the phone on the floor. Justine grabs me by the shoulders, shaking me wildly. And here I stand. Motionless. Soundless. Tears welling up in my eyes. She follows my line of sight to the phone, my eyes unwilling to look away as I stare in a mixture of disbelief and anger. She bends down and picks it up, but by now, the line has gone dead.

"Cassidy. Hey! Can you hear me?" She shakes me once again. I don't reply, but rather sink to the floor. "Who was on the phone? What happened?"

She lowers herself so she is sitting next to me, her voice soft, yet laced with concern. "Talk to me!"

"Drew," I choke out as I turn to face her, her figure blurred with my tears.

"What about him?" She pulls me close, and I allow myself to melt into her side. Bile rises in my throat and I fight to swallow it back.

"He…"

My phone rings again, silencing the words that are about to spill from my lips. I reach out, taking the phone from Justine as she looks on worriedly.

"Is that him?" she asks, and all I can do is give a small nod in reply.

"Don't answer it!"

"I have to." I swallow hard, as I press the screen to accept the call. "H—hello?"

Justine grabs at the phone, trying to pry it from my hands, but I don't relent. When she realizes she won't win, she settles for pressing the speakerphone.

"Cassidy?" Drew's voice comes through the speaker.

I try to speak, but the words come out in a garbled mess. Clearing my throat, I try again. "Yes?"

"Oh my god. It's you. It's really you!"

I choke back a sob at the sound of his voice. I can't let him hear the way it affects me. When I say no more, he speaks again.

"Say something. Please."

288

"What do you want?"

"You, Cassidy. I want you. I've always wanted you." Each word he speaks slurs into the other, but I can still understand what he's saying. And it hurts. Like a thousand daggers piercing my heart. "Ending things, walking away from you—from us—it was the biggest mistake of my life."

"Don't…" I'd longed to hear him say this for so long. I'd prayed every night for months on end that he would come back to me, but he didn't. Instead, I was left broken. The pain had been unbearable, the wound re-opening each time I'd had to see a new article about how Drew Sterling, the new big rock star, had been seen out with a different woman every night. Pictures of him smiling, laughing, and kissing woman after scantily-clad woman, had been a daily reminder of how much he didn't care how he'd hurt me.

"I miss you Cassidy…" There's a loud bang from the other end of the line, followed by a long stream of profanity, as he drops the phone and it tumbles to the floor.

"You okay, baby?" A second voice sounds through the phone—a woman's voice, her words just as slurred as his. "Who are you talking to?"

"No one." Those two words cut me deeper than anything has. I am no one to him. "I'll be right there."

"Don't make me wait too long." She giggles, and my blood begins to boil. "The bed's cold without you in it."

How dare he!

"Is he fucking kidding me?" Justine barks out, her voice laced with hatred. "Give me the damn phone and let me give him a piece of my mind."

I hold my hand up to silence her, knowing I need to handle this on my own. She shoots me a look, but when she sees the anger radiating off me she backs off.

There's some rustling around before Drew speaks

into the phone again. "Babe?"

"Do *not* call me that. You are a real piece of work, Drew. I don't know what you thought you would accomplish by calling me, but don't you dare do it again. Ever!" My hands shake as I yell into the phone.

"C'mon Cassidy, don't be like that. You know I…"

Justine reaches for the phone, and this time I let her. She taps the screen, effectively disconnecting the call before Drew can complete his sentence. Whatever he had been about to say, I know I don't want to hear it.

Chapter Four

IN THE DAYS that follow, Drew has calls over ten times, leaving messages that I don't bother listening to. Instead, I delete them, un-played. There is nothing he can say that will change things, and for once I don't want them to change. I can finally say that I no longer want anything to do with Drew Sterling, but that doesn't mean it hurts any less.

Liam continues to text, wanting to re-schedule our date, since I cancelled on him after Drew's initial call, but I just can't bring myself to go. It wouldn't be fair to him when I have wounds that have been re-opened.

"Hey, girl." Justine enters the room, tossing her purse on the floor and plopping down next to me on the couch. "What are your plans for Saturday?"

"Hmm. Well, I was thinking of having a date over…"

"You finally agreed to get together with wolf boy?" Her face lights up.

"No, not Liam." I roll my eyes at the ridiculous nickname she has given him.

"Then who? For the past few weeks, you've been moping around, so I know you haven't been talking to anyone else." She shoots me a skeptical look.

Keeping my expression as serious as I can, I look to her and reply. "Ben and Jerry." When she just stares at me blankly, I hold up my pint of ice cream so she can see the label.

"You are such an ass." She grabs the decorative pillow next to her and throws it at me, nearly knocking my delicious treat out of my hands.

"Hey watch it! Don't hurt Ben. Or Jerry. They have been good to me." I scoop a spoonful into my mouth and give a little moan. "Mmm… So good!"

"You are so stupid." She laughs. "But seriously. A bunch of us are having a party down at the beach Saturday night. Bonfire. Drinks. Music. I was thinking, maybe you could invite wolf boy to come. It'll be fun!"

"Justine, I haven't even been on a date with him. Hell, I've only ever seen him on the tour. I'm not bringing him to some party where he won't know anyone…myself included. Besides, I don't really feel like partying."

"Then let him take you on that date. Give him a *chance*. Get to *know* him."

"I can't." I look into my ice cream and swirl the spoon around, my appetite for sweets having diminished.

Two years ago, Drew broke me when he ended our five-year relationship seemingly out of nowhere. We had been high school sweethearts, together through our first year of college, but then he'd suddenly ripped my heart right out of my chest and crushed it. The pain he caused had been unbearable and it had taken me a while to get back on my feet after that. He never did tell me why he'd done everything, but my guess is that he'd wanted to be free to live the rock star lifestyle. He certainly has been doing just that from the looks of all the pictures and articles I'm unable to avoid seeing—a different girl on his arm in each one.

"Why not Cass?" I feel her eyes boring into the side of my head, but I can't bring myself to look at her. "It's been almost three weeks since Drew called."

I flinch at his name, and she takes the ice cream from me, placing the container on the coffee table, taking my hands in hers.

"I know he hurt you. What he did… it was a real dick thing to do. And I know him calling stirred up memories and emotions you had done so well to move past. But not every guy is Drew. There are good guys out there, and you deserve to find one of them. You deserve to be happy, but for that to happen you have to take a chance."

Her words tug at my heart, and a lone tear slips down my cheek. It's not that I miss Drew anymore. No, those feelings have long gone. But in their wake, it has left me with fear—the fear of letting anyone in again.

"I—I don't know if I can, Justine. What if I do that? What if I take a chance with Liam and he ends up hurting me the way that Drew did…or even worse? I don't think I could survive that kind of pain again. My heart wouldn't be able to handle it." Tears fall steadily down my face now, and I raise my eyes to look at her. She pulls me into a hug, gently combing her fingers through my hair.

"You can't live your life hiding from the *what if's*. I know it feels like the safe choice, but it's not. If you do that, then you are never truly *living*, you're merely getting by. Life is all about taking chances. Don't you think it's about time you took one?"

"I don't know…"

"Listen to me." She pulls back, her hands gripping my shoulders and her eyes never leaving mine. "You've been hurt, and the possibility of it happening again is terrifying. I know this. But, Cassidy, you can't keep your heart sheltered forever. One of these days you have to break down the barriers and let someone in."

Chapter Five

I WIPE MY sweaty palms on the side of my pants as I check my hair and makeup in the mirror for the umpteenth time. Other than my cheeks being flushed a slight pink from nerves, everything is still in tact. The clock reads 4:58 p.m.—exactly one minute since I last checked, yet it feels as if hours have passed. I begin to pace our living room once again, my hands twisting the hem of the gray lacy overlay Justine picked for me to wear on the date a few weeks ago—before I had chickened out.

Through the window, I see a car pull in front of the house, and I halt in place, my body frozen. My heart begins to race, and I feel my throat start to close. Liam exits the car and walks up the path. The closer he gets, the harder it is for me to breathe.

I can't do this!

"Justine!" I croak out, her name shaky and distant-sounding as it leaves my mouth.

In an instant she is beside me, arms wrapped around

me in a tight hug. "Hey, calm down, Cass. You're going to be fine. Just breathe. In"—she takes a deep, slow breath—"and out." She releases it and repeats again.

"I—I can't go through with it. I can't…"

"Yes, you can. And you're going to have a great time. I promise you. It's just a date. *One* date. Now breathe. In…and out."

The doorbell rings, but she doesn't move. Instead, she continues repeating those words until my body begins to relax, and my breathing slows to a normal pace.

"See? Everything will be fine. You got this girl!"

A knock sounds from the door this time, and Justine pulls back to look at me. "Well? Are you going to leave him standing out there all day?" She spins me around and gives me a gentle nudge towards the door. "Go get your wolf boy!"

I take a final calming breath and shake out my hands in an attempt to release as much tension as possible.

You got this Cassidy. You can do it.

Making my way to the door, one foot in front of the other, I focus on my breathing. The knob turns in my hand, and I swing the door open. The sight before me knocks the wind from my lungs, but this time in a good way. Liam stands there in khaki cargo shorts, and his navy-blue polo shirt hugs his body in such a way that it outlines the muscles underneath. He looks hot!

"Wow, Cassidy. You look beautiful." His eyes rake over my body, and I swear I can *feel* his gaze upon my skin.

"Thank you." I smile up at him shyly.

"You ready to go?"

"Yeah, just let me say goodbye…" I turn to wave to

Justine, but she is nowhere to be seen. She must have snuck off to her room once she saw I was actually going to open the door. "Never mind. I guess she already left."

Stepping through the door, I pull it shut and turn. Liam has his arm held out and I link mine through it. Our skin touches and the electrical current races throughout my body once again. His body shivers next to mine, and I know he feels it, too.

We make our way downstairs and to his truck. He reaches out and opens the door for me, waiting until I climb up and get situated before gently closing it and making his way around to the driver's side, joining me inside.

"So," I ask. "Where are we going?"

"I've already told you. It's a surprise."

"Liam, you know I don't…"

"You don't like surprises. Yeah, I know." He puts the truck into drive, but leaves his foot on the brake. "I'm hoping to change that, though. Can you trust me?"

I turn to him and meet his gaze. His eyes sparkle with excitement, and his dimple makes an appearance, giving him a boyish look. I let his words sink in for a minute as I chew my bottom lip—something I do when I am deep in thought. Can I trust him, this complete stranger who I've only met once before?

I sit here silently contemplating his question when he reaches forward, pulling my lip from my teeth with his thumb. He leaves his hand there for a moment, gently rubbing his thumb across my bottom lip. Where his finger touches it feels like fire kissing my skin.

"Please, Cassidy?" His expression turns serious. "Trust me when I say I would never have you do something that would make you uncomfortable. I wouldn't ask this of you if I weren't positively sure that it's something you will love, and the surprise is a big part of it all." He lowers his hand and places it on the seat between us, palm up. "Will you trust me on this?"

I take a deep, calming breath and place my hand in his. "Okay," I reply.

He gives my hand a squeeze, causing my heart to flutter in my chest, the smile returning to his face.

He brings his focus to the road and pulls away from the curb. The excitement radiates off of him, and I have to admit it's a bit contagious. As we begin our drive to destination unknown, I can't help but feel more at ease than I have in a long time. All doubts I've had these past few weeks are erased and replaced with an excitement of my own.

Liam and I talk the whole ride, and I find myself no longer worrying about what his surprise is, which is extremely unusual for me. I am so lost in conversation that I don't even realize where we are until he stops the truck.

"Stay here for just a second. I'll be right back." He hops out of the truck and walks to open the gate before us. It's then that I finally look around and my eyes widen as I see the sign: Lone Paw Sanctuary.

"Oh my God!" I screech as he climbs back in. By now I am bouncing in my seat, excitement coursing through me. "Are we going in?"

"We are." He flashes me the biggest smile I have ever seen. "Is that okay?"

"It's more than okay!" I beam at him. "It's perfect! So this was the surprise, huh?"

"Yes. Well, part of it anyway."

"Best surprise ever!" I can barely contain myself at the knowledge that I'll be able to once again see the wolves. I'd not expected this.

"Trust me, the best is yet to come."

Liam pulls into the lot, which is empty except for us, and parks in the spot closest to the hill we will have to make our way up. Before he's able to climb out of his side, I'm already rounding the front of the truck.

"So much for chivalry." He chuckles, shutting the door behind him. "I was going to get the door for you."

"I'm sorry. It's just I'm so excited to see them! I didn't think I would ever have the opportunity to again. At least, not for a long time."

"You really love wolves, huh?" Liam takes my hand in his and intertwines his fingers with mine as he leads me towards the hill where the wolves live.

"I do. They've always fascinated me, ever since I was a little girl. It's one of the reasons I decided to go to school to become a vet. While I love domestic animals, I'm hoping that one day I'll be able to work with wolves and exotic animals. That's my dream, anyway."

"Wow, that's pretty impressive."

"I wouldn't say impressive." I shrug. "It's just what came naturally to me, you know? I can't see myself doing anything else."

"I know what you mean."

When we get to the top, I go to follow the path from the tour, but Liam tugs my hand gently and guides me down a smaller path to the right—one we hadn't walked down last time.

"Liam, where are we going?" My eyebrows knit in confusion as we stop in front of a small shed.

"To the second part of your surprise." He unlocks the door and swings it open. "Wait here for just a second. I'll be right out." His form disappears into the dimly lit shed, the door squeaking shut behind him.

A minute later, he reappears with a plastic bag in one hand, and a backpack slung over his shoulder. "Ready?" He takes my hand in his again, leading me down a narrow path behind the shed. "There's someone I want you to meet. Well, two someones actually."

"Umm…okay…"

"Don't worry." He smiles down at me when he sees my concern. "You're going to love them. Trust me."

"You sure have been saying that a lot." I look down at my feet, my hair falling into my face.

He stops then, moving to stand in front of me. "Hey." He reaches forward and tucks my hair behind my ear. His finger slowly trails down my jawline until it reaches my chin, tilting my head up so I have no choice but to look into his hazel eyes. "Have I let you down yet?" Warm breath fans over my skin, his face mere inches from mine.

"No." My response is instant. I don't even need to think about it before answering. "You haven't."

"Well, I'm not about to start now." His gaze moves to my lips, for only a second, and I'm paralyzed in place. "I promise."

We stand there for what could be hours for all I know, as time has come to a complete standstill. His scent surrounds me, woody and musky, and I lick my lips as they suddenly feel dry. When his eyes follow the movement of my tongue I notice they turn a slightly darker shade. The realization hits me that he wants to kiss me, and I'm shocked by the fact that I *want* him to.

My phone chimes with a text and the moment is lost. Liam clears his throat and takes a step back, shifting the strap of the bag on his shoulder. I fumble in my purse until I find the intruder and see a text from Justine.

"I'm sorry. It's my roommate, Justine, checking to

make sure all is going well." I laugh nervously as I send her a quick reply letting her know everything's fine and that I'll text her later, then drop the phone back in my bag. "She's my best friend, but sometimes acts like a second mother with me."

"Nothing wrong with that. It's good to have people in your life that care about you in that way."

"Yeah, it is." I smile thinking just how lucky I am to have her in my life. "So, shall we head on to this big surprise of yours? I'm eager to see what it is."

"I thought you don't like surprises."

"I don't know. I think I may be starting to come around."

We continue along the path that leads us farther and farther from the enclosures we visited on the tour. A large field opens in front of us and stretches on for as far as I can see. The chain link fence continues along on our right and once we come to a gate, we stop. Liam reaches in his pocket and pulls out a set of keys, flipping through until he finds the one he needs. He pushes it into the lock and turns, the click of it opening loud in the silent air.

"Ready?" His eyes twinkle with excitement as if he's the one receiving the surprise. Before I can answer he pushes the gate open, pulling me through, and shuts it behind us, the latch clicking into place.

What does he have up his sleeve?

I follow him to the middle where a number of large, flat rocks are positioned in a line. He climbs up and takes a seat, drops the bags next to him, and outstretches his hand. I take it, and he helps to pull me up, so I'm seated next to him, my legs dangling over the edge.

"So, um…where are these people you wanted me to meet?" I look around, but see no signs of anyone. "Will they be here soon?"

"They're already here." He chuckles, and I stare at him in confusion. "Most likely sleeping over there." He turns and points to a small wooden hut that looks like an oversized doghouse with a ramp leading up to the roof.

My eyes wander over the surrounding area, taking in everything I failed to notice when we entered. The fence surrounds us on all four sides. Trees, bushes and rocks spread throughout the grassy area, and I gasp as I realize we are inside an enclosure, one much bigger than any of the others I've seen.

"Liam, are we…"

"Onyx! Ayla! Come on out!" Liam calls, and my heart takes flight in my chest.

My eyes dart back to the hut and anticipation runs wild. A shadow moves across the doorway, followed by a head popping through, ears perked up to the sky.

"There you are boy. Come on, I have someone special I want you to meet."

At the sound of Liam's voice, a large black wolf, who I presume to be Onyx based on his color, emerges from the hut. When he spots us, he trots over with his head held high and looking mighty happy to see Liam. He slows as he approaches and nuzzles his head against Liam's side. Liam gives him a little scratch on his head and he sits, leaning his weight into Liam and looking over at me.

"Onyx, this is Cassidy. Cassidy, meet Onyx."

The beautiful creature leans forward and sniffs the air. I tentatively reach out, palm facing up, allowing him to smell my hand. His warm, wet nose tickles as it brushes against my skin and releases little puffs of air. The desire to pull my hand back and scratch it is strong, but I resist the urge, not wanting to frighten the wolf and ruin this moment.

In one swift motion, Onyx moves his nose underneath my hand and pushes it up. When I remain still, he moves closer, stepping his two front paws onto Liam's thighs and does it again, nudging my hand closer to his head.

"Go on, don't be scared," Liam encourages. "He's not going to hurt you. He just wants you to pet him."

"I'm not scared. Just being cautious since he doesn't know me."

I extend my arm further and turn my hand so my fingers brush along the somewhat coarse black fur on his head. When I reach the area behind his ear, he presses his head into my hand in a movement that resembles a dog when you find a good scratching spot on it. I press my fingers deeper into his fur, the bottom layer softer than the top, and I give a good scratch. Onyx seems to approve and lays himself across Liam's lap while I continue.

"So, I'm going to go out on a limb and guess you like this surprise?" Liam smiles at me and looks completely at ease, leaning back on one hand while petting Onyx's back with the other, as if having a giant wolf on his lap is natural. Maybe it is for him. I wonder how long he's been doing this for.

"Like it? I love it! I mean, simply bringing me back here so I could see the wolves again is amazing enough. But this? Actually being inside one of the enclosures with them… This is beyond incredible. It's like nothing I've ever experienced." My words come out fast, something that happens when I'm excited.

"I'm glad." He laughs, the sound quickly becoming one of my favorite things to hear, and I find myself inching closer to him until our shoulders touch.

"Seriously, though. There are no words to express how thankful I am for what you've done."

"No need for thanks." His hand comes up and rests on my cheek, causing my heart to give a little jump in my chest. "Seeing that beautiful smile on your face is more than enough for me." His thumb rubs gently along my cheekbone, his expression turning serious as we sit there staring into each other's eyes. He leans in ever so slightly, our lips inches apart. I know what's about to happen, and I wait for the fear and uncertainty to kick in but, it never does. For the first time in a long while, I'm not afraid of opening myself up to someone. Instead, I lean into his touch and close my eyes, waiting for the kiss that I'm certain will take my breath away.

Something rough and wet runs across my cheek, causing me to shriek, and jump back. My eyes fly open only to find a big white head of fur in-between Liam and me. I gasp as I realize it's another wolf, and it just licked me!

"Ayla!" Liam chuckles. "Now you decide to join us?" She wedges her way further between us, licking Liam's face all over. "Glad to see you, too, girl, but you couldn't have waited a little longer?" She gives him a final lick before nuzzling into his side.

"Well, hello there, beautiful." I bring my hand out, just like I did with Onyx, and allow her to smell me.

Once she has given me a few sniffs, I begin petting her. Ayla's fur is slightly softer than Onyx's, and is the polar opposite color wise. While Onyx's is Jet black, Ayla's is completely white. Seeing the two of them next to each other reminds me of a yin yang symbol.

"Well, now you've met the two I wanted you to meet. Onyx and Ayla are my favorites here. Just don't tell the others that or they may get jealous." As he speaks, I see the adoration he has for them across his face. He loves these wolves, and it's obvious they return that love.

"Well, don't you worry. Your secret is safe with me." I give a little wink. "So, what's their story? How did they come to live here?"

"About three years ago, a man was hiking in the forest and came across them. He could see Ayla was injured, but couldn't tell how bad from his distance, and he didn't dare get any closer. He did note there was a lot of blood when he called the police. They immediately called us, so we sent a team down to help. I was one of the people on that team.

"When we got there, Ayla was unconscious and had lost a lot of blood—more than we ever could have imagined. Her beautiful white coat was covered in red. Onyx was lying next to her, whimpering and licking her as if trying to wake her up. It was obvious they were very close. The guys sedated Onyx and secured him in the van, while I stayed back to tend to Ayla. She had been shot in the stomach, and her leg was caught in a bear trap. While I worked to free her she didn't once wake—not even for a second. Her breathing was so shallow; I wasn't sure she was going to make it."

"Oh my god! That's horrible! Why would someone do that to her?" My heart breaks for this beautiful creature and I dig my fingers deeper into her thick fur. The pain she must have gone through is something I can't even begin to imagine.

"Beats me. I'll never understand why people do some of the things they do. My guess is a hunter shot her and she took off running—must have gotten away from them, but run into the trap on her way. Snapped her bone right in half. Luckily, we have an excellent vet, Dr. Roldan, who dropped everything and immediately met us back here to treat her. Two surgeries, and six hours later, she was stable.

"She remained unconscious for two days before finally coming to. Poor Onyx was a mess. He would cry and pace back and forth in his enclosure all day, looking for Ayla. It got so bad that we had to start bringing him in to see her once she was well enough. Needless to say it was a long road to recovery, but as you can see she pulled through with flying colors, and luckily there have been no long-term effects from her injuries."

"That has to be one of the saddest stories I've ever heard. I'm so glad it ended up having a happy ending. These two are the sweetest."

"Yeah, they're pretty great, aren't they?" He ruffles the fur atop Onyx's head. "Hey, I almost forgot. Are you hungry?"

I haven't given it much thought, but at the mention of food my stomach gives a loud growl. "Yeah." I laugh. "I guess I am."

Liam reaches around Onyx and takes out two large bones from the plastic bag and both wolves sit up, suddenly alert, with their ears perked up to the sky. He tosses them to the ground below us. Ayla and Onyx leap down off the ledge, and settle in below our feet, chewing happily away. Grabbing the backpack, he opens it and pulls out two sandwiches, some fruit, and a couple bottles of water.

"Um, Liam? Shouldn't we eat outside of here? Aren't you worried these two may get a bit aggressive over our food?"

"Nah, it's fine. We fed them right before I left to pick you up, and they are more than happy having their bones as a treat. Besides, I eat lunch in here with them almost daily. They're used to it and seem to enjoy the company."

He hands me a sandwich and I happily dig in, hungrier

than I thought I was.

We eat our meal and make small talk, getting to know one another. The conversation is light, and I feel completely at ease around him. All too soon, the sun starts go to down. The blue sky darkens and turns shades of orange and pink, signaling our time here must come to an end. We say our goodbyes to Ayla and Onyx, and make our way back towards Liam's truck.

As I climb in, my chest constricts, and my heart feels heavy. It's funny the way life works sometimes. Just a few weeks ago, the thought of going on this date had scared me beyond belief. I'd almost let my past run my life once again, and I did all I could to avoid this day. Now that it's here and just about over, I wish we had more time. Today has been…perfect.

The drive back takes far less time than I'd like. Before I know it, we pull up in front of my apartment and park alongside the curb. Without a word, Liam hops out of the truck and meets me around my side as my feet hit the pavement. He takes my hand in his, our fingers intertwining, and walks me to the door. I pull out my keys, unlock it, and turn back to him.

It's dark now, the sun having set, and the small, outside light casts a dim glow across his face. The way the shadows fall make him look more handsome than ever—if that is even possible.

"Thanks for today, Liam. It, undoubtedly, has been one of the best days of my life."

"I'm glad. When I saw how you reacted to the wolves while on the tour, the look you got in your eyes, I knew I had to bring you back so you could actually go in with them. I'm just thankful that you gave me the chance to take you today."

"It was an experience I'll never forget."

"Yeah, those animals are pretty amazing, aren't they?"

"Not just the wolves. The company was pretty amazing as well."

"You think I'm amazing?" he asks.

My cheeks heat, and I avert my eyes so I'm looking anywhere but at him. I can't believe I just said that.

"Hey. Don't be embarrassed." He takes a step towards me, and I can feel the heat from his body, despite the cool air and the small distance between us still. "Cassidy, look at me."

My body is happy to oblige, although my mind tells me I've just made a fool of myself. My head tilts up until our eyes meet, and the emotion I see behind his is enough to steal the breath right out of my lungs. I can feel the pull between us, the unseen electric current crackling and sparking as our bodies press against one another, closing the final gap.

"I think you're pretty incredible yourself." His hand finds its way to my cheek and he gently strokes his fingers over it. My body shivers in response and I wrap my arms around his waist.

The world around me fades away as his lips gently press against mine, and everything else ceases to exist. The kiss deepens as my lips part, yet he keeps it slow and sweet. I've never known that a single kiss could ignite one's body the way Liam's has done to mine.

All too soon, he pulls back, ending what was the world's most perfect kiss. I want to protest—demand he kiss me again and never stop—but it's getting late, and I know we both have to be up early in the morning.

"Goodnight, Liam." I step back and open the door. "Thanks again for today. I had such a great time."

"I did, too." He smiles at me. "Goodnight."

I turn and step inside, running a finger over my tingling lips. Before I can close the door, I hear him call out from halfway to the street. "Hey, Cassidy?"

"Yeah?"

"Can I see you again tomorrow, in the evening, after work?"

"I'd love that." My stomach flutters as if a hundred butterflies have decided to take flight in it. "See you tomorrow."

The door shuts quietly behind me, and I make my way upstairs to my apartment. A huge grin spreads across my face when I pull out my phone and see the screen light up with a text.

Missing you already.

My heart swells with happiness, and for the first time in a long time I'm able to look forward to what the future may bring.

THE END

Punishment & Pleasure

ELLE M THOMAS

Chapter One

THE CRUNCH OF the snow beneath my feet sounded amazing. I liked the snow, the freshness of it always made me think of new starts, a do over if you will. Although, the fact that it was coming down like a blanket was less appealing. There had been the odd shower forecast last night, but nothing like this. For the first time since my car refused to start that morning, I was pleased that I'd been unable to drive to work because I would have struggled to drive back in this.

"Shit!" I squealed as I turned the corner of my street and lost my footing, almost ending up on my behind in the white stuff.

With a deep breath and my heart going ten to the dozen, I straightened myself and continued the short distance to my home. Looking up, I came to an abrupt standstill. A blue sports car sat on the opposite side of the road, but still outside my house, and not for the first time.

I knew I'd sounded paranoid when I told my friend,

Harlow, about the car hanging around. It had started a few weeks ago. It would just appear, park and stay there. The windows were slightly tinted, so from my house I couldn't make out the driver. I'd given it little thought the first time, nor the second or third, but beyond that, it had begun to creep me out, which is when I'd told Harlow. She'd reassured me that it was probably nothing: someone looking at moving into the area and checking it out at different times, or maybe somebody had a regular lift. She even suggested he could be a private eye looking to catch out some cheating partner, but this was getting to be more than any of those things and was now freaking me out.

As I got closer, I decided that enough was now enough and I needed to confront whoever this was. I ignored the voice in my head telling me that if he was a serial killer, I was going to end up in his boot and never be seen again because I was fairly certain that any serial killer worth his weight would be less obvious than this.

Finally, and with my heart hammering away with nerves, I came to a stop next to his car. Leaning down, I tapped my knuckles against his window. The sound of an electric motor coincided with the darkened glass lowering.

"May I help you?" I sounded like a bloody shop assistant rather than an authoritative resident.

"No." His reply wasn't rude, just blunt.

"Are you waiting for somebody?"

"No."

I arched a recently threaded brow at him as the snow continued to fall, some of it beginning to enter his car through the open window.

"Are you lost?" My tone was a little pissy now because he was giving nothing, and I had a right to know what he was doing here and why.

"No. I know exactly where I am."

I huffed and decided I might need to get a little threatening, even with his use of extra words.

"Well, if you can't offer a reasonable explanation for your presence, I am going to assume your sole intention is to stalk me, so…" I turned my back on him and headed for my front door, my hand already in my pocket and retrieving my phone.

I had almost reached my house when I felt a hand tightening around my arm. I could feel my legs go from under me and the ground coming up to meet me. I felt sure, even with the softer landing of the blanket of snow, that this was going to hurt my arse when I landed.

Fuck! I had not thought this through: if he was a serial killer, I had now shown him where I lived and, as I was returning home, I had keys on me. Now, as he grappled me to the ground, I was a dead man walking, well, not a man, nor walking, but still. I cursed myself for walking into this trap. I had watched enough episodes of Criminal Minds to have avoided the rookie mistakes and, not only had I made them, I'd added to them tonight.

My arse hit the floor with a thud and as my back threatened to join it, I noticed my movement slowing. He was guiding me down to break my fall until I lay flat out in the snow with my serial killer looking down at his next victim.

"Sorry, I didn't mean to startle you."

I stared up at him with a dubious expression. "You are stalking me, so forgive me if I don't quite believe that claim."

He laughed. "Stalking you? Is that what you think?" He laughed again. I did not, but I did allow him to help me up so that I stood before him. "You live here?"

I rolled my eyes and gave him a stony stare that was intended to tell him that I had his number and that the nice, innocent guy routine was wearing thin.

"No, I don't live here, but thought that as you were going to murder me tonight after stalking me for weeks, I'd try the decoy move and be slaughtered in someone else's home rather than my own."

I watched as he bit back a smile, although his eyes didn't get that message because those deep pools of warm, rich chocolate were clearly laughing at me.

"I am not a murderer, nor a stalker…" His expression changed and, in a flash, he reached forward, pulling my woolly pom-pom hat off my head.

"But a hat thief!" I accused, snatching my hat back.

He did absolutely nothing to hold back his laughter or smile now.

"What the fuck is the matter with you? Stalker, murderer and now hat thief?"

I should have remained silent because the man, this very attractive man, already saw me as a source of amusement and possibly had concerns about my mental stability. I didn't remain silent, instead I made things worse. "Serial killer."

"What?" He seemed to choke on air but quickly recovered. "You used to be a blonde."

I stared at him, actual fear creeping in now because I had been a blonde, briefly, two years ago when Harvey and I moved in. I considered trying to run for it, to a neighbour's house, or to just scream at the top of my lungs, but I didn't. Instead, with a quiver to my voice, I asked, "How long have you been watching me?"

I was scared of the answer, fearful of why I had only recently noticed him hanging around. His reply wasn't any of the ones I thought he may have offered.

"For the last time, I am not watching, never have watched you, stalked you, planned on killing you. Nor am I a serial killer."

I mean, I was sure if he were any of those things, he wouldn't readily admit them, but there was something in his expression and tone that made me believe him.

With a nod from me, he continued. "I used to live here, with my wife. You bought the house from us—you and your partner. You were blonde, and now you're not."

I studied him more closely and he did look familiar. It had been a couple we'd bought the house from, and the man had been attractive—they both had. "Right." I wasn't sure if his explanation made this situation better or worse.

"You look much better as a brunette by the way."

I giggled at his compliment and found I was twisting and twirling my hair around my fingers as a red blush crept up my face. That is when I noticed a thick layer of snow on and in my hair and all over the man opposite me who wasn't wearing a jacket, never mind a coat. He shivered as he shook the snow from himself, and that move made me shudder, too.

"Would you like to come in? I could make some tea and you could dry off."

"Thank you. That's very kind of you."

What the hell was I doing? Just because I had met this man before, two years ago, I still didn't know why he parked outside my house on a regular basis. He could still be the serial killer I had suspected him of being just a matter of minutes before.

Chapter Two

AFTER PASSING COMMENT on the changes that had been made to the downstairs of the house while I made us tea, the man who I was now certain wasn't a serial killer, Jackson, began to remove his wet clothes.

He pulled off the thin sweater he wore, briefly rucking up the T-shirt beneath it, too, revealing a bronzed and toned torso that all too soon was covered by his very tight muscle T-shirt stretching across it once more.

I stared, my mouth hanging open at the glorious sight of this Adonis. I could feel myself flushing and heating up as my body reacted to the sight of a near naked man in my kitchen. I reminded myself that he had only removed one item of clothing meaning he wasn't actually anywhere near naked, but the way my body was reacting to him, he may as well have been. Then he kicked off his heavy boots and placed them on the mat near the door.

I was seriously disappointed that he didn't unbuckle the belt that held his well-fitting jeans up—not that they were especially wet.

He took the cups from me, and with a smile that suggested he had enjoyed my ogling of him, he said, "You might want to take yours off, too."

I said nothing but flushed even more at what I perceived to be his suggestion for me to get naked with him.

"You're wet, Gracie," he said with confidence.

I wouldn't have gone that far, but my lady parts were certainly dampening at the sight of his thick muscular arms and flexing chest. Plus, his first utterance of my name, Grace— although he had made it his own with his use of *Gracie*—had my pulse picking up pace. I could feel it hammering away in my neck. I could feel it hammering away everywhere.

His laugh broke my thoughts. "I promise to be good and guard the tea while you put some dry clothes on."

Shit! What was the matter with me? Embarrassed, I nodded and ran upstairs where I quickly changed into leggings and a long sleeve T-shirt that hung off my shoulder. I returned to the lounge to find Jackson looking through my books.

"Romance and rom-com?" There was no judgement or mocking in his voice.

"Yeah, sorry. I'm a bit of a girl," I said, remembering that my choice of books, films and music used to irritate Harvey no end. He would always mock me for it, especially in company, so I found myself apologising for it whenever it was mentioned.

"Nothing wrong with romance and laughter."

I smiled across at him, taking a seat at the opposite end of the sofa to him.

We chatted for a while about the house, books, music

319

and movies. Strangely enough, the subject of his presence outside my home didn't come up before the inevitable topic of our other halves did. After all, when we had met, he'd lived in this house with his wife and I had been planning to move in with my boyfriend.

"Is your boyfriend likely to have a problem with you luring me in here with offers of hot tea and removing clothes?"

I laughed at his words but more at his expression and comedic wiggle of the eyebrows. "I don't have a boyfriend, and if you mean my ex, Harvey, I doubt he'd care."

He looked a little shocked and then something else filled his face: pleasure, happiness, relief…But why?

"And your wife? Does she know you've been stalking me for weeks?"

He laughed at my stalking reference, but somehow, when I watched him throw his head back as he properly belly-laughed and his neck stretched, I wished he had been sitting in the street and watching me. He was very attractive, and I could really go for him. The truth was that since Harvey, I had only had sex with one person, which had been very disappointing, but then that decision had been made by shots and vodka.

"My wife, my ex-wife—much like your ex-boyfriend—wouldn't give a shit, although she would probably assume the reason I've been spending time here, looking at this house, would be because of her and my inability to move on."

I was shocked at just how honest and open we were each being. "And would she be right?"

He looked shocked, too, but by my question more than anything else I think. He shrugged. "Maybe to begin with."

This honesty thing wasn't working in my favour if he was sitting in his former marital home thinking of his ex while I was fighting the urge not to imagine him naked.

"We were happy in this house, or so I thought. We moved to start a family. That had always been the plan. After about nine months, nothing had happened, and we'd been trying for six months before we moved from here."

I nodded, although if this was about to go down the infertility route and the pain of not being able to conceive a child, I was unsure what I'd say because I had never been ready to start a family with Harvey—maybe that should have occurred to me before buying a house with him—and I had never actively tried to get pregnant. In fact, the one time my period had been late, Harvey had been beyond angry with me and I had cried for a whole day, horrified at the prospect of being stuck with him forever. Harlow had come to my rescue with a pregnancy test that confirmed I was not pregnant. The relief had been immense. Clearly, despite my love of romance, Harvey had never been my happy ever after.

"I suggested seeing a doctor for tests, and that was when she told me there was no need. She was still on the pill and had no desire to have a baby with me."

"I'm sorry." I was sorry he had been hurt but was also glad he hadn't had a baby with her, or he wouldn't be here now.

He waved away my attempt at sympathy. "It seems a lifetime ago. Anyway, that was the end. You can't really go back from that. I couldn't."

"Yeah, I get that. Harvey and I never even discussed children. I'm not sure we ever discussed anything long-term. I loved him, or thought I did, but I'm unsure if I could have if the relief I felt when he said he was leaving me was anything to go by. I tried to be everything he wanted in a woman, that's why I went blonde, but I guess the truth was that he never wanted me, so I was never going to be enough."

"You're still better brunette," he said then cocked his head to the side slightly. "He cheated?"

"Yes, a lot, and with several people. He even left me with an STD when he finally went."

Jackson looked horrified at that particular gem.

"Don't worry. I'm all clear."

Why the fuck did I say that? He didn't need to know that, did he? I mean, he wasn't a date or anything. He wasn't someone I planned on sleeping with.

"That's good, really good."

I stared across at him. He seemed far too happy with that knowledge, so maybe he did need to know.

"And your ex-wife? I don't mean did she leave you with an STD…" My voice trailed off because I really needed to stop speaking before I embarrassed myself further.

He laughed and moved along the sofa until he was sitting next to me. "She didn't. As far as I know never had one. She does, however, have a new husband and a baby on the way."

"Sorry." That's all I had but meant it because that would have to hurt.

"Water under the bridge."

"So, why did you start sitting outside my house?"

"I didn't," he replied. "I started sitting outside my house."

"Does that make it our house?"

Fuck me, if I hadn't just turned up the heat and intensified the charge between us in that one question.

"It probably does." He edged even closer, his eyes never leaving mine. The dreamy pools of liquid chocolate boring into me. "But I was driving nearby the first time and just wanted to take a look at the place. "You've ruined my front garden by the way."

My mouth opened to speak, but no words formed.

"Took me over a year of TLC to get that fucking grass to grow without patches and now it's paved!" He genuinely sounded horrified.

"Harvey's idea. I liked your lawn."

His eyes were darkening by the second, and I no longer knew if we were talking grass and gardens.

"Harvey's a fucking idiot then, for more than just my lawn."

I had the definite feeling he was referencing my ex-boyfriend's treatment of me.

"I vetoed the suggestion to remove the bush." I even pointed in the direction of the jasmine bush that still grew beneath the window. "I ensure it's always well-tended and trimmed."

Jackson looked as though he was either about to burst out laughing or combust. "Good. I approve of a well-trimmed bush."

Shit! He was talking bush-bush, not an actual bush, and I was becoming turned on by it. Our gazes were fixed as he moved closer again, our legs touching, and I had a feeling he was going to kiss me, knowing I would offer zero resistance.

"It smells divine." I needed to stop speaking because I was just making this whole exchange more mortifying by the second.

"Hmmm." He reached up and with his thumb brushing over my cheek, he continued moving until his hand was in my hair, cupping my head and bringing it closer to his. "Divine."

My eyes darted between his eyes and his lips that were full, pink and looked soft. They parted slightly, allowing his tongue to dart out and lick across them.

"Jackson…" I had nothing else to add, but I noticed his breath seemed to hitch when I uttered his name for the first time.

"Divine," he repeated. "I bet it tastes better than it smells: the bush. Addictive I imagine. One taste of you and I will be hooked."

Fuck! He wasn't even pretending to be discussing his garden, my garden anymore…well not unless you counted my lady garden!

"Jackson," I repeated but still had nothing beyond his name.

He shook his head. "The next time you say my name will be when you call it as you come on my tongue."

Oh, yeah, all pretence disappeared in the second he touched me, and I was totally unprepared for what to do next. Jackson on the other hand was not.

Chapter Three

I WATCHED AS his mouth headed for mine and I swear I considered holding my breath. Who'd have thought that this was how my night would develop when I confronted the stranger parked up on my street. Not me, that's for sure.

Soft lips landed on mine and with zero resistance, my mouth opened, welcoming the invasion of a tongue that was gentle, probing and working against my own. Jackson appeared to be in no hurry as he continued to kiss me while running his fingers through my hair, occasionally tugging against the strands. His other hand had made its way around me, settling in the small of my back, and it was from this position that he manoeuvred me, so I was lying flat out with his body blanketing mine.

I felt giddy, like a teenager finally getting to kiss her crush. In fact, we were both like adolescents, kissing, touching and making out for countless minutes, and it felt amazing. I could feel his hard arousal, pressing into me and knowing that he was getting off on this as much as I was caused my desire and longing to intensify.

Eventually, Jackson broke our kiss leaving us both breathless.

"That was seriously fucking hot."

I was unsure if he needed a response to his words. Clearly not as he leaned back in and began to kiss me again, but this time he littered kisses along my jaw, down my neck and across my shoulder that was still bare, courtesy of my top hanging off one side. His kisses began gently and then became a little more insistent before turning into nips that were moving down across my chest. Jackson had one hand cupping my behind while the other was pushing my top further down my arm until it could go no further, or so I thought. The sound of fabric tearing startled me until I realised it was my top that literally hung off me now, my lace covered breasts revealed.

"Is this what you wear for work?"

Jackson's mouth and hot breath caused my stiff nipple to bead further until it was painful. He closed his mouth around it and began to suck.

"Yes," I moaned, unsure whether I was encouraging him to continue or answering his question.

He released my nipple but flicked against it with his tongue. "Hmmm. Does it make you feel pretty, sexy, powerful?"

I was unsure how it made me feel—I'd never thought about it and certainly never analysed it, but now that I had, yes, all three.

"Yes," I repeated, but it was more of a moan as it coincided with his teeth grazing my sensitive peak.

He continued his assault for another minute or so, and I was relieved at the reprieve, albeit momentarily. His mouth moved to the other side while his free hand reached up and began to squeeze and roll the first nipple.

The sensations were exquisite: pleasure crossed with pain; the need for more and yet less; feeling hot and cold…My skin was alive in its own right coming up in gooseflesh that felt over-sensitised.

My moans grew louder, and his erection swelled against me. With one nipple being squeezed firmly and the other in his mouth, I was delirious and then, with no warning, he bit down into my flesh. My back arched, my legs tried to close, but with Jackson between them, that was impossible. I cried out as the warm tingle of pleasure flooded through my body and brain.

Looking up from the fog of arousal, I found Jackson up on his knees, staring down at me, his eyes and expression dark, angry almost, but not quite.

"Did you just come?" He fixed me with a stare that made me nervous.

"I don't know."

He cocked his head. "You don't know? Have you had an orgasm before?"

I nodded, almost bashful, which was ridiculous considering I had a virtual stranger kneeling between my splayed thighs.

"So, let me ask again, did you come?"

Clueless as to why, with an apologetic expression, I nodded again.

"Have you done that before?"

We'd established that I knew what an orgasm was and that I had experienced one before, so I could only assume we were now talking about an orgasm without sex or clitoral stimulation.

"No. Never."

A ghost of a smile momentarily crossed his lips.

"I approve of that, but what I don't approve of is you coming without permission."

My mouth dropped open, but no words came.

"In the future, you will ask."

I nodded and wondered if he had other kinks besides this dominant lover thing he had going on. It wasn't something I'd experienced before, but it was kind of hot.

"If you don't ask, you'll be punished."

"Punished?" At least I'd regained the power of speech.

"Yes, punished. I might spank you or fuck you without making you come. The possibilities are endless."

What the fuck did that actually mean, and where had the light-hearted banter from my very own serial killer gone?

He looked down at the space between us, specifically at my covered sex that was aching and pulsing. I was turned on now at the idea of him spanking me, if not orgasm free fucking.

"Are you wet?"

We were no longer talking from the snow.

I nodded.

"Use your words."

He was speaking to me like I was a five-year-old. I reckoned I could deal with that, but at the first suggestion of calling him Daddy, I was out.

"Yes."

He smirked. "I can see you are."

I flushed crimson that my arousal may have escaped and made my clothes damp.

"Do you ache?" He pressed his hand against the seam of my leggings, and I moaned loudly.

"Yes," I cried, pressing down against his hand.

"Is your pussy squeezing and tightening against the emptiness there?"

"Yes," I repeated, distressed to see him move his hand from me.

"Good."

Bastard. I liked 'not a serial killer' Jackson—he was hot and funny—but Jackson the dominant lover? He was an arsehole of the highest order, and I liked him even more.

He moved from the sofa and stood over me, offering me a hand to stand. I had no idea what might happen next but got to my feet and stood before him with my aching, wet pussy, torn top, and breasts spilling over the top of the lacy bra I still wore.

"Are you sorry for coming earlier?"

What sort of stupid question was that? Who in their right mind would feel sorry for that? I mean, it wasn't the best or most intense orgasm I had ever had. It had kind of felt like aftershocks of an orgasm, but before a big one, so, not the best, but it was the most unexpected, arriving with no warning.

I wanted to explain that to him so he understood why I wasn't sorry—that I'd had no choice. Instead, I opened my mouth and gave him one word. "No."

His face suggested he hadn't expected that response but didn't look entirely disappointed by it. His hand cupped my chin, and he tilted my face up towards his.

"You will be, Gracie. Go upstairs to your bedroom and strip down to your underwear and wait for me."

I swallowed hard, fear creeping in.

Maybe he sensed it because he leaned down and landed a gentle kiss near my ear.

"Time for your punishment."

I was fixed to the spot staring up at him.

"Punishment?" Maybe this was a huge mistake. I wasn't equipped for this experience and had no knowledge of how this might work. Nerves thrummed through my whole body and I could hear evidence of it in my voice.

He leaned back in and this time took my ear between his lips and I assumed he picked up on my nerves too. He licked the shell, breathing heavily with his own desire. "Hmmm. Punishment, and then pleasure."

The final word was accompanied by a nip and my reaction to it all was a moan and more moisture escaping my body, adding to the slickness already there. So, maybe this wasn't a mistake and even if I didn't understand it, perhaps my body was entirely equipped for this.

Chapter Four

I HEADED INTO my bedroom and was initially unsure what I should do. Was there a protocol for this? Waiting to be punished for coming? If there was, well, I had no clue what it was. Should I remain dressed or take my clothes off? Sit, stand, kneel? Maybe I should have asked before coming up here.

"Take your clothes off."

Looking over my shoulder, I found Jackson standing in the doorway, watching me and allowing his eyes to take in the room.

"Just down to your underwear. I can take care of that for you."

I began to remove my clothes, focusing on the bed in front of me while my back was turned to him.

"I like what you've done with the room. It was always my favourite."

"Mine, too. Harvey preferred the bigger room, but I like the lighting in here."

This was surreal again: here I was, stripping to be spanked by the man whose former house I now lived in, and we were discussing decor.

"I always loved how bright this room is. The way the sun comes up and shines through in the morning."

I nodded. I liked that, too.

"And how quiet it is."

The other bedroom at the front had the noise of the road outside, a nearby dual carriageway and the railway line that ran alongside it.

"It won't be quiet for long."

I had no idea if he was suggesting I'd make noise when I was punished or when we had sex.

My thoughts distracted me from him moving until he stood behind me while I was dressed only in my underwear. The feel of his breath on my neck caused a hitch in my breathing and my whole body to shudder.

"Bend over."

He pressed a hand between my shoulder blades, encouraging me to fold over the end of the upholstered bedstead with a high headboard and a lower footboard.

Compliantly, I obliged.

"Good girl."

I felt him move away briefly, taking in the sight of me bent over the bed, my arse presented to him. His hands came to rest on my hips before lowering, smoothing over my cheeks, caressing the globes of my behind that were on show courtesy of the tiny white thong that matched my lace bra.

"I'd have stalked you much sooner if I'd known how sexy you'd look like this."

I stiffened beneath his touch, concerned that maybe my first thoughts, fears of him, were correct.

He felt the change in my demeanour. His back covered mine, his mouth coming to rest near my ear.

"Ssh. It's okay. I'm a very friendly stalker."

I sensed the smile on his face and immediately relaxed again as kisses gathered on my neck, shoulders, back. They moved lower until he ended up on his knees, my behind directly before his eyes while his hands roamed my cheeks, coming to rest on the waistband of my underwear.

Slowly, he dragged my thong down my hips and past my thighs where he released them, allowing them to drop, landing on my feet.

"Better," he muttered before moving in closer until his face almost touched me.

A single kiss landed on my behind where my cheeks met, and then his hands were there, spreading me wide open. I gasped and shuddered as his mouth moved in closer, kissing my leaking core before his tongue dipped inside me, the same tongue that then spread my arousal up towards my puckered opening.

I froze, fear and nervousness coursing through me until the sensation of his mouth returning to my sex relaxed me. Jackson used this distraction to move a well lubricated finger against my behind, applying enough pressure so that the tip of his finger momentarily slipped inside. My insides clamped around him, making him chuckle against my sensitive folds.

"We might need to work up to that."

Unsure whether he required a response from me or not, I remained silent, but pushed back against him.

"You taste divine, but I reckon it will be even better when you come."

My response was more silence.

He set about teasing me with his tongue and fingers

333

that stroked me inside and out until I was sweating, panting and struggling to remain standing. Time ceased to exist, and I was clueless as to whether we had been up here minutes or hours. Every time I was on the brink of release, he withdrew just long enough before resuming his torment of my body.

Within seconds, I was back on the precipice, and this time he didn't pull back. With his tongue circling my clit and two fingers inside my pussy, I felt another digit enter my behind, his thumb maybe, and that is how I came in a haze of moans, screams and tremors that rocked me off my feet—the most intense sensations I had ever known.

I was unsure if I actually blacked out, but I became aware of him holding me upright whilst he feasted on me, licking, lapping and consuming my juices until the aftershocks of my orgasm began to reignite, threatening to develop into another.

"Jackson." My utterance of his name was meant to stop him from causing my already delicate tissue from becoming even more over-sensitised.

He clearly didn't get that from my whispering of his name as he began to fuck me with his mouth.

"Jackson, please."

The amount of genuine pleading in my voice must have seeped through because he stopped, got to his feet, spun me around and he kissed me.

I could taste my own flavour on his tongue and lips and, whilst a little alien, it tasted good, sharing it with him. His hands laced through my hair that he was beginning to pull, a little pain joining the pleasure I felt.

He broke the kiss.

"Punishment time."

He spun me around again and repositioned me to

bend over the end of the bed.

"I almost forgot you'd been a naughty girl."

I heard the sounds of him removing his clothes and ignored the ridiculousness of his words.

"You need to stay very still, okay?"

"Yes."

"Can I tie your wrists?"

I hadn't been expecting that and had no idea what I should say because as much as my rational brain was telling me that this man was a stranger, I couldn't deny that I liked the idea of him restraining me.

"Just my wrists?" Unsure where the question came from, I was more surprised by the fact I sounded disappointed that it might be just my wrists.

He laughed again. He'd heard my disappointment too.

"This time."

The words were barely out when I felt something cold wrapping around my wrists that he'd held bound in one of his hands. I realised it was his belt securing my arms in the small of my back. With a couple of minor adjustments, a nudge spreading my legs wider and a gentle push to lower my face and chest to the bed, I felt his nakedness press against me.

"You're fucking gorgeous. I noticed how beautiful you were the first time I saw you."

I absorbed his words and was reminded of my faint recollection of our first meeting. The truth was that my first thought of him was that he had scared me. He had been the scary, intense owner of this house and his wife had been soft and warm. It was similar to how I had often felt when meeting friend's parents as a child: the stern, more serious dad and the kind, gentler mum. I pushed thoughts of his wife, ex-wife away as I returned to thoughts of him, the dark man.

"Are you ready?"

My reply was a simple *yes,* and before I could brace myself or question if I was, the first smack landed. Heat radiated from my right cheek. Clearly, he wasn't playing. Another landed to the other side, heating the whole of my behind. Then another, lower. He spread the spanks around my rear, and as more were delivered, the heat intensified and spread, but the pain and discomfort lessened as it morphed into something else—into a strange, dark kind of pleasure.

"Your arse looks amazing with my handprint on it. I want to fuck you so hard." He groaned out the words. "Do you want that? Would you like to feel my dick inside you, stretching and filling you while I spank your arse?"

Everything below the waist was clenching, my body's own affirmation to what he was suggesting. He paused, maybe waiting for an actual confirmation from me.

"Yes."

The sound of foil was the next thing I heard and then, with one hand on my hip, his other hand was guiding his erection to my entrance. I was wet so I had no concerns that this would be painful. However, it had been a while since I'd had sex, and as he began to inch into me, I knew he wasn't small. The stretch of my skin burnt, but it was a strangely pleasurable burn. He entered a little more, paused, pushed forward and paused again. He continued like this until he had filled me all the way.

A few seconds passed when all I could hear was his deep breathing and then he withdrew before slamming forward, rocking me slightly but also causing my sex to contract, almost objecting to the invasion at speed.

His hand on my hip tightened, preventing me from

escaping him—not that I wanted to, although, instinctively, my body tried to inch forward.

The other hand, the free one, caressed the skin of one cheek, almost tracing what I imagined were the lines of his handprint, and then it was gone as he pulled back again. This time when his cock re-entered me fully, the other hand landed a smack to my behind. I cried out in shock more than anything, but as soon as the sting and burn registered, pleasure took over, pleasure that caused moisture to leak from me, coating him and easing his movements further.

"Fuck!" He groaned his appreciation of my body's reaction and really began to let me have it.

Every withdrawal left me feeling bereft, but as each surge back inside was accompanied by a smack that warmed and softened me further, I felt more fulfilled than I could ever recall feeling during sex.

His pace quickened with every thrust and I was so focused on his movements and my body's reaction to them, the familiar sensation of an oncoming orgasm seemed to creep up on me.

"Oh God!" I cried, knowing I was going to come very soon, whether he wanted me to or not.

He spanked me again, harder. "You know what you need to do," he hissed from between gritted teeth.

He wanted me to ask for permission to come.

I resisted the temptation to point out that not asking for permission was what had got me where I was now.

"Please."

He landed another smack that really stung. Clearly, I wasn't very good at asking for permission.

"Please, can I come? Let me come for you."

I was unsure which of my attempts spoke to him best, but one, if not both of them, had.

"Yes, now, come. Gracie. I'm coming," he roared, and together we crossed the line.

A few minutes passed and once we had each gathered our thoughts, he undid his belt from around my wrists and we crawled under the covers of my bed.

He leaned over me and lowered his lips to mine. I was unsure if he was about to embark on round two, or if I was even capable of it, when his phone rang.

Quickly, he scrambled for it, and after a couple of panicked sounding words that he was on his way, he hung up, threw on the clothes he had up here then turned to me.

"I have to go."

I made as if to get up.

"No, you stay. I'll grab my things from downstairs."

He turned to leave but paused in the doorway.

"Thanks."

Chapter Five

A WEEK HAD passed since that night with Jackson, and sometimes I had to pinch myself to believe it had really happened. I had heard nothing from him since his 'thanks' that had left me feeling cheap and used.

I knew he hadn't got my number, but he knew where I lived. He could have dropped in or put a note through the door. The way my arse stung the following day, some flowers would have been nice.

He had been my second one-night stand and would be my last because both had been disastrous for different reasons. I had no expectations of Jackson or of a future with him and I had got precisely that. I had been left with nothing but a sore arse. Okay, a sore arse and some hot sex, and if he had been honest and up front about that, it would have been fine. Perhaps not fine, but I would have known what I'd been agreeing to. A shag. A quick bunk-up. An enjoyable way to spend an evening. The thing was that I hadn't been privy to what it was. He had barely finished coming when his phone conveniently, almost too conveniently, rang and he had to leave in a hurry leaving a very bad taste in my mouth.

I had been ashamed for a few days and then I got pissed off before revealing all to my friend, Harlow. She had suggested a night out to cheer ourselves up—not that she needed cheering up.

I checked out my appearance before leaving the bedroom and I looked good. I wore a black sequined minidress with bare legs and a pair of heeled ankle boots. My hair was down and straight and my make-up was simple and sheer.

My phone pinged to say my taxi had arrived, and as I ran down the stairs, I was looking forward, to dinner, cocktails and dancing.

We ate at a local tapas bar before moving on to an actual bar. There was a DJ and music ringing all around us, and after the first couple of drinks, I was beginning to buzz.

Harlow and I danced for a while and then headed back to the bar before a trip to the ladies. We followed this little routine over a couple of hours, and it was as I was leaving the bathroom that I saw him.

On the other side of the bar, talking to a woman was Jackson. She laughed at something he said while I silently fumed.

The sight of him brought back my feelings of shame. He could have told me he was looking for an evening of meaningless fun. I might have still gone along with it, but he hadn't given me the choice: he'd simply used me.

"Hey."

Harlow came to stand next to me and followed my gaze.

"I can see the attraction, but he appears to be with

someone," she said.

I spun and glared at her.

"Yes, he does, doesn't he? And yet just over a week ago he tied me up, bent me over and fucked me!" I was shouting. So much so that a guy who was passing by came to a standstill and grinned at me. "Not tonight arsehole."

He walked away, but still smiled.

"That's him? Jackson." She whispered his name.

"Yes."

"Shame he's a bastard when he looks like that."

Harlow and I were different. She was adventurous and game for anything. She never went in for regrets, and I had never known her to feel shame. Tonight, I really envied her that. The worst part of the night was that as ashamed as I felt when I thought about what I had done with Jackson, I couldn't bring myself to regret it.

I was about to reply when he looked up. His gaze cast across the bar and settled on me. We each stared at the other, and when I saw him make to leave his companion and head for me, I dashed for the dancefloor.

With Harlow's hand in mine, I forged a path into the middle of the floor and once there began to dance. The man who had overheard the brief summing up of my night with Jackson was there with a friend. He smiled and I smiled back. He took that as his invitation for him and his friend to join me and mine to dance.

Probably only a few minutes passed before our dancing was interrupted by Jackson.

"Gracie," he began.

I turned my back on him and continued to dance with my new friend.

Jackson moved around so he was in front of me once more.

"Let's talk," he said now, but his earlier calm tone was already beginning to disappear.

"No."

He looked stunned by my response.

"I said let's talk."

I recognised the darkness in his eyes and the edge to his voice, and as panty melting as I still found it, he was pissing me off.

"I said no."

I turned again but this time took my dance partner with me and went so far as to drape an arm around his waist, as if to pull him closer.

With a few mutterings of curse words behind me, I thought Jackson had gone.

He hadn't.

I realised that when I felt an arm snake around my middle and pull me back. Startled, I faced Jackson who looked absolutely fuming.

"And I said, let's fucking talk."

The next thing I knew, I was being dragged from the dancefloor and down a corridor, past the bathrooms and into some kind of storeroom.

The door slammed shut, and Jackson stood with his back against it, staring at me and breathing heavily.

"Grace! Are you in there? Shall I call the police?"

Harlow.

Jackson stared at me. "Should she? After all, if I am the stalker, she must be the rescuer. Do you want rescuing, Gracie?"

I should have wanted rescuing from him, but I didn't. I wanted him to explain why he had been an arsehole, meaning I had no cause to feel ashamed of what we did.

"I'm fine," I called to my friend, who I was sure

laughed.

"Okay."

Then she was gone.

"Just the two of us," Jackson said and had the audacity to smile at me.

I shook my head at him. "Say what you want to. I have a dance partner to get back to."

That wiped the smile from his smug face. He stalked towards me, his long strides meaning he was before me in the blink of an eye.

"No. You don't."

His sexy little alpha routine had been attractive, a turn-on, just over a week before, but now it was pissing me off. He had been a one-night stand. I had been convenient—a casual fuck, no more, and that had been his doing, not mine, so his bossy, possessive routine was inappropriate.

"Fuck you!" I spat.

"I'd like that almost as much as fucking you."

The sound of a loud smack rang around us.

He seemed to wobble his jaw, as if checking it was in one piece, then he stopped dead and stared at me. "I find your angry streak very attractive."

I rolled my eyes. He really was a dickhead.

"Angry?" I laughed at him. "I am fucking fuming. You walked out on me with a 'thanks'—at least if I were a whore, you'd have thrown me some cash down—and then nothing: no call or note, not even the courtesy of an appropriate thank you for a decent shag."

He stared at me and said nothing.

"I even wondered if your phone call was a friend who gave you a set amount of time and then gave you your get out." It was my turn to laugh now. "But I dismissed that. I thought you were unlikely to be that much of a cold, calculating arsehole, right up until I saw you all over whoever was in line to be tonight's tied up, fucked and spanked party guest. Do you even know her name?"

He frowned. "My call was genuine."

His head lowered towards mine, and as I inhaled his scent, the good memories from our night together resurfaced.

I instinctively closed my eyes, which was long enough for his lips to meet mine. He kissed me hard, no sign of nervousness or insecurity in what he was doing. I immediately responded, kissing him back, my arms wrapping around his neck while his closed around my middle pulling me to him.

Before anything else registered, I found myself pinned against a wall with my legs closing around him.

Releasing my mouth, his lips travelled along my jaw to my ear.

"I'm sorry."

My reply to his apology was a low mewl, but I was desperate to believe him.

With his body pressed against mine, his hands became free and while one moved to my head, positioning it to allow him greater access to my neck, throat, ears and face, the other dropped between us and settled against the fabric of my underwear that was already warm and damp.

"Yes, yes," I moaned as a finger slipped beneath the lacy fabric and travelled along my seam.

"Fuck!" he growled as his finger slipped between my wet folds.

My body immediately began to quake when his digit possessed me. I clenched around him when a second filled me, my arousal growing as he began to fuck me with his fingers.

I was going to come, and there was no way I was going to ask for permission, or even tell him. He had used me first time round and now, I was going to return the favour.

His thumb skimmed up and that was all it took to see me coming fast and hard. I could barely see, think or breathe.

When I opened my eyes, he was watching me, possibly preparing to speak. Maybe the threat of punishment was on his mind.

I didn't think so.

With my legs lowered, he placed me back on my feet.

I straightened my dress and walked to the door that I opened, briefly looking over my shoulder.

"Thanks."

Chapter Six

I COULDN'T BELIEVE the bloody snow was back. After the night I met Jackson, we'd had a bout of dry, sunny days that had melted everything and now, less than a fortnight later, it was back and worse than last time.

It was falling at a rapid rate and despite my big coat, hat, scarf and boots, I was wet and cold as I made the journey from the bus stop home.

Turning into my street, I did think how beautiful it looked and as it was now dark, the fresh snow was barely disturbed. The change in direction meant it was blowing directly into my face, blurring my vision. I dropped my head and focused on getting home where I could shed my wet clothes and put on something dry and warm.

As I passed my neighbour's house, something caught my eye in the street.

A car.

Jackson's car.

I considered walking straight to my house and locking

the door behind me, but something stopped me—my desire not to do that stopped me.

Slowly, I made my way to his window and tapped it with my knuckles. The sound of an electric motor coincided with the window lowering, just as it had the first time.

"May I help you?" I think that was what I'd said before, and I suspected this was his attempt at making amends and possibly starting over.

"No." His blunt reply was exactly the same as before. I bit back a smirk.

"Are you waiting for somebody?"

"No."

This was déjà vu alright.

"Are you lost?" My tone had been a little pissy by this point last time, but now I was struggling to be anything but amused and optimistic at his presence.

"No. I know exactly where I am."

I arched a brow.

"Well, if you can't offer a reasonable explanation for being here, I am going to assume your sole intention is to stalk me, so…" I turned my back on him and headed for my front door, my hand already in my pocket to retrieve my phone.

I realised that my memory of our first encounter in the street was perfect, and I suspected that his was, too.

I had almost reached my house when, just like last time, I felt a hand tightening around my arm. and I allowed my legs go from under me so the ground was coming up to meet me. As it did so, my hat flew off. I felt sure he'd save me from the fall. He didn't disappoint. With control, he guided me down until once more, I lay flat out in the snow with my serial killer looking down at me.

Staring down at me he offered me a small but very sexy smile. "You used to be a blonde, but you look much better as a brunette."

I'd loved that he'd remembered that about me and loved even more that he preferred my natural colour, so I played along with the replay of our first night a while longer. "How long have you been watching me?"

"Not nearly long enough."

He offered me a hand and pulled me to my feet, leaning down to brush the snow from my hair. I reached up and reciprocated.

"Would you like to come in? I could make some tea and you could dry off."

"Thank you. That's very kind of you."

The first time I'd made that offer and he'd accepted, I'd questioned what I was doing, but now, I knew exactly what I was doing.

With the door shut behind us, I headed for the kitchen, put the kettle on and removed my coat and boots. He followed me and stood before me where he began to remove his wet clothes. His jumper came off first, then his boots.

I stared at his naked chest—taut, muscular, bronzed—and my mouth dried.

"My call last week was genuine."

He stepped closer and reached for the bottom of my jumper that, with a little help from me, he pulled off.

"The woman in the bar was my sister; she is the one who called me."

He pulled me to him and kissed me, long, slow and deep. Then he reached for my trousers and undid the button and zip, allowing them to fall down in a pool around my feet.

"Our mum suffers with confusion. She lives in sheltered accommodation. Supported living," he explained before undoing his jeans and pushing them down. He stepped out of them and lifted me from mine.

I smiled when he reached down and pulled off our socks—his own, then mine.

"When I was here with you, I had no intention of leaving, not unless you'd wanted me to. I'd planned to stay and do inconceivably dirty things to you."

He smirked and I could only grin back.

"But my sister called to say the people at her home had been in touch. Mum had gone walkabout, and nobody knew where she was."

"Sorry." I wasn't sure why I was apologising. Maybe for assuming the worst of him, which I had.

"No need. I should have explained, but I panicked and needed to go and find her."

"Is she okay?" That seemed the most important thing here.

"Yeah. She'd gone back to our old family home. Thought it was still her house."

He smiled while speaking about his mother and that made me like him a little more.

"She'd had a rough week, which is why I didn't come to see you. My sister and I took it in turns to stay with her until she was settled again, and then when I was in the bar, we'd decided to have a night out while one of our cousins spent the evening with her."

"Sorry," I repeated. "I didn't know."

He nodded. "Because I didn't tell you, so please stop apologising for that. I was telling my sister all about you when I spotted you."

"If you'd told me in the bar, in that room, I would

have been less angry."

He laughed but pulled me to him again, roughly taking my mouth this time. "I told you, I liked your angry streak."

He nipped my lower lip making me yelp slightly.

"So, shall we try again, Gracie?"

"Yes, but no running out on me."

"Absolutely not. Nor 'thanks', without cash."

I couldn't keep the huge, dazzling smile from my face. A small squeal escaped me as he lifted me up and placed me on the edge of the kitchen counter. He stood between my legs and landed a gentle kiss to my temple.

"I think you do owe me one apology though."

The furrowing of a frown on my brow must have conveyed my confusion.

"At the bar. You came. Without permission."

"But you ran out on me—"

He cut off my words with another kiss, this one saw his tongue bypassing my lips, leaving me breathless and his fingers made circles around my nipples over my bra. The lace fabric of it only serving to abrade the pebbling peaks until they were hard, aching bullets that were desperate for more attention.

"You came. Without permission," he repeated.

"Sorry."

He cocked his head, possibly trying to figure out if my apology was genuine or not.

"I think somebody needs to be punished."

I said nothing but could feel the heat of a crimson flush covering my face, neck and chest while heat and moisture gathered low in my body, my sex clenching and pulsing with anticipation.

"I think somebody needs to be tied up, spanked and fucked, don't you?"

I made no reply. I kept my eyes on him, reached forward and through his underwear palmed his length, pumping it slowly.

"Definitely time for your punishment."

His glance was dark as he watched me, on shaky legs, drop from the countertop and saunter to the doorway where I paused and looked back at him over my shoulder.

"Punishment?" I remembered he'd said first time that punishment could be spanking or not coming, although with Jackson, I doubted I'd ever manage the latter.

"Yes, punishment. Punishment and pleasure."

THE END

Buttercup Eyes

LYNDA THROSBY

Chapter 1

DARKNESS SLOWLY PERVADES me yet again as my eyelids slowly close. I don't want them to; I try to fight it. It's no use: I've succumbed to it.

"No, no, leave me alone," I shout in panic. I turn to run away, the yellow eyes now entrenched into my memory. I need to move fast; I need to run. I'm panting, my arms flailing, but my feet won't move. What the hell is wrong with me?

I look down and see I'm in sand. I'm confused. I've been here before, doing this exact same thing: trying to escape the yellow eyes but not being able to move—being stuck in sand, sinking fast.

I look around me. There's a train at my side. How bizarre… I could have sworn it wasn't there before. How did I not notice it? I'm on a station platform, stuck in quicksand. The train suddenly blows its whistle; it's so loud I cover my ears with my hands. Steam spews from it. How odd that it's a steam train, like it's 1920 or something.

I think I need to get on it—to get away from here and him. I start to panic that whoever is after me is closing in on me. I look behind me but there's no one there. Why am I running if there is no one chasing me?

The yellow eyes… The yellow of buttercups.

Just then, the train starts to move out of the station. I watch as it disappears into the distance and leaves me here, stuck and scared. I feel tears falling down my cheeks as the silence suddenly deafens me.

I try to lift a leg but it's no use: it will not budge. I bend to try pull it with my hands and suddenly hear a whooshing noise before feeling wind. I bolt upright, my long blonde hair falling onto my face. I move the strands aside and I listen. I stand like granite, not daring to breath, just like a statue. I hear and feel the whoosh again behind me. I turn my torso quickly but there's nothing there. My eyes scan every nook and cranny, but I don't see anything. There is no one anywhere: it's just me, all alone, on a deserted platform. It's just me.

I move the loose strands of hair from my face again and I slowly turn back to face forward. I scream and fall backwards as I try to move, but I can't. I'm sitting on my arse, shaking like a leaf as he bears down on me. Those yellow, buttercup eyes are unnatural, yet I'm mesmerised by them. Although I'm shaking, scared, I'm not petrified like I feel I should be. I find myself gravitating towards him.

His face is abnormally pale; his chiselled, high cheek bones are almost pointy; a sharp chin protrudes slightly giving him a rounded jawline that is so smooth; and his dirty blonde hair is messy and long. But it's those eyes… It's like staring into a field of buttercups. They're not natural. His pupils are like slits, elongated rather than being round like normal people.

He stops moving closer and raises his eyebrows. It's me who is progressing closer to him. I lean forwards. I want to reach out and touch his face, to see if he's real, to see if it's as smooth as it looks. He furrows his beautifully arched brows, confused as he watches me raise my hand. I hesitate, only for a second, as if maybe asking for his permission, until he smiles. I gasp, dropping my hand to my lap.

His teeth are pure glistening white, but he has fangs—actual *long fangs that look sharp. Everything about him is sharp edges. I lean back, withdrawing from his space, putting my hands behind me in the sand. Only they start to sink. I move them quickly before they get stuck like my legs. Why hasn't my whole body sunk? How bizarre. But isn't everything about this situation bizarre and not right?*

He smiles again, seeing the confusion on my face. He starts to move his face back towards mine, only this time, he uses his hand to stroke the side of my neck. His touch is ice cold. He gently tilts my head to the side slightly, exposing it to him. He suddenly leans in and licks down my jugular vein, then back up again. I have goose bumps all over—I think more from the coldness of him than what he's doing to me. He proceeds to then pepper my neck with feather-light kisses. It's then I start to pant at his cold touch. I should be terrified, but I want him to carry on—I want him to do more, to touch me more.

Suddenly he bears down, sinking his teeth into my neck. I scream and scream as he sucks what feels like my life, draining it from me. There's no one around to hear my screams. His hand starts to wander down my throat towards my chest. I scream, trying to thrash. It's no use, I'm stuck. I suddenly stop moving.

"Hey, Shar, wake up. Wake up. You're doing it again."

I'm being shaken hard. My eyes flutter open. I'm gasping for breath, holding my neck and I'm hot and sweaty. It's my roommate, Liz. We don't get on very well. I know she's getting fed up with my nightmares, as am I, but they feel so real. I dread going falling asleep. It's the same every night almost, just with some slight variations. I catch my breath, looking up to the ceiling trying to make sense of it all. I do this most mornings.

I sit up and watch as she stomps around her side of the room, getting ready for class. I look at my Apple Watch and see it's still really early. I'm not sure why she leaves so early: first class doesn't start for another two hours. I hear her muttering to herself as she grabs stuff and shoves it into her bag. She's angry. It's not my fault. It's not like I can help what I dream about.

Liz is an artist. She's weird, but in a good way. I wish I were brave enough to be like her. She's a goth with jet black hair that she wears in high pigtails most days. She only lets it down at night when she's going out, and even then, she styles it amazingly. She wears black lipstick all the time. They are even black in the mornings. In fact, I'm sure her lips must be stained black by now. Her eyeliner is always so precise and cat-like making her eyes elongated, and more often than not, she has different coloured contact lenses in. She's got her black fishnet tights on today with a short, tartan skirt, her black Doc Martins that have skulls all over them in silver glitter and her black bomber jacket that is full of zips, buckles, safety pins and padlocks.

She turns to me. She must feel me staring at her. It's then I notice she has yellow eyes. I gasp, and my hand flies to my throat. She scowls at me, raising her eyebrows, giving me the evil eye. I gasp for breath. Her eyes look just like his, from my dreams.

"You're weird. You know that, right?" she snaps at me. She grabs her bag and heads to the door. She turns back to me. "And they all call me a freak. They should try sharing a room with you." With that she leaves, slamming the door behind her. I lay back down and stare at the ceiling again. I don't get what the dream is about. I'm always stuck in quicksand that only sucks up my legs; I'm always on a platform with a steam train; and he always bears down on me, sucking on my neck. I'm enamoured by him, but he's fictional: I made him up. I try to decipher what my dreams mean but I can never work it out.

I get ready for class. I'm not one of the popular girls

at Uni, thankfully. I hate any attention. I don't have any friends and never have really. I'm an introvert so prefer my own company. I don't go out: I keep myself to myself. I've been here for two semesters now, and I still struggle with being away from home. My dad's not so good, and he's all I've got. My mum left us when I was nine. She ran off with the neighbour.

She dumped the neighbour and got a new fella, but he gives me the creeps. He used to comment on how mature I was getting and how my breasts were really developing perfectly. Every opportunity he got, he would make a snide comment at me, about my breasts or my 'tits' as he called them. I was thirteen the last time I ever stayed at mums, and I haven't seen her since.

I remember it like it happened yesterday. Without going into too much detail, my mum's creep of a boyfriend, Gerard, unlocked the bathroom door one day as I was in the bath. I screamed and shouted at him to get out. He wouldn't budge. The window was ajar, and I thought the more I screamed the more likely it would be that someone outside would hear me and come to see what was happening.

He'd slapped me hard across the face to stop me screaming. The bubbles in the bath had dissolved, so he'd been able to see everything. I tried to cover up with my hands and arms as best I could, but he stood leering at me.

I watched in shock as he dropped his sweatpants while standing in front of me, and he proceeded to play with his cock. He'd wanted me to play with it. I'd stood up and pushed him, only slightly, to get him out of my way. I was no match to his bulk, but to my surprise he'd stumbled backwards. I'd thought because his sweatpants were around his ankles, it made him lose his balance, he fell, smashing the back of his head on the sink. Then he'd rolled to the side and fallen to the floor, cracking his face on the toilet as he went down. Served him right, the pervert. I'd been able to feel rushes of wind from the window and was cold and goosepimply. I had to get out quick.

The thing was, as I'd left the bathroom, wrapping the towel I had grabbed around me, my mum had just stood there in her bedroom doorway with what looked like a cigarette hanging from her mouth—I say that because I'd been sure it was a spliff. I remember being so confused and scowling at her: the fact she had been there while I was screaming for help. But all I'd wanted to do was get my things and leave that house. As I left my room, she'd stood blocking me from going down the stairs. I hadn't been able to understand what she was doing until she opened her mouth and it all clicked.

"Did he do you then?" she asked.

I didn't know what she was talking about. I was so angry, hurt, annoyed and confused.

"Did he fuck you?" she shouted at me.

I remember being stunned, thinking who was this woman? Why hadn't she come in when I was screaming? Why hadn't she come in to help me? Why was she being a bitch to me? Had she wanted him to fuck me? So many questions had spun around in my head.

I'd wiped the tears that were streaming down my face as it dawned on me: she'd let him do what he did, and God knows what else he would have done if I hadn't shoved him. I had to ask her: she was my mum and I needed to know.

"Why didn't you help me, Mum? Why did you let him come in there? Did you want him to 'do me', to rape me? You're as sick as he is. Don't ever get in touch with me again."

I'd shoved her out of my way and ran down the stairs, leaving that house for good.

I'd cried my eyes out for days. My dad had been upset that I was upset. I'd just told him I was poorly with lady's problems. I couldn't tell him what had happened: I was too afraid of what he might do to them both, and I didn't want to lose him.

That had been the end of my mum.

I'm now twenty and haven't seen her for seven years. I don't even know where she is or what happened to her. I don't really care after that day. It changed me. It made me very conscious of who I am and how I look, hence why I have never dated anyone. I'm an introvert and I like it that way.

I also have to think of my dad. He's developed CoPD—a lung disease. He manages okay without needing oxygen, only on the rare occasions it gets bad, but it can get worse if he isn't careful. I didn't want to leave him to go to Uni, but he made me go. He said I had my life to live and he had his. He's got a new lady friend, which helped make my decision. I'm happy he's happy at the moment.

Chapter 2

I'VE CONTINUED TO have the same dream every night. In fact, I've had them for such a long time now, Liz throws things at me if I wake her. I've been considering taking drugs of some kind to knock me out so I don't dream, but I don't want to become addicted, so haven't gone there. I've even considered going to the doctor's to ask for help with sleeping tablets. I've also been having strange feelings during the day. I feel like I'm never alone, that someone is watching me, but whenever I look around, I don't see anyone out of the ordinary or anyone looking suspicious. It's really starting to get to me.

I have an exam coming up soon. I'm studying history, so I need to do a lot of research in the library. It means staying late and not getting back to my room until after 10 p.m. All this week, I've had the feeling someone's been following me home after I leave the library. I'm starting to get really scared. It's starting to affect my work.

I decide to get the books I need during my lunch—as

I'm always in the library anyway—and take them home with me to study. After what I think is only a few hours, I look at my watch. It's 11.59 p.m., wow where did the time go? Liz isn't coming back, tonight. In fact, she hasn't slept here the last week. I assume it's because of my nightmares.

Leaning back in my chair, I have a stretch, and a yawn. I see something move out of the corner of my eye at the widow and jolt my head in that direction, but there's nothing there. I get up and slowly walk to the window. I'm three floors up, so it's not like anyone can be walking outside and there are no stairs or anything close by. I lean against the window and look out, but there's nothing there. Just then, I hear a small tap on the door. I turn and just stare at it, like it's going to open or explode or something. I don't move. It can't be Liz: she's staying out and she has her own key. I hear the tap again, slightly harder this time.

I move slowly to the door. We don't have a spy hole, so I can't see who it is.

"Who is it?" I shout. I wait and listen.

There's nothing—no sounds at all. I'm just about to walk away when there is a light tap again.

"Who is it?" There is no way I'm opening up unless I know who it is. I put my ear to the door to see if I can hear anything; there's nothing.

It's now gone midnight, so most students will be in their dorms, but there are usually a lot still milling around the corridors until the early hours. I don't hear a thing. I move back from the door and they tap again.

"Please go away. I'm not opening the door, so you're wasting your time." I move and sit on the edge of my bed. My hands grip the edge tightly and my legs bounce with nerves. I stare at the door like it's going to magically open or something.

Imagine my shock when it does.

Holy fuck.

I watch with wide eyes as the door very slowly creeks open. I grip my bed so tightly, my fingers are hurting.

I need to call security. I look around for my phone. It's on my desk. I open the phone app on my watch and start turning the dial to search for security. I've never had to phone them before. The door isn't fully open, but I see a black shoe come into view. I start to panic and hit the wrong things on my tiny stupid watch.

"Don't come in; I'm calling the police," I stutter to whoever it is. It would be far quicker to call the police than try find the number for security. I'm fumbling with my watch, trying to get the emergency SOS button up, when I look up and freeze at what I see standing in the doorway, his back to the now closed door. How the hell did he get in and close the door so quickly and without me knowing?

It's the boy in my nightmares.

It's the yellow, buttercup eyes that have me mesmerised, as they always do.

But he doesn't exist—only exists in my head.

I can feel myself start to panic. I must have fallen asleep whilst working and not realised, and now I'm in a nightmare again, only this one has escalated to my room.

That's it. It's the only explanation. In fact, there are no other explanations. I screw my eyes shut and pinch my leg really hard. I squeal and open my eyes, but he's still there, looking bemused, watching me.

I raise my hand with the watch. "One more swipe and it connects to the police. Leave me alone. Get out." I am just about to swipe the SOS to connect me when he's got me on my feet with my hands wrapped behind my back. He doesn't hurt me. In fact, he's very gentle.

His face is in mine. We are almost nose to nose. I can tell he's crouching slightly to get into my face, which means he is tall. His hands are ice cold as they hold mine behind my back. He doesn't breathe, the complete opposite to me, who is panting with panic, but not just panic, something else—something I don't quite understand.

My heart beats out of my chest. I feel like I'm going to hyperventilate. He's so close. I could just edge slightly forwards and kiss him. I huff out at my thought. Kiss him. I've never even been kissed. How the hell did he get to me so quick, before I had chance to connect the call? I didn't even see him move, just a woosh of air.

I stare into his eyes and I feel myself calming. My breathing starts to even out and my heart palpitations start to slow. I'm scared, but he has such a calming effect on me. This has to be a nightmare. They always feel so real, just like this. Only this time, I'm not stuck in quicksand.

I try to move, to wriggle out of his grip, but without any impact, he is far too strong for me.

"What do you want? Why are you in my nightmares? Why are you doing this to me? I need to wake up."

He doesn't speak; he smiles. His chiseled, pointy cheekbones are so prominent when he does, and I kind of melt. He opens his mouth slightly, and it's then I see his fangs.

My eyes widen. He's going to bite me again.

He leans in and rubs his nose on mine, softly. His cold forehead rests against mine as he stares into my eyes. I'm shocked at how he makes me feel. I start to melt into him, my chest resting on his solid one. He lets go of my hands and takes hold of both my cheeks. He then bends my head very slowly and gently starts to lick, then kiss, up the side of my neck. I know this routine: it usually ends up with him biting me.

He continues to kiss and lick. I'm waiting with bated breath for the bite, but it doesn't come. He pulls back and stares into my eyes with his bright, buttercup ones. They are strange but beautiful. They must be contact lenses like Liz's: no one has eyes like that. His fangs must be fake as well. Unless he's had them filed down like that. I've heard of people who do that. Strange people.

"What do you want? I need to wake up."

"You," he whispers into my mouth just as his lips crush mine. He holds my head tight at the sides, so tight, I think he may crush my head. I try to pull away, but he grips tighter and he presses harder into my mouth. I slap at his arms, trying to get him to release me. He hasn't closed his eyes, and he must see the panic on my face. He lets go and steps back.

"You arsehole. You nearly crushed my head. That hurt and you crushed my lips. They feel bruised now." I shout at him as I stroke my fingers over my lips. "If this is a nightmare, why do I feel the pain? Why haven't I woken up already?"

"It's not a nightmare, Sharlene. This is my reality and now yours." He whispers with a voice that is so velvety smooth, my name, pronounced in full, from his lips sounds like it's crooned to me.

What does he mean by that? No one ever calls me by my full name, well except my dad sometimes. I scowl at him. I don't know who he is, this man-boy. He looks young but acts old, if that makes sense.

I step back, but he grabs my arm, gently. He's freezing. I try to pull free. "You're so cold. Why are you cold? Do you need to get warm? Do you need a blanket? Let me get my duvet for you." I try to move, but he still has hold of me.

"I am fine, I am always cold. Do you need to get warm? Are you cold?" He looks concerned for me. This is different. I feel the pain, the cold, and he hasn't bitten me. This isn't how my nightmares go. I don't understand what's happening. Maybe I have some kind of chemical imbalance in my brain and I conjure up this man when I feel low. Maybe he's just my imaginary friend—I mean a lot of kids have them, so maybe adults do, too. I nod my head to let him know I am cold. The reality is I need to sit down. He lets go of me and I sit on the bed. I wrap my duvet around my shoulders. He stands in front of me looking down at me. I look up at him

"They are really cool contacts you have there. My roommate wears different contacts all the time. How did you get your teeth like that?"

What the fuck am I doing? Why am I asking such stupid questions? I feel like a pathetic little girl crushing on someone much older than I am.

I put my head down in embarrassment.

He lifts my chin up very gently with a fingernail. Did I mention his nails are longer than mine?

"Don't be shy, Sharlene. I can see your embarrassment. These are not contact lenses, and my teeth are all natural."

I scowl at him. Now he's taking the piss out of me.

I huff out, tightening the duvet around my shoulders. "Yeah, right. You must take me for a right fool. No one has eyes that colour."

He smiles and I melt, yet again. When I stare into his eyes, I have these feelings all over my body, like he's controlling me. If he asked me to do something stupid, I would probably do it, like he commands me. This nightmare needs to end. It's going to start going places I've never been in my life if it doesn't.

"You can leave now, erm, what's your name? Or do I get to name you as you're in my head and I made you up. Yes. Let's call you Ridley. Yes, I like that, and it suits you. You're like a riddle to me."

He laughs at me—I mean really laughs—showing me his sharp fangs. "Well if you want to call me Ridley you can, although my name is actually Prescott Stanhope. Nice to meet you, Sharlene Upton." He bows, like actually fucking bows, with one arm over his tummy and the other round his back, like you see in old historical shows on TV. I watch them all with being into history. It makes me smile at his gesture. Then I scowl.

"How the hell can you have a name when I've made you up. No, that's not right. You cannot have a name." I am so confused. Nothing makes any sense, and I now just want to wake up from this nightmare. He scares me, but he doesn't. I have feelings for him in the romantic sense, but then I don't because he scares me. I am all a dither. Maybe I banged my head or something. Did I fall off my chair? I look at the chair and it's upright. Maybe if I just lie back and close my eyes I will wake up and he'll be gone.

I do just that, wrapping the duvet around me tighter to ward off the ice cold I feel. I put my arm up over my eyes to block out the light from my lamp. I lay like this for what feels like an age. I don't hear him. He doesn't speak or move. I don't move again. In fact, I think I actually fall asleep.

Chapter 3

I WAKE UP, the light shining through the window telling me it's morning. I look at my watch. It's 9.43 a.m.

Shit.

I'm late for class. I've never been late. I'm wrapped up in my duvet, which is how I was in my dream. That's so weird. It seems so long ago, yet I feel like I just had the best night's sleep in, well, forever. With no dreams, but it was all a dream. My head is hurting with all this confusion. I don't know what's reality anymore, yet I remember everything about the dream like it was real—I was convinced it was real.

I get up gathering my stuff to head to the communal bathroom to get showered. I'm just about to unlock my door when it opens easily. It's not locked. I know I locked it, knowing Liz wasn't coming back.

I head to the bathrooms, which are empty, thankfully,

with it being so late. I finish my shower, dry and dress then go to do my teeth. I put the toothbrush to my mouth and see my lips are a funny colour. I touch them and they hurt. I remember in my dream telling him my lips felt bruised. I softly run my fingers over them and lean in closer. They are bruised. How can that be?

I'm in a daze the rest of the day. Liz finds me in the library at lunch and tells me she won't be back again tonight and probably not all week. She has a new boyfriend and is enjoying him while she can. That's fine by me. I like having my own space—introvert to a tee.

I grab a sandwich and an iced latte from the coffee shop near the library to take back to my dorm. I have a lot of work and research to do. I'm juggling my much too heavy bag full of books from the library, with some in my arms, as well as my latte when suddenly the books in my arms and then my bag are being taken from me. It's dark out, it's about 7 p.m. and I look startled at the figure to my left—the figure who has removed my items so fast, I don't have chance to protest, shout or scream. I don't have time to process what is happening.

I look horrified at the hooded figure until he lifts his head slightly, showing me his buttercup eyes. Prescott. I gasp at his face. He's here, out in the open with me. I know this isn't a dream. I touch my lips, and I see him follow my hand. He smiles a very slight smile, but I see it.

"It's you. But how?" I have no idea what is going on.

"I saw you needed some help, so here I am." He smiles wider, showing me his fangs. I find myself leaning in to get closer to him.

Just then it starts to rain.

Shit.

I don't have an umbrella. He suddenly takes my hand and before I know it, we're standing outside my dorm door, dry as a bone.

"I definitely have a chemical imbalance, if my imaginary friend can do that," I say to myself, trying to find my key to unlock the door. But he's got it and has the door open whilst I'm looking in my pocket for it. I shake my head and he smiles that smile at me.

He gestures for me to enter first, like a noble man, bowing as he does. He follows me inside and places the books on my desk and my bag on the floor next to it. I just stand, staring at him as he moves with such fluidity around my small room. He has my coffee placed on the desk and my jacket hung on the back of the chair before I realise. I'm still standing in the same spot, mesmerised, just trying to comprehend what is actually happening.

This is the boy from my dreams, or nightmares, or whatever the hell they are, so how the hell is he here in my room helping me? He sits on my bed with his back to the wall and his long legs dangling over the edge. He's removed his hoodie and is sitting with a goofy smile on his face.

"Why are you here or not? How are you here or not? I'm so confused. You move so fast and without any effort, just like the wind, you're cold to the touch and you mesmerise me. Are you even real? I just reckon I have this chemical imbalance that seems to conjure you up." I'm talking to myself with my head hung.

In the blink of an eye, he's standing holding my face in his palms, tilting it up so I can see his face. He lowers and gently kisses my lips. No force or harshness like in my dream last night. My lips are very tender, but I don't care. This time, it's soft and I open my mouth to receive him. He starts to tighten his hold slightly, until he feels me pulling away, which makes him loosen his hold. He slips his tongue into my mouth and deepens the kiss. He gently moves his hands round the back of my neck, still holding my head with his thumbs on my cheeks. I put my hands on his hips and gently pull him into me as the kiss deepens. Our tongues duel.

"Ouch." I pull away. I can taste blood in my mouth. I must have cut my tongue on his fangs. I see his eyes narrow to slits and his buttercup yellow eyes turn a darker shade of yellow. His tongue comes out, licking his lips. He looks at me like I'm his next meal, with his lips curled up at the sides, he looks menacing.

I turn my back on him. He's scaring me, and I need to take a breath. It's like he doesn't need to breath at all. I turn back and he looks normal as though the last few minutes never happened. I shake my head. He looks confused as I step away from him

"What's wrong?" he asks.

I'm bewildered. I have this strange boy in my room; I have no idea who he is. Any boy in my room would be strange. I don't do this. I'm convinced he isn't real—he doesn't even look real. He looks more like a vampire, only I thought they had black or red eyes not yellow cat like eyes. I've watched enough films to know they are usually cold and move fast but they are mythical, everyone knows that. He scares me, but not in such a bad way, more in the way I'm enamoured by him. He's definitely been in my dreams. There is no way they were real, well because they were so weird being stuck in quicksand on a platform with a steam train...

He takes my face again and gently kisses the tip of my nose. "I'm sorry if I came on too strong. I've been wanting to kiss you for so long. You have no idea. Now I have shown myself to you I just cannot help it."

I tilt my head staring at his face. He is so handsome and chiselled. In fact, he's beautiful. "What do you mean you have wanted to do that for so long? How long? What do you mean now you have shown yourself to me? Tell me this is not real. How can you be real? Vampires are fictional."

He laughs out loud, taking me into his arms. He hugs me to his chest. He has to loosen his grip once he realises he is holding me tight. "Sharlene, I have been in your life for many years. I have stayed hidden, but I have been there. Yes, I have been in your dreams—it is one of the things I can do: project into the mind. I had to stop you from running away from me, hence the quicksand. I had to make you believe it was all a dream. I have been there protecting you from many mishaps, like the time you were about to cross the road when you were eleven, you had your nose stuck in a book and you didn't see the car. I stopped that car hitting you, the one that beeped at you, and you didn't know why.

"I was there the day your mum's boyfriend entered the bathroom. You thought you had pushed him; it was me. I was outside when I heard you scream. When I saw he was in the bathroom with you… Well, let's say if my blood could boil it would have. I don't know how I didn't rip his heart out right there and then. You couldn't see me: I had not shown myself to you at that point. It was me who pulled him back and smashed his head on the sink and his face on the toilet. Then, I heard you talking to your mother and she had been standing there all that time. I'm sorry, but once you left, she had an accident. She's still alive but she's in a rehabilitation home: she is paralysed from the waist down.

I didn't mean to push her down the stairs, but she would have let him rape you. She didn't deserve to live. Please forgive me, I know she is your mother. There have been so many other occasions that I could reel off. Do you remember the time you were on your bike riding on your own by the canal when you were nearly seventeen? You hit a stone that twisted your front wheel and it catapulted you into the dark, dank, canal water. You were so disorientated. You kept disappearing under the water. It took me a couple of attempts to get you out."

I'm stunned into silence, trying to process all he is saying and thinking back to all the times I've done something and somehow been okay. It was him all this time.

"You've been following me like a stalker for all these years? Do you even age? Does that make you a pervert for stalking a little girl? You must have seen me naked that day in the bathroom. Oh my god, are you always around when I'm naked? I feel sick. I can't take this in."

He laughs at me. I scowl at him.

This isn't funny. Finding out someone has been watching you for years. No, not funny. I don't know why, but I slap his chest. I regret it the moment I make contact. He's like granite and my hand hurts.

"Ouch, that fucking hurt. You need to leave, Prescott, whoever the fuck you are. You need to leave me alone. My brain can't function with you around, and I feel so angry right now."

I'm on the bed, laying on his chest, before I even have the chance to blink. I try to pull up, but he won't let me move.

"Prescott, let me go. Please leave before I have to call the police."

He loosens his grip on me, but only slightly. I still for a few minutes. It's then I realise I don't hear a heartbeat whilst lying on his chest. I can hear my own pulse in my ears—it's a little bit erratic—but… Wait, I'm sure that was a beat. I listen hard and it's minutes before I hear it again. I lever myself up to look into his face. I really look. I should be terrified by eyes like that and knowing he has fangs, but I'm not. He's beautiful.

"What are you?" I whisper.

"A fantasy," is all he says, smiling at me.

That doesn't help and angers me more.

"Leave now. I don't want you here. I don't want you around me or even near me." I watch as his smile fades, and he looks hurt. It pulls at my heart. The fact I could even hurt him. This being—this thing—holding me, I'm sure could rip me apart right now if he wanted to, yet I can hurt him. He lets me go and I get up. He sits up on the bed and very slowly gets up himself. Grabbing his hoodie he makes for the door. He doesn't turn to look at me

"If you need me for anything, Sharlene, just say my name. I will be at your side in an instant." With that, he's gone like the wind just left.

I sink to the floor and lean against my bed with my arms wrapped round my pulled-up knees. I feel the tears flow down my cheeks.

I think I'm going mental. I think I have a problem.

I don't know what this is, and it sure as hell all feels real, but he isn't real; he can't be real. Maybe something happened to me and this is my way of my brain keeping me going.

I don't get any work done, I'm not in the mood for reading about history. I spend most of the night researching vampires on my computer. There is nothing I don't really know, but there are some things about Prescott that are different than the normal. He says he's been there for years and saved me from so many things. I remember all those things he mentioned, so I know he's not lying. I get into bed and eventually fall asleep.

Chapter 4

AS I START to wake up, I yawn and try to stretch my arms but hey feel confined. Now that was the best night's sleep ever. I know I said that about the previous night but this one truly was. I feel like I've slept forever: no dreams or nightmares. In fact, nothing.

Not opening my eyes just, I lie there for a little while. The first thing that pops into my mind is buttercup eyes.

I suddenly hear a beeping noise seeping into my head, followed by other distant noises and voices.

There are voices. What the hell? Has Liz brought someone back to our room?

I try to open my eyes, but for some reason, they won't. I manage to free a hand, there is resistance, and start to rub my eyes. I feel someone touching my hand, stopping me. I jump. It startles me. Liz isn't here, or she wasn't, she's staying at her boyfriends. Don't tell me Prescott is back. I panic. Why won't my eyes open?

"Prescott, I told you not to come back. Now leave." I

freak out, realising quickly that I haven't said the words out loud, only in my head because there's something in my mouth. I'm going to choke; it's in my throat.

Oh my god what is happening to me.

I become frantic and try to move my hands again to get whatever it is out of my mouth, but they are being held.

Just then a female voice is at my ear.

"Shhh, Sharlene, it's okay. Don't panic. Try to stay calm. We need to get this tube out of your throat. Please stay calm for me, okay. My name is Liz. I'm here to help you. No one is going to hurt you. Nod if you understand me?"

I nod. It's Liz—my roommate, Liz—but she sounds different. Why have I got a tube in my throat? What's happened to me? What has Prescott done to me now. Oh God. The beeping, it sounds like a hospital machine. I've seen them on the TV when I've watched medical programmes. Oh no what's happening?

Just then, I feel something being removed from my eyes. Were they taped shut? What the fuck is happening? I feel my heart rate getting erratic like it did with Prescott last night. I'm scared.

"Shhh, calm down, Sharlene. You're going into a shock. Your heart monitor is running wild. Calm down for me. Now, try to open your eyes. It might be bright at first but I can't dim the lights until we have examined you properly. Can you nod for me and try open them?" It's the same voice.

I start to peel my eyes open. She's right, it's bright, and I squint. I very slowly make them into slits and try to focus on something. I turn my head slightly and I can see the outline of someone standing by me. I see some colour. I see yellow, buttercup yellow. I try to smile.

"Can you see me?" I hear his voice and I nod slightly. I'm relieved he's here. I know he will protect me. I try to open them wider, tolerating more and more light, but my focus is off.

"Okay, that's great, Sharlene. Now, we are going to pull the tube out of your throat. It will be uncomfortable at first and it might make you cough or even be sick, but don't worry, we've got you. Okay, stay as still as you can while we remove it."

I lay like a statue, all the while opening my eyes wider and wider till they are fully open. I feel the tube sliding up my throat. I want to gag. I start to choke. There are hands holding my shoulders down and one holding my forehead so I don't move.

"That's really good, Sharlene. It's almost out, just a little more. There you go." It pops out, and I immediately sit up and wretch. Nothing comes up. I sit for a minute with my eyes closed. Someone is rubbing my back. The hand is cold. It's Prescott.

"Prescott, please don't leave me again. Please stay with me. What happened?" But no words come out of my mouth. I move it but there's nothing. I lift my head. My vision is blurry, but I can see outlines of several people standing around me. I can safely say I am not in my dorm room, and I have no idea where I am, how I got here or even how long I've been here. I try to concentrate on my vision. I stare hard at each outline, I can see them moving around.

"Sharlene, can you see anything yet?" It's Liz.

I shake my head.

"Here. Take this straw into your mouth and sip on the water. Your throat will be dry, and this will help." She places the straw to my lips, and I suck up the cold water. It hurts to swallow but I manage to do it. It feels cool sliding down my throat. I sip more; I'm thirsty. "You're doing great. Now don't panic about your vision: it can take a little while to come back. Here, lay back slightly and try to relax. I know you've been doing that for a long time but now you're awake."

I scowl at what she just said. What does she mean it's been a long time? I was in my dorm with Prescott last night. I lay back and close my eyes.

I'm not sure how long I fall asleep for, but I feel a hand rubbing up and down my arm. I turn my head in the direction, and when I open my eyes, I see my dad standing there with tears streaming down his face. I can actually see him. My vision is back.

"Hi, Dad," I croak out and he smiles.

"Hey, poppit. How are you feeling?" He's rubbing my arm without realising it.

"I feel tired, Dad. I don't know where I am. Why am I here? How long I've been here?"

He looks confused as he wipes the stray tears.

"Hasn't anyone told you?"

I shake my head. I'm thirsty. "Water, please, Dad." I'm so croaky and my throat hurts. He puts the straw to my mouth, and I sip. "Tell me what's going on, Dad. I was in my dorm last night and then woke up here."

He looks really confused.

"Poppit." He takes a breath and looks down to my arm where he's stroking it.

"Dad, what is it?"

He looks back to me. "You had an accident, Poppit. You nearly drowned just over three years ago. You've been in the hospital all that time. You never regained consciousness. Poppit, when the hospital phoned me this morning to tell my you had woken up, I couldn't believe it. I've never given up hope. I knew you would come back when you were ready."

Wait, what? What is he talking about? "Dad, I'm in university. I have a dorm with a roommate called Liz. I'm studying history. How can I have been here for so long? How old am I now?"

"You're twenty, Poppit. You were on your bike and somehow you fell into the canal. They say you drowned, and no one has any idea how you got out. It was a jogger who found you on the footpath. Do you remember anything about it?"

I shake my head. I don't remember much of it, apart from Prescott telling me about it last night and him telling me he saved me. He never said I had drowned, or that the life I thought I was living was only in my head. Was he even real?

I Suddenly feel like my world has just lost its bottom finding out he isn't actually real. Was that all just my imagination along with everything else? But it was all so real. I was living it. How do I know?

Mum.

"Dad, where's Mum?"

He looks confused. "You haven't seen her since you were thirteen when you came home upset. I found out not long after that she had an accident. She fell down the stairs. Something happened with her and her boyfriend and he was injured and ended up in a coma and your mum ended up being paralysed from a fall down the stairs and has been in a rehabilitation home with her not having any relatives to look after her. I was shocked when I found out, but I didn't want to upset you any more than you were."

I gasp. Prescott had told me all that last night. How would I know if he didn't tell me? He is real, he has to be.

Just then, the door opens and in walks a doctor. I gasp, again. It's Prescott. It's definitely him, but he looks different.

"Ah, Miss Upton. Nice to see you awake. It's been a long time. I'm just looking at your chart here, and I'm pleased to say everything is looking really good. How is your vision now? Can you see clearly?"

I don't say or do anything. I'm stunned just staring at him. It's him, only he has brown eyes. He's still pale, he still has the pointy, chiseled cheek bones and prominent chin. He even has the same voice and mannerisms; I know it's him. He's beautiful.

"Miss Upton, are you okay? Can you speak? Can you see me now?"

I nod slightly, and I see a very slight smile on his face. He knows I know. I also know there is a double meaning to his question.

"Yes, Prescott. I see you clearly now," I say, and he smiles. I just confirmed I know.

"Doctor Stanhope here has been looking after you ever since you were brought into the hospital, Poppit. He's taken very good care of you—always there to answer my questions and reassure me you would wake up one day."

I look at the admiration on my dad's face for Prescott, and it melts my heart. Just like Prescott does. He truly melts my heart.

He comes over to me. "I'm just going to shine a light in your eyes, if that's okay. If it's too bright, let me know."

I nod. He shines the light in my eyes, and in doing so, he touches my face as he lifts an eyelid up. I take in a deep breath from his touch. He's icy cold. I know now he's wearing contacts to hide his buttercup eyes. He's smiling at me because I know. He does a few more tests, still touching me—on my arm, my leg, my head—and every time, I take in a sharp breath. It seems to amuse him.

"Perfect, Miss Upton. You amaze me. You would never know you had been in a coma for three years. We need to rehabilitate you—get you mobile and learning to walk again. That's going to take a bit of time, but I will be here to oversee it and help you as best I can."

I just nod and thank him. Dad stays for a little while, telling me things I've missed, even though I don't feel I've missed anything because I've been going through it all in my head. I must fall asleep as he's talking because the next time I wake up, it's dark.

I nearly scream when I see movement in the corner of my room. Suddenly Prescott is at my side, stopping me.

"You scared the shit out of me. Why are you hiding in my room?"

He shrugs. "It's habit. It's what I've done for the last three years. Every night, I sit here watching you—never leaving you."

I'm shocked, and I feel myself blush. Luckily, it's dark and he can't see.

"No need to be embarrassed, Sharlene. I would do anything for you. I love you. I have loved you since the first time I saw you when you were five. I'll never forget that day. It was the 23rd December and they had taken you to the theatre, I think to watch a pantomime. I was walking down the street just as you came out and it was instant, the clinch. My family had told me it would happen one day. I'd given up as the centuries passed and nothing ever happened. Then I saw you, happy and laughing. Your father swooped you up into his arms and was pretending to eat you up. You were so giddy, squealing. I followed behind at a distance, and I laughed at your laughter. I've been there looking out for you ever since—for fifteen of your years."

I feel a little weird knowing that, and what the hell is a clinch? I must look confused.

"There is much to learn and much for me to tell you. The clinch is when we instantly know who our life partner will be, it is a form of seal that we feel to a person. You are mine."

This isn't the time for all this, and the fact he said it's been centuries hasn't gone unnoticed, but I'm tired. If what he's saying is true, we have a long time to get to know each other. I don't feel scared at all. I feel safe. He makes me feel safe. I fall asleep with him sitting next to me, holding my hand.

Funnily enough, he's not making me cold, he's making me hot. Something else to baffle me.

Epilogue

IN MY NORMAL years, I'm now two-hundred and twenty-six, but in Prescott years, I'm still twenty-six.

A lot has happened since I woke up from my coma. As you can tell from my age, I am now like Prescott, well to some extent, and we are in fact happily married with our own beautiful family: one son and two daughters. I had Joseph and Dorothy when I was human. It was hard, and both nearly killed me, but Prescott made sure it all went smoothly, doing whatever it is he does with his sorcery, as I call it. I had no idea Vampires could actually reproduce, but apparently when you are not only Vampire and have sorcery in you, then you can do almost anything.

What is Prescott? Well, he's full of surprises that's for sure. He is six-hundred and thirty-one years old. I couldn't even comprehend that the first time he told me. It just baffled me. He has powers and can do things with magic. He amazes me all the time. He helped me recover from my coma and my rehabilitation. It turns out every dream/nightmare I had with him, was really him in them. He can enter people's minds and make them see him. I could make a long list about the things he can do, but even I'm still learning.

He is a Vampire, as I knew, but he is also magical. His mother, Selene, is a direct descendant of the Goddess Hecate. I started to study the Greek Gods and Goddess's and Hecate is the Goddess of magic, witchcraft, necromancy and boundaries—amongst other things. Selene means 'the goddess of the moon and mother of vampires' so with the necromancy, I suppose it explains the falling in love with Prescott's father, Heathcliff, who is a full-on Vampire, she bewitched him, or so the story goes.

Prescott is a mixture of all sorts, but he only ever uses it for good. He doesn't practice dark witchcraft. Selene makes sure he has never ventured down the dark side.

I, on the other hand, haven't discovered any other powers. I'm supper fast, strong, pale and ice cold. Oh, and I can have babies, which apparently normal Vampires cannot, so that's a plus. We could have so many. I was a virgin until Prescott, and let's just say that once we'd done the whole sex thing, I was addicted to him. I never ever thought it could be so amazing, to make love, but apparently with Prescott it is.

Our thirst for blood is very controlled, and we mainly drink the blood of animals before they are slaughtered for meat. We run a cattle farm—how convenient. We help feed our faction. There are more of us than anyone realises, which is why our farm is the largest in England.

Heathcliff is so ancient that Prescott says he doesn't have long to live. Yes, apparently Vampires have a life span. I never knew that, but Prescott's idea of not having long to live could be thousands of years.

My dad took a turn for the worse with his CoPd and he passed away before my twenty-sixth birthday. He was happy. He got married to Anne, his girlfriend, who I thought was made up in my coma, but apparently, he'd started dating her whilst I was in my coma. Prescott had added some realities to my dreams so I was prepared. They had a good few years together, and he got to spend time with Jo and Dottie. His proudest moment he told me was walking me down the aisle on my wedding day. After he passed, I asked Prescott to turn me. It was the right time.

We stay on our farm, the children grow fast and I'm pretty sure we will be having many more.

Life is pretty spectacular right now.

THE END

Acknowledgements

What can be said about the year 2020?
We've had ups and downs; we've laughed and cried.
Although time alone has sometimes been a blessing, it's
been hard for so many to see a way out of isolation.
Finally, we are in a place where the light at the end of the
tunnel is visible.

Thank you, Eleanor, for everything you've done to
organise this anthology: from bringing us all together to
edits. Thank you for making an amazing cover and for all
the other graphics that go along with it. You're amazing at
what you do, and we wouldn't have been able to do it
without you.

A huge thank you to Phoenix Book Promo for all the
hard work spent in the promotion of this anthology—
such a fantastic support.

Thank you to all our beta readers and editors for their support and dedication to these stories.
Thank you to the amazing team of authors who have brought this anthology to life; it's been an amazing venture to work on together.

Most importantly, thank you to all the readers who have purchased a copy. We hope you enjoy these stories as much as we have loved creating them.

With love from the Dandelion Authors

Printed in Great Britain
by Amazon